RED MAN WHITE MAN

BY HARRY C. JAMES

ɪE NAYLOR COMPANY - SAN ANTONIO - TEXAS - 1958

PRINTED IN THE UNITED STATES OF AMERICA

FIRST EDITION

LIBRARY OF CONGRESS CATALOG CARD No. 58-10424

SHIPOLOVI
WALPI
MISHONGNOVI
POLACCA
KEAM'S CANYON
SHONGOPOVI
COLORADO
RIMMY GUS
INDIAN WELLS
WINSLOW
HOLBROOK

RED MAN WHITE MAN

DESIGNED AND DECORATED BY DON PERCEVAL FO

Dedication

To the traditional leaders of the Hopi, whose stubborn integrity has preserved the Hopi people.

THIS IS A WORK of fiction yet it is, in a way, a "true" story. The incidents — with possibly one exception — really happened, but they happened to a variety of people, at different places, and at various times. The characters and their names are entirely fictitious and any similarity to any person or persons, living or dead, is purely coincidental.

— HARRY C. JAMES
(Honauwayma)

Contents

Prologue

I*N THE OLD HOPI Indian village of Shongopovi, ragged patches of wet and dirty snow are melting into puddles of mud here and there in the narrow streets between the long, uneven rows of one-and two-story stone houses. The winter sun fails to bring any sparkle to the drab and spiritless northern Arizona landscape, or any heartening warmth to the cold rock of the mesa top. A few cur dogs crawl listlessly to follow its shifting rays. Several young children idle through the town, too dispirited even for play. An occasional man or woman walks with leaden steps from one house to another on some necessary errand. But no tom-tom throbs the rock. No song is lifted to the gods.*

The *now almost horizontal rays of the December sun disclose a curious figure walking toward the village on weary feet. His face is encased in a green mask with painted eyes and mouth and diagonal lines, its top decorated with a spreading tuft of feathers. He wears a long white cotton shirt and a cotton kilt. Down his back dangles an old and battered fox skin, and from a cord around one shoulder hangs a shabby leather pouch. In one hand he carries a dance rattle and in the other a cluster of bows adorned with feathers.*

He totters through the streets to one of the central open spaces. There he performs a little faltering dance and in a high-pitched, quavering voice he sings a plaintive song. Some of the children gather round and exchange smiles at the grotesque antics of the old man, but their smiles are feeble and there is little joy in them.

The dancer shuffles along the street with the unsure footsteps of the aged, coming to rest beside the entrance to a kiva. Here he deposits his feather-decorated bows and again performs his feeble dance and sings his querulous song. There from his pouch he takes corn meal and with it he draws lines upon the ground, trails of sacred meal radiating from the ceremonial chamber to the north, to the south, to the east to the west.

At this point Nemtaka, the village chief, comes forward. He hands the ancient dancer some prayer feathers and corn meal and receives in exchange the pouch and the dance rattle. With the corn meal left in the pouch he marks upon the ground another trail, one leading away from the village towards the south. The masked figure, still with palsied steps, follows this trail and slowly disappears into the distance.

To the desolate village, wrapped in the gloom and cold of winter, this traditional ceremony bears the promise that the sun will return from its southern journey and bring with it longer days and warmth. The masked dancer is the Soyal Kachina, *the first of the spirits to return to the Hopi from their winter homes. His corn meal trails will guide his fellow Kachinas when they come to initiate the new ceremonial year.*

The sun drops slowly beyond the mountains to the west. The chill air of night sweeps through the streets. Darkness falls swiftly. Thin wisps of smoke rise from many chimneys. Dim light comes from the small windows of the houses. High on the mesa, back of the village, a coyote trots across the rocks. He halts and sniffs the wind, but he is hungry and cannot stop to sing.

I

"HELL – WHAT A ROAD!" muttered Jim Talastewa angrily as the old Ford hit a deep chuck-hole, filled with dust as light and fine as talcum powder. The tires literally squirted it out of the ruts, and the truck was enveloped in choking clouds of it that filled the eyes, ears and nostrils of Jim and his companion. They snorted and coughed and spat mud to clear their throats. The truck stalled, and the driver fumbled the shift as he tried to start it again.

"Hey, guy, you're not driving a Navy truck now. This old bus cost me a lot of dough. Let me drive. I know this road."

Tom Nesviki, the owner of the truck, a short squat Hopi, with a red *banda* around his square-cut hair, slid over into the driver's seat as the other Indian opened the door and stepped out to look at the tires. He, too, was a Hopi, but rather tall and slim for one of the tribe. His Navy "blues" looked incongruous on an Indian and doubly so against the desert landscape.

They had taken the road north from Winslow to the Hopi towns. Ahead of them was the fantastic landscape that

George Herriman so loved to use as a background for his Krazy Kat cartoons. Beyond, spreading in a great and gentle arch all across the horizon, were the Hopi buttes, their triangles, rectangles and other odd geometric shapes clean-lined black figures against a cloudless Arizona sky. It was like no other skyline in the world.

The older Hopi, now driving the truck, was anxious to be on his way.

"Come on, General Pershing, you'll have lots of time to look at the country. Let's get home; I'm hungry."

"Hey, boy, I was in the Navy, not the Army," protested Jim Talastewa.

As he climbed back into the cab of the truck, he pulled out a package of cigarettes and passed it to his companion.

"Here, Tom, have a fag."

Tom did not take his eyes off the road as he reached for the cigarette that Jim lit for him. For several minutes nothing more was said. The truck lurched from chuck-hole to chuck-hole, and a comet's tail of dust stretched a hundred yards behind them. His cigarette finished, Tom began to hum a Hopi song, beating out the rhythm against the battered floor boards with his free foot.

"What song's that?"

"Why, sailor, don't you remember the Long-haired Kachina Song? Just before you enlisted, we all went over to Moencopi to see that dance. You heard it all day long. You ought to remember that one, Jim."

Jim sensed from Tom's tone that he was hurt by the younger man's failure to remember. As clan brothers, they would know the same songs and be expected to remember them forever.

"Hell, Tom, I've been away since 1917! A lot happened in those seven years. I've been a white man all that time, Tom. Maybe I should never have come back. What the hell will I do out here?"

"You can grow corn like the rest of us. You said you had some money saved up. You can buy some good sheep. You will be better off than the rest of us Hopi farmers!" There was a shred of envy, even of antagonism in the older man's voice.

"What a life that would be for a guy! To eat mutton and corn and mutton, day in, day out, day in, day out, year after year to plant corn, only to see it wither and die for lack of rain—to raise sheep for the Navajos to steal! What a life for a guy after all the places I've seen! God, I can't even remember my own language! I was just a little over sixteen when I enlisted. Boy, how we all lied about my age!"

Although Jim seemed to direct his words to his companion, he really was musing aloud in the fashion so typically Hopi. Tom sensed this and smiled to himself.

"Why have you come back to us, Jim? To show off how much like a white man you have become? To tell all the boys and young men how often you were drunk and how many white girls you were able to get in New York and Los Angeles?"

"Don't get sore, Tom. I didn't mean anything by shooting my mouth off in Winslow. Lying there on those two dirty cots in that filthy shack after I got off the train made me sore. Hell, after seven years in the Navy, they wouldn't rent us a room in a decent hotel or boardinghouse! No, a filthy shack was good enough for filthy Indians!"

"Nobody said that to us, Jim."

"No, they didn't need to say anything. The signs outside those two decent places both said *Vacancy,* but when we wanted to rent there was no vacancy! I got the idea—they didn't need to say anything! The officers on the ship didn't treat me like a dirty Indian. It's hard to come back to Arizona and run into that again. When I went into that beer joint last night, the guy there wouldn't serve me. 'We can't serve Indians here, boy.' Then he takes me to one side and whispers to me about a joint on the other side of the Santa Fe tracks! 'There,' he says, 'you can get all the beer you want and they've a couple of swell Mexican girls, too.' Christ! Now I'm back in Arizona and I'm an Indian again. Christ!"

"Can't you say anything but 'Christ!' Jim?

"Have you become a Christian, too, since you went

away?" The older Hopi laughed bitterly.

"No, I have not become a Christian. I have become nothing. I believe in nothing but myself. Don't expect me to dance around with a snake in my mouth thinking the snakes will make it rain. I'm too smart for that old stuff. And don't let any of those damned missionaries come around me, either, telling me that Jesus is coming. They've been saying that since I was a kid. Why didn't He come and stop the damn war?"

The older Hopi had no reply. Jim passed him a cigarette, hoping that another smoke might bring some better feeling between them. As boys, he and Tom had been great friends. They had gone on long rabbit-hunting trips together. They had worked together in the fields. The older boy had taught the younger one not only how to throw the boomerang-like rabbit stick and how to hoe weeds, but also an endless variety of Hopi songs. As they lay together under a brush shelter near the clan corn fields, Tom had recounted to Jim the traditional legends of the Hopi people.

Jim was five years younger than Tom, but Tom looked old enough to be his father. Hopi life is hard. Tom's deeply lined face was that of a serious, wise, mature man, while Jim in his neatly cut Navy uniform looked like a college boy in his teens.

An hour or so passed in complete silence. Tom held his eyes to the road, but Jim gazed in all directions, taking in the land which he had not seen for seven years. They passed some Navajo children herding sheep just a few hundred feet away from the road. Still farther back was a log and adobe mud hogan with smoke sifting through a smoke hole in the conical roof.

"I didn't remember any Navajo hogans along this road," remarked Jim.

"No, there weren't any here when you went away. The Navvies have moved into this part of our reservation only in the past few years. The old men say they didn't use to be in this part of the country at all."

"It must make it sort of tough to have their reservation all around ours."

"Yes, it does. They seem to stand in better with Washington than we Hopi do."

"Can't our chiefs do anything about it?"

"What can they do – go to war against the Navajo? Don't forget – we're people of peace."

"There were a couple of Navajo kids at our training depot – swell kids."

Tom grunted.

At noon, they stopped near a small spring not far from the road and washed the dust from their faces and hands. Then Tom produced from a white cotton bag some of the blue wafer-like Hopi bread called *piki* and a handful of dried peaches, so leathery that Jim could hardly eat them. Then they had another smoke and dozed a bit in the sun before driving on.

Eating the *piki* brought back to Jim a flood of memories. What would his mother think of him now? He had worn the uniform to show it to her. Could he remember enough Hopi to talk to her? He tried to recall some words. . . .

"Hey, Tom – *Ingu-u* –that's the word for mother, isn't it?"

"Yes, *Ingu-u,*" Tom replied.

Jim repeated it two or three times and the repetition of the word brought back added memories. He remembered the warmth and tenderness of his mother's arms, when she had carried him home the day he fell from that little cliff above their clan spring. He had been cold with pain and fear until she had found him and borne him swiftly, but gently, up the steep trail to their home. He remembered, too, how her two older sisters, the aunts who were almost as close to him as his own mother, had examined his leg with intelligent fingers, to be sure that there were no broken bones, and how they had comforted him. He was just about to ask Tom about them – if they were still alive – when the truck climbed a slight ridge and there, directly before them, across the wide, almost level desert valley, were the Hopi mesas. Tom brought the truck to a halt and the two of them sat there, drinking in the sight.

They could just make out the doors and windows of the

houses of their own village, Shongopovi, on the middle mesa. The houses built of the same rock as the mesa, seemed one with the cliffs. Only the black squares and rectangles of the windows and doors and an occasional plastered wall betrayed the fact that there really was a village on the mesa top. They could see their road sweeping away across the wash and then climbing steeply up the mesa. Away to the east, on another arm of the mesa, were the twin villages of Mishongnovi and Shipolovi, but they were too far away to be clearly discernible.

Prominent in the west was the conical-shaped butte which served as a landmark for the ancient village of Oraibi. The village itself merged with its mesa rock. Only the church of the Christian missionary stood up like a defiant exclamation point against the sky which already was being colored with the pageantry of an Arizona sunset. Here and there could be seen the sandy corn fields, bare at this winter season. In small orchards, close to the mesa, a few dead-looking peach trees struggled for survival. Still farther to the west, loomed the purple and rose bulk of the mountain massif of the San Francisco peaks — to the Hopi, the home of their Kachinas, the intermediary spirits between them and their gods.

For some time, great white clouds had been piling up and now they dominated the scene — huge, flat-bottomed masses of cumulus touched with tones of red, yellow, and orange. Beyond these a band of olive-tinted clouds with vivid streaks of yellow and red swept across the sky in dramatic contrast.

The two Hopi continued to stare at the spectacle without exchanging a word. Tears came to Jim's eyes. This was his homeland. How beautiful it was! In spite of his doubts and misgivings, he knew that somehow he *did* belong here.

A tiny wisp of white cloud just above the topmost peak of the mountains of the Kachinas turned for a brief second a glorious molten gold. Jim breathed a faint, *"Lolomi! Lolomi!"*

Tom smiled quietly. No "Hell!" this time, only "Lolomi!" the lovely Hopi word which implies that all is beautiful and peaceful, sometimes uttered in greeting, sometimes in heartfelt prayer.

Tom knew that for all his errant talk, Jim was still a Hopi.

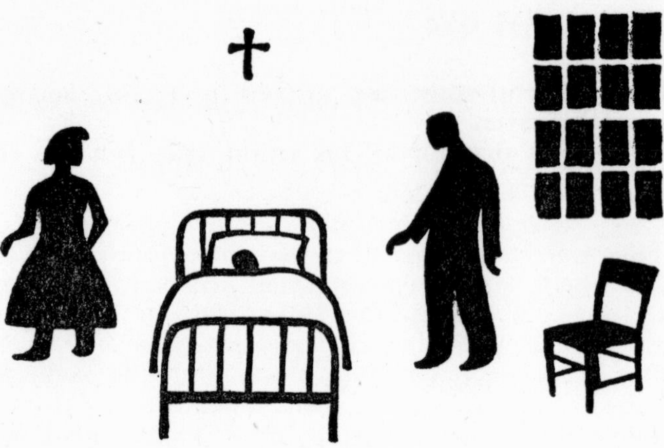

II

THE BOY'S ROUND HEAD was black against the dead white of the hospital sheets. His face was a sickly olive-brown, and his frightened dark eyes followed the nurse apprehensively. He had never been in a hospital – he'd heard all kinds of stories about them. Anything could happen in a hospital – doctors cut people open there – people died there. The one somewhat reassuring fact was that the nurse was an Indian like himself – she looked like a Hopi, even – one of his own people. But he was too feverish to think clearly.

As he lay there, it was hard for him to believe that he was really not very far from home. But he had never been to Keams Canyon and the twenty miles there from Shongopovi had seemed endless to him. This quiet place frightened him. The nurse in her stiff white uniform was like no Hopi woman that he could remember.

Now she was coming back to him, in her hand a small hypodermic. His eyes dilated with fright and he cringed away from her. Her hands were warm and kind as she took his arm, swabbed it quickly with alcohol, and expertly injected a sedative. She laid the hypodermic and cotton on a table, then sat down on the edge of the bed and smiled at him.

"What is your name?" she asked in Hopi.

"Leonard," he replied.

"No – what is your own name, your Hopi name?"

They were not supposed to use their Hopi names at the Indian School. He remembered that first morning when the white teacher had made them stand up one by one as she gave them names to suit her fancy.

"Sequa-Honau." The boy pronounced the name softly and slowly. He was beginning to feel drowsy.

The nurse repeated it after him, *"Sequa-Honau* – Blue Bear."

At that moment the door opened and a young doctor came in. He, too, was all in white, and he wore glasses that sparkled in the bright light of the room. Drowsy as the boy was, he stirred uneasily as he looked up at the doctor.

Kathleen Lensa, the nurse, stood up and put her finger to her lips.

"I think he is almost asleep," she whispered. "He is very frightened. I just gave him a sedative."

She and the doctor walked slowly away from the bed and Sequa-Honau, reassured, fell asleep.

"I've been up at your village, Kathleen, watching the Soyal Kachina arrive. Some day you must tell me what it's all about. But what happened to this youngster?"

"I'm not too sure. It seems he collapsed in school and the teacher had him brought here. In a note she explained that he has just come to Shongopovi from Bacobi to live with an aunt, because his mother died. She thinks he hasn't been having enough to eat."

Tears came to Kathleen's eyes as she spoke. She brushed them away with a quick gesture, then looked over at the sleeping youngster and turned down the light. In silence she and the doctor walked into an adjoining office.

"Why isn't more done about all this sort of thing?" she burst out passionately. "Here it is 1924 and there are still Indians on the reservation that have not enough to eat. It's time the noble white man –"

"Kathleen, you must pull yourself together. I agree with you completely, as you know, but right now we have patients to consider. What have you done for this youngster?"

"I'm sorry, Don. He was so pathetic when they brought him in that it still upsets me. I am sorry — I've not done much really, besides trying to make him comfortable. I bathed him — he's skin and bones — and, as I said, I gave him a sedative."

They walked back into the ward. The boy awoke as Kathleen adjusted the covers. When he saw the doctor he shrank away.

"This is Dr. Cummings, Sequa-Honau."

The boy looked at him shyly.

"Let's see if he can take a bit of food," suggested the doctor as he sat down on a chair by the bed. "I like that name," he said to the boy with a smile.

In a few minutes the boy relaxed and his apprehension began to fade. Dr. Cummings reached over and took his pulse. By the time Kathleen returned with something for him to eat, Sequa-Honau was telling the doctor all about his home in Bacobi.

Kathleen fed him slowly. When he finished, the youngster smiled at the two of them and slid down into the bed with a little sigh of content.

"See you in the morning, Mr. Blue Bear," Dr. Cummings called back as he and Kathleen turned off the light and left the room.

"He'll be all right, Kathleen. He'll be back at Shongopovi in a few days, none the worse for wear."

"But, Don, we ought to find out a little more about him and this aunt that he has just come to live with."

"Well, I'll drive him there myself when it's time for him to go home and see what the situation is. Do you remember her at all?"

"I've been away from the village so much these last years that I don't know all the families any more."

"Well, don't worry. We'll see that Sequa-Ho — some of these Hopi names of yours stump me," he laughed. "Anyway, we'll see that the Blue Bear is well taken care of."

"Oh, that will be fine, Don!"

"Dr. Cummings to you, young lady. Come here."

He took her in his arms.

"Do you still insist that you must marry a Hopi one of these days? I still think that you and I could make a fine go of it."

Kathleen gently pulled away from him, then looked directly at him and said, "You are wonderful, Don. You are the only white man I have ever known who talks to me and looks at me as if I were just like any other woman and not an Indian squaw in a nurse's uniform – a queer sort of curiosity. But, Don, it just can't be. I know now, even more than I ever have known it, that my job is to stay here and help these people as a Hopi. I can really do that only by becoming one of them, by taking my place as a married woman and a mother in my mother's clan."

"But, Kathleen – you are a nurse. You can't go back to Shongopovi and live on corn and mutton. You could not be content to be the wife of a Hopi farmer making, maybe, two hundred dollars a year! What kind of life would that be for you?"

"I know, Don. I know only too well that it may very well be impossible. It seems impossible to me when I think about it. The young men of my age have nearly all been away from the reservation – in the Army or Navy. They come back here with a taste for liquor and manner of living that is completely foreign to our Hopi way of life. The ones who have not been away seem so dirty and so superstitious – I don't know how it will work out, Don. Maybe I'll just have to become an old maid public health nurse like – oh, well, some day I'll know the answer."

"But, Kathleen, couldn't we get married and go away from here – maybe to some other reservation? Every Indian tribe I know of in this Western country needs medical help. We could be transferred up to the Blackfeet at Browning in Montana or to the Arapaho and Shoshone at Wind River in Wyoming. I love you, Kathleen! More than anything else in the world I want you to be the mother of my kids!" With a sudden movement he seized her in his arms once again and kissed her. "As I watched you feed that poor half-starved youngster in there I realized what a wonderful mother you'd be. Kathleen, please – please!"

"No, Don." She released herself slowly. "No. You are the finest man I have ever known. The fight you made against Superintendent Lyons, who thinks that Hopi women belong over their grinding stones and not in the uniform of a nurse, was wonderful. I shall always be deeply grateful to you for that. I shall never forget your endless kindness to every Indian that has been brought here. In a way, Don, I do love you, and I respect you – but I have made up my mind and –" she looked up at him directly, "you know how stubborn we Hopi people are!"

•

III

THE TRUCK WAS BROUGHT to a stop against a pile of piñon and juniper logs. As the two men clambered down, Tom pointed to the wood and remarked, "Our food supply may be low, but at least we'll be warm this winter."

They walked toward the low irregular block of houses clustered along the edge of the mesa. To the south they could see the Painted Desert with its irregular buttes and the dusty stretch of road over which they had just driven. As they entered the first plaza between the houses, Hopi children stared curiously at Jim. Two or three very young ones decided he was a stranger and scampered to their homes, while the older ones laughed in a sort of embarrassment, covering their mouths with their hands as they did so.

The houses of Jim's mother's clan were in the last block near the mesa's tip. An old burro flapping its ears in the dusk might have been the same one that stood in that very place when he was a boy. Nothing seemed changed. The familiar wooden door of his own house was shut, but from the old chimney, made from three large pottery cooking pots, with the bottoms knocked out, wisps of smoke sailed off in the gentle breeze. Tom called out something in Hopi which Jim did not understand. A woman answered from within and the door opened almost at once to reveal the short chunky figure of Nasayungti.

Jim experienced a moment of relief at recalling his mother's Hopi name — a good name in their village, he knew. The woman stood there, wiping her hands on her cotton skirt, her round, kind face wreathed in smiles. Jim found he was pleased that she still dressed her hair in the old Hopi fashion with two large bound rolls on either side of her face.

The first moments of shyness over, his mother came quickly to him and greeted him in a torrent of Hopi. Jim put his arms around her and started to kiss her, but he stopped in confusion as he realized that kissing would be foreign to her. She patted his sides with her hands and laid her face against his chest. She seemed almost pathetically small as she looked up at him and smiled and talked. He could think of nothing to say to her in Hopi. Why could he not remember some words? His halting English phrases were incomprehensible to her, he knew, but in her excitement at his return nothing he was saying, or trying to say, would have had much meaning.

From the house next door came another woman, older than his mother, her face seamed and wrinkled. Her wide grin displayed almost toothless gums as she came up to him in voluble greeting. She, too, patted him in obvious delight at his return.

Tom helped out. "She is your aunt. They both say you are welcome home."

As his mother led him into the house, she looked up at him with such tenderness and joy that he found himself deeply moved. Why had he written so few letters to her? Someone would have read them to her. Why should she be so proud to have him back after his long silence and all his neglect? That she was proud it was easy to see as she patted his arm and timidly spoke, as if to herself, a few words of her limited English, "My boy! My boy!"

They stepped into the square room with its hard adobe floor, unevenly plastered white walls, and pole-and-brush ceiling. Jim's eyes took in its sparse furnishings. No doubt he had used most of them before he went away. The usual pile of sheepskins and blankets lay folded on a low seat that ran along the back wall. There were odds and ends of small boxes and stools, worn smooth and shiny with much use. An old wood-burning cook-stove stood in one corner, and in another a battered table held a large kerosene lamp and a few dishes. Prayer plumes of eagle down hung from one of the roof poles, protection for the house against disaster. Coral, shell, and silver necklaces decorated the wall near the table. On another wall, into a coarsely-woven wicker mat, were stuck some old and faded photographs.

Nasayungti picked up one of the pictures and with a laugh handed it to Jim, repeating, as she did so, her little English phrase, "My boy!" It was a snapshot one of the white teachers at the school had made of him when he was twelve years old. What a frightened-looking kid he was! It had taken great courage to have his picture taken in those days. The old Hopi had told him – and he knew they really believed it – that when someone took your picture he took something of your soul away with him.

As he put back the picture, he noticed on the opposite wall three highly colored, carved wooden dolls – *kachina* dolls. The feathers were bedraggled and the paint in many places was peeling off, but he suddenly recalled them completely. One of his uncles had made them for him and presented them to him at one of the great ceremonials.

When his mother saw him looking at them, she pointed to them one by one and repeated their names for him, "*Anga Kachina, Koyemsi Kachina, Tawa Kachina.*" Then she pointed back to the first doll and said in English, "Long-haired *Kachina,*" and to the others in turn, "Hopi Clown *Kachina,*" and "Sun *Kachina.*"

She laughed as she spoke, as if she found her knowledge of English very amusing. Jim sensed that she was treating him as if he were a very small boy who had to re-learn his Hopi language and customs.

Tom had brought Jim's things, a duffel bag and a suitcase, and then he had left. Jim's old aunt, too, had returned to her dwelling. He and his mother were alone. She showed him where to stow away his possessions, and as he put them away he watched her prepare supper.

He was reassured to find that everything in the house was clean. His mother herself looked scrubbed and her cotton dress was neat and well cared for. For days he had been worrying about this. There were no toilets at Shongopovi, he remembered — in fact he could recall sharply the smell of urine in the streets. Could he accept the dirt and lack of sanitation which seven years in the spick-and-span Navy had made him loathe? Well, the house was O.K. Maybe in spite of the lack of an adequate water supply things might not be as bad as he feared.

His mother set the simple food on a bit of clean oilcloth spread upon the floor and pulled up two little stools for them to sit on. There was a bowl of mutton stew, some strange-looking gobs of corn meal something like dumplings, *piki,* stewed peaches and a pot of strong black coffee. None of it was particularly inviting, but he knew that from the Hopi standpoint it was an opulent meal. He thought of the food on the ship, and he had no appetite for this. Again reassuring himself that it was clean, he forced himself to eat. It didn't taste too bad, and he managed to eat enough to satisfy Nasayungti.

As she cleaned up and put things away, he pulled out his cigarettes and had a smoke. He wondered if he could ever get used to eating nothing but that sort of grub. What were the fellows back on the ship eating tonight? — she'd still be in San Francisco. What movies would they be showing on Market Street? He'd be missing all the fun. God! It was only now really dark — and what was he going to do the rest of the night? — go to bed?

IV

JIM HEARD SOMEONE at the door, but before he could reach it it was pushed open and Tom entered.

"Come on over to the *kiva*. We're practicing for a Buffalo Dance."

"But I don't belong –"

"I talked with Nemtaka and it's O.K. for you to come."

"Nemtaka?"

"He's village chief now. Come on. All the young people will be there. They want to say hello to you."

His mother had caught the words "Buffalo Dance" and "*kiva*," and she nodded her agreement.

As Jim was going out the door he suddenly remembered the name of those dumpling-like things he had had for supper – *hurucucki*. They tasted better now that he knew their Hopi name. Outside he stumbled after Tom until his eyes got used to the darkness. He could dimly make out several others bound in the same direction. Some of them exchanged guttural words of greeting with Tom. The *kiva* was only a few hundred feet from his house. He recalled the large rectangular room excavated in the solid rock of the mesa with only about two feet of the wall above the mesa level. It was as old as the village itself.

They could plainly hear an occasional drum beat, as if someone were playing it just for idle amusement, but by the time they reached the entrance the drum had stopped. The entrance was a small square hatchway from which projected the two long poles of a ladder. Jim was used to the darkness now, and he looked up to see the sky powdered with stars. Tom went down the ladder first and Jim followed him, somewhat uncertainly feeling around with his feet.

As he turned from the foot of the ladder he found himself looking directly into the expressionless faces of about thirty young men and women. For a moment there was an embarrassed silence. He felt completely out of place in his Navy uniform. Here he was, surrounded by the boys and girls he had gone to school with, but none of them looked familiar to him. What was he doing in this place anyway? Why hadn't he re-enlisted? Right now he'd be walking down Market Street with some of the fellows from the ship and they would have some time of it. Now here he was, looking like a damn fool in his Navy blues, with a bunch of dirty Indians at the bottom of a hole in the ground, waiting to thump a drum and sing a bunch of songs he didn't remember — and didn't want to remember — the words of. He *was* a damn fool.

His unhappy thoughts were interrupted by one of the young men stepping forward and addressing him in Hopi. When it was obvious that Jim did not understand, the speaker switched to English.

"We are glad to see you back, Jim. I am your Uncle Hubert. Don't you remember me?"

The man was at least five years younger than Jim, but Jim recalled enough about the intricacies of Hopi relationships not to be surprised at this. Yes, he did remember Hubert now. The little kid had gone along on the last rabbit hunt just before he enlisted. He took Hubert's proffered hand.

This gesture broke the ice. The others crowded around

him with laughter and comments and joking. Shortly afterward a few old Hopi men entered, then the younger group found seats around the walls of the *kiva* and settled themselves to rehearse the various songs of the Buffalo Dance. One of the old men took the drum between his knees and softly began to tap out the rhythms of one of the songs.

At that moment Jim looked up and saw a girl coming down the *kiva ladder*. Two steps from the bottom she turned and jumped lightly to the floor. Although Jim could not understand the words with which they all greeted her, there was no question about her popularity. When she saw him she spoke directly to him, "Welcome home to Shongopovi, Jim. We are all glad that you have come back. You don't remember me? My name is Kathleen." She shook his hand and then turned to join the group along the walls.

Jim watched her as she talked and laughed with them. Like himself, she was slim and tall for a Hopi. She was dressed like a Hopi girl, from her moccasins to the coral beads at her throat, but her brilliantly-colored print dress fitted her well, accenting rather than distorting the grace and suppleness of her body. She had a sparkle of animation that set her apart from the other young women present. He had always thought that Hopi girls were the most attractive of all the Indian ones he had known, and Shongopovi had long boasted that its women were the most beautiful of Hopi women. He had no remembrance of her as a young girl. How could he have forgotten her? Even as a child she must have been beautiful.

The old man with the drum now began to pound out the rhythms so that in the narrow confines of the *kiva* the chatter of young voices was almost drowned out. One of the other old men started a song, and the young people once more settled themselves to the purpose of the evening. This first song was one they all seemed to know and soon their voices swelled to its impelling rhythm. They sang full-throated and with joy. The elders beamed their approval.

Jim found that he, too, was beating out the rhythm with his foot. The song began to come back to him, and he joined in the singing. They went over it a second time. Now he remembered it all, and he found himself singing with the joy and abandon of the rest of them. He observed that they were looking at him and nodding and smiling. Across the *kiva* Kathleen was singing, but her eyes were closed and her face seemed masked by sadness. As he watched her she opened her eyes and nodded to him and slowly smiled.

Why had she looked so sad until that moment? Why had she such assurance in English when the others used it so timidly? Yet she had spoken Hopi to the group. As the evening wore on he found himself constantly watching her, but she seemed oblivious of him. Their eyes did not meet again. He decided she was one of the most beautiful girls he had ever seen. Girls had been easy to get when he was in the Navy. Well, here was one that might make life interesting at Shongopovi — things might not be so dull back on the reservation after all!

It was midnight when the rehearsal was over. As they emerged from the fetid humidity of the *kiva* into the sparkling, cool night air, it was like taking a deep cold drink on a hot day. Jim hoped for a word with Kathleen as she came up the ladder, but somehow in the darkness she escaped him. Tom and he walked home together in silence, and Tom bade him goodnight at his door.

His mother had left the lamp turned down. She awoke and smiled up at him from her bed of sheepskins and blankets on the floor. He went over and patted her. Then he dipped some water from a full bucket near the door and washed himself in a small basin, throwing the dirty water out into the street. He made his bed in a corner of the room, but before lying down he took out a pair of blue jeans, a denim shirt, and work shoes and set them beside his bed. In the morning he would fold up his uniform and put it away.

•

V

IT WAS STILL DARK when Jim awoke. In the vague distance he could hear a man calling out in a sort of singsong cadence. He was astonished to find that he could distinguish many of the Hopi words: "Everyone awake! Arise! Become children of light, vigorous, active, and filled with joy! – Today the men of the Bear Clan will hoe weeds in the corn planting of the clan mother."

His mother's clan was the Bear Clan and his mother was the head woman of that clan. They were going to hoe weeds in her corn field. Why? Where was his father? He had wanted to ask that question as soon as he returned. His father had gone away when he was a very small boy and Jim could remember him only vaguely. What had happened? He searched his memory for the Hopi word – *ina-a,* that was it, *ina-a,* father.

He turned over and saw that his mother was already up. The stove was lit. He could see her moving in the faint light that was coming through the small windows. He pulled on his new clothes and washed up. Then he went to his mother and, pointing to her, said, "*Ingu-u,* my mother."

She nodded and laughed and repeated, *"Ingu-u,"* and then in English, "Mother."

Then he questioned, *"Ina-a?"*

His mother's face changed and she said simply, *"Maski."*

The word was unfamiliar to him, but he sensed that his father was dead.

Breakfast consisted of more mutton stew and strong coffee. He yearned for a plateful of ham and eggs. Before he had dwelt on this long enough to feel sorry for himself, Tom entered. He joined them at breakfast and gave Jim a simple explanation of the day's plans in which he would be expected to participate.

"You will come with us to clear the ground for your mother's corn planting. Today we will need to hoe brush there so as to clear the fields to be planted next year."

"Sure – I'll go. But what happened to my old man, Tom? I know he wasn't around much when I was a kid. He just sort of disappeared one day. What happened to him?"

"Oh, he went off to Winslow to work for the Santa Fe," Tom replied. "For a while he came back now and then for one of the big ceremonies, and then he stopped coming back. Nobody knows what happened. Your mother divorced him, so we look after her corn for her."

Two older men, several young ones, and a boy whom they called Sequa-Honau now entered. Jim's mother exclaimed with delight at seeing the boy, and Tom explained that the youngster had been in the hospital at Keams Canyon where Dr. Cummings had taken good care of him. Now he was living with an aunt in Shongopovi because his mother had died.

Jim's mother had coffee for all of them before they started off for her fields. She provided him with a small cotton bag with food in it such as most of the men were carrying. Sequa-Honau had a Boy Scout canteen filled with water, and one of the old men carried a pottery water jar with the end of a corncob stuffed in as a cork. They all carried heavy hoes, and Tom had found an extra one for Jim to use.

The sun was just rising as they left the mesa top. They

trotted down the narrow winding trail between the great blocks of rock of the talus slopes on the west side of the mesa. It was easy enough going down the steep trail, but when they reached the sand hills of the desert Jim had a hard time keeping up. Even the old men and the young boy continued without the least sign of fatigue, but he was winded before they had gone a mile.

He finally called to Tom, "Hey! Stop for a while and let me get my wind."

They all stopped and laughed at him, but it was a friendly laugh – it did not hurt – and he found himself laughing with them. He found that more and more of his language was coming back to him, and he timidly ventured a few words. He hated to say things incorrectly and have them laugh at him, but he didn't mind this group so much – they were the men of his mother's clan, his clan uncles, and they were friendly to him.

It was a good three miles out to where the next year's corn was to be planted, and they had to stop for him four or five times on the way. He felt that he had already done a good day's work by the time they arrived there.

After placing their food and water in the shade of a little brush shelter the group set to work. They located four patches where the corn would be sure to get the moisture it needed. It had been some time since this area had been planted, and there was plenty to do. They separated out to the different patches, and soon the rhythmic flailing of the hoes was the only sound to be heard.

The sun was high now, and the sweat ran down Jim's back. He took off his shirt as the others had done and worked in just his blue jeans and Navy shoes. After about two hours had passed, one of the old men let out a yell which was the signal for them to gather in the shade for lunch. The scanty meal was soon finished and, after they had all taken turns drinking from the canteen and the pottery jar, Tom produced a package of cigarettes, and all except the boy had a leisurely smoke.

As one of the old men finished his cigarette he turned and addressed Jim, who found that it was not hard to understand the drift of what was being said — more and more of his language was coming back to him.

"We are happy that you have come back to us, but you have been away so long that it is as if you came back to us a white man, not a Hopi. You do not speak Hopi with us. You do not think like a Hopi. You must now talk Hopi with us, and soon you will again think like us."

The old man paused. Tom passed him another cigarette which he lit and puffed on for a few seconds before he continued.

"Our life is hard out here on the desert. It is not easy to live as we Hopi live. You have eaten well and lived well among the white people. It will be hard for you to be a Hopi again. But you will find that the white man has not all the truth — all the wisdom — in the world. You will find something here with your own people that you never found when you were a white man. We here are all your uncles. I am your uncle and I am also your father."

Jim looked at him in surprise.

"No, I am not your real father — he has gone. But when you were a very small boy you once were very sick. As is our Hopi way, your mother gave you to me as my son so that I could cure you. I am a Hopi doctor, so I adopted you and cured you. Now I will be a father to you again. I will help you in your ceremonies. You will soon be a Hopi again."

Jim looked curiously at the old Hopi as he finished speaking. What a dirty-looking old guy, he thought, but he somehow remembered the courtesy expected of him and murmured, *"Askwali."*

They all roared with laughter, for Jim had used the form of *"Thank you"* that is used only by Hopi women. He realized his mistake at once and searched his memory for the right form, then he joined their laughter as he corrected it, *"Qua-qui."* The old man, Lololomi they called him, patted him on the back as they all got up to return to their hoeing.

By the middle of the afternoon, Jim's back was cracking in two. He tried a short rest, but after it he was so stiff that he could hardly straighten up. The trot back to the village and the stiff climb up the mesa nearly killed him. He had to stop repeatedly, and always the young boy stayed behind with him and joked him. A brat of a youngster, he thought. As he climbed over the edge of the mesa he was suddenly aware of three girls sitting on the cliff's edge. Kathleen was one of them. They called to him, laughing at his fatigue.

"Oh, so you have become a Hopi farmer again!" It was Kathleen's voice that mocked him.

He wiped the sweat and dirt from his face as well as he could and walked over to them.

"Are we to go to the *kiva* tonight?" he asked in faltering Hopi.

Kathleen's mockery disappeared and she replied, "Yes. It is only a week until the dance and there will be rehearsals every night."

"Well, I'll see you there," he called back as he started for the house.

Stiff and sore as he was, he certainly could eat some of that damn mutton stew tonight!

When he got to the *kiva* that evening Kathleen was not there. When he asked one of the girls about her, she giggled and said in broken English, "Kathleen gone to the hospital at Keams Canyon, she a nurse there."

Although he knew his questions would cause gossip among them, he had to know. "Will she come back for the dance?"

The girl giggled again and this time she replied in Hopi, "She will be in the dance."

That night all the words of the songs came back to him. He found that he was strangely exhilarated when the old man with the drum told him to get a costume ready for the ceremony.

VI

JIM SPENT THE FOLLOWING DAY visiting clan relatives and talking with other young men throughout the village. Many of them had been in the armed services, but none of them had been away as long as he had. They all spoke of how hard it was to readjust to Hopi life. Their talk soon turned to the booze fights they had had and the girls they had known. Hopi-like, there was no mention of the fighting in which they had had a part.

During the afternoon old Lololomi joined in one of their conversations. After smoking in silence for a long time, he turned to Jim and asked, "What work are you going to do with us? Are you going to plant corn and be a farmer? Will you have sheep? Are you going to work for Washington?" This last was said with evident distaste and disapproval.

Jim realized that the other young men were eager for his answer. He considered for a while and then, as if he were thinking aloud, he replied, "I remember that there was a Hopi over at Old Oraibi who had learned from some Navajo how to do silver work. He made some very beautiful necklaces, bracelets, rings, wrist guards such as we wear in the dances — all kinds of things. When the white people came out at Snake Dance time he sold them and got good money for them, too. I would like to do silver work like that. I —"

The boy, Sequa-Honau, who was listening to all the talk, interrupted him, "That is Bill Lanta. He is my uncle. He still makes things of silver. He no longer plants corn. He has another man do that for him and he pays him with money he gets from selling the silver."

Old Lololomi smiled at the lad's eagerness. "Yes, we all know Bill Lanta. He is a good Hopi. He is now showing other Hopi how to work in silver. I am sure he will be glad to teach you. It is work that is good to look at, and it is good for the heart of the man who does it. You should go to Oraibi and see Lanta."

Jim nodded as if in agreement. When he was a small boy he had liked to draw. The teachers in school had given him paper and pencil and crayons to encourage him, but for years he had not thought about it. Maybe he could design silver. Maybe what he had just spoken of was a real desire, though he had said it more because Lololomi expected some sort of answer to his question than for any other reason. He could not have explained why he suddenly thought of the old silver craftsman.

As the group broke up there was desultory talk of village affairs, of corn planting, of sheep. Jim was suddenly aware that Sequa-Honau was looking up at him eagerly. "If you ever have sheep may I herd them for you?"

Jim laughed, "Well, I've only been back a few days. Maybe I will have some sheep some day, and if I do I'll remember you."

The youngster scampered off and Lololomi looked after him with an affectionate smile on his old face.

"We are glad to see him well again. He tells everyone how good Kathleen and Dr. Cummings were to him in the hospital. He follows Kathleen all the time. Now he will follow you, too."

Jim wandered off by himself and sat down on the edge of the mesa, pondering the afternoon's talk. What *would* he do out here? He had plenty of money saved up — he didn't have to decide right now. Maybe he would plant a little corn, enough for himself and his mother, and maybe he would get some sheep or some cattle. He'd be a lot better off than most Hopi. Maybe he could do some work on the government buildings or on the road and make a little extra money. Maybe he would learn to make silver. But why should he stay out here where life was so hard, where there was so little fun to be had? He could get a good job in Frisco. He had skill with tools. He could make good money in the city.

He began to wonder about Kathleen. What sort of girl was she, anyway? Nurses had to be smart. They made good money, too, a lot more than some men. Why was she back on the reservation? They needed nurses in all the big city hospitals. What was it that had drawn them both back to this place? Did she have to get easy with the Hopi language again? Would he ever come to feel as much at home at Shongopovi as she seemed to?

He heard a foot scrape on the rock and he looked up to find Kathleen standing above him. The professional small black leather bag which she carried and her stiff white nurse's uniform startled him momentarily.

"Don't look so surprised, sailor," she smiled as she spoke. "It's just me, Kathleen, the girl in the *kiva* night before last."

"Sure, I know — but I didn't expect to see you here in — in that outfit. I — I — didn't hear you come."

With her free hand she brushed off the rock edge and sat down.

"Why did you come back here, sailor? You made quite a record for yourself in the Navy, I hear." She spoke in Hopi, using only such English words as *sailor* and *Navy* for which there were no Hopi equivalents.

"Don't know exactly. Why did *you* come back? You could get a job as a nurse in town."

She looked far out over the desert. Some minutes passed before she replied. He could see her face cloud. Evidently it was hard for her to answer. "I do not know just how to answer, Jim." He was pleased, somehow, that she did not call him "sailor" this time. "I had a good position in Phoenix."

She continued, Hopi-like, in deep absorption, yet speaking her thoughts. "I was head nurse in the surgical ward of the hospital. There were three other Indian nurses there, too. The doctors and the white nurses were kind and really friendly. They didn't treat me like an Indian – I was just like any other nurse. But, somehow, I never felt as if I really belonged. I wanted to be with my own people. At night I would remember the drums reverberating in the *kivas*. Sometimes in the middle of the night I would wake up remembering the wonderful smell of juniper and piñon smoke. One day I suddenly knew that more than anything else I wanted to come back and take part in the ceremonies and feel that I was truly a Hopi again."

She seemed to have forgotten that Jim was there. As she looked far out over the desert the sadness that Jim had noted in the *kiva* again masked her features. At length she turned toward him. "And what about you?"

Jim could not speak as freely as she had, but he was aware that she had just voiced the very feelings that had haunted him time and time again during the years when he was away.

"Yes, I often felt that way, too. But how can you dance in the ceremonies? Do you honestly think that putting on crazy costumes and singing words we hardly know the meaning of can bring rain and good crops? Do you really believe the snakes are our brothers – that when the Snake Men free them after the dance they will go to the Underworld and persuade the gods to be good to the Hopi? Do you believe such things?"

His voice had risen in impassioned inquiry. Kathleen did not reply at once. Again she seemed off in a world of her own. When she did speak her voice was low and earnest.

"No, I don't believe the snakes will send rain. I don't believe that the *kachinas* that dance in our streets are gods — you and I were shown long ago that they are our own people dressed up. I believe none of these things, Jim, and yet, for some reason I find it hard to explain, I believe it is good for us to have the Snake Dance and the other ceremonies. When I was last here for one of them it was wonderful to see how it united every person in the village in a sort of community prayer. I felt part of that unity, one with the village, one with all Hopi!"

Deeply moved by her eloquence he turned as if to touch her. She failed to see his gesture, and her voice took on a different tone when she again spoke.

"When I was in training in Phoenix I often went with the other nurses to their Sunday church services — but it was not for me. I guess I'm nothing but a heathen Indian squaw!"

There was bitterness in her final words. She stood up to go.

"What *are* you going to do out here, Jim? Or maybe you aren't going to stay?"

"I don't know yet. I came out here to try to think it out."

"Oh, I'm sorry to have interrupted." Her words were genuine.

"You didn't interrupt; you have helped me. You know what it means to come back."

She nodded in understanding. Jim started to reach for her hand, but he stopped. Somehow it seemed wrong to touch her. Was it the white uniform that made her seem like one apart? Someone honked a horn.

"That must be Dr. Cummings," she said. "I am going with him to see some children at the Oraibi school." And she started to run toward the village.

He called after her, "Kathleen, will you be my partner in the Buffalo Dance?"

"Sure! Can you get the costume?" Her shouted reply was a challenge.

"I'll have it ready!"

He was not any too sure that she had heard him, but with a lightened heart he went home to supper. Somehow supper was a satisfying meal. Even the mutton stew seemed to be flavored better than usual. Nasayungti smiled at his improved appetite. He ventured to ask her about the costume he would need for the Buffalo Dance. Her reply showed that she understood.

"Lololomi comes tonight. He will help."

Even as she spoke there was a knock at the door and Lololomi entered. He knew enough English to supplement Jim's still halting Hopi.

"See – I have gotten for you the costumes you will want; for Kathleen, too, you must have one."

Was there a hint of a twinkle in his eye? How did this old fellow know that Kathleen would be his partner? Lololomi's words confirmed what Kathleen's last question had meant. He recalled that in some of the dances the man is supposed to supply his own and his partner's costume. Kathleen must have a fine one, on that he was determined.

His mother and the old Hopi were carefully sorting out the things that the latter had brought and some other items that his mother produced from the storeroom. Already on one pile lay the costume he would wear. It was, they said, complete and in good repair. Eagerly he turned to the one they were assembling for Kathleen. He could not make out what it consisted of but his mother's fingers seemed nimble and sure as she worked on a white embroidered blanket and some brilliantly colored plumes. Only the white buckskin moccasins and leggings seemed not to satisfy her.

"Take these," she said, "and whiten them."

"In the *kiva*," explained old Lololomi, "you will find white clay. Not tonight. It is late. I must go."

Jim was amazed to find how late it was – too late to go to the *kiva* for the rehearsal, he decided. Anyway, it was important to get the costume business settled. He'd do those buckskin things the first chance he got. He chuckled as he slipped between the blankets. From machine tools to white buckskin moccasins! He dozed off, wondering at her bitterness when she said, "nothing but a heathen Indian squaw." He found that he, too, hated that word "squaw."

VII

IT BEGAN TO SNOW early the next morning just as Jim was returning from the *kiva* where he had gone to get the clay for whitening the moccasins and leggings. He was glad to have some reason for sitting in his mother's warm house throughout the cold and blustery morning hours. His work was done by noon, however, and he grew restless for companionship. He decided to walk over to the house of Allan Lemtewa, one of the young men he had been talking with the day before. The snow had turned into a cold driving rain which made the narrow streets of the old village seem more forbidding than ever. Even his heavy Navy jacket failed to keep him comfortable.

He found Allan warming up an old dump truck and he asked what was up.

"Gotta go into Holbrook for a load of coal for the school," Allan explained. "Why don't you come along?"

Jim protested, but even as he did so he knew he would go. He had to get away from the reservation for a while anyway.

"Come on," urged Allan. "We'll get there before dark and spend the night in town and have a good time. In the morning we'll load the coal and be back here by noon." As Jim still seemed to hesitate he added by way of extra bait, "This is Saturday and there's lots doing in Holbrook on Saturday night."

"O.K. Wait till I get some dough."

Back at the house, Jim took two ten-dollar bills out of his suitcase. Maybe I ought to take all this dough into town, he thought, and put it in the bank. Then he remembered it was Saturday and the bank would be closed. He told his mother where he was going and that he would bring her back some wood. He sensed her displeasure that he was going into town. She said nothing, however, and he closed the door hurriedly, annoyed to find he had a disturbing feeling of guilt. But he was no kid who had to have mama's permission to go to town — he couldn't hang around home all the time.

"All set, Allan. Let's go," and the two of them piled into the cab of the truck and were off.

On the outskirts of Holbrook they stopped at a hamburger joint. Two Navajo and a couple of Mexican section hands were eating at a counter. Two girls were waiting on tables, and an older girl was frying hamburgers on a smoky gas plate in a corner back of the counter.

She turned as they opened the door and called out to Allan, "Welcome to our city, big boy. Make yourself at home. Who's your new friend?"

She looked Jim over appraisingly, noting the clean, pressed Navy jacket — just out of the service and with a pocketful of money, no doubt.

"Take care of Allan and his friend," she called to the waitresses as the two men sat down at one of the small tables. "Allan's a good Hopi!"

Without asking, the girls brought coffee and took their orders for hamburgers. One of the Navajo put a nickle in the slot, and a scratchy jukebox began to squeak out a record of *Toot Toot, Tootsie, Good-bye.* The Navajo listened to it in poker-faced silence. One of the girls went over to talk with them, but they did not seem very friendly now that some Hopi were there. In a few minutes they paid for their coffee and sandwiches and stalked out without a word.

As soon as they were gone Allan pulled one of the waitresses into his lap. At her giggles the older girl scolded, "Leave her be, Allan! Eat your hamburger and drink your coffee like good little boys 'til we close up the joint – then we'll have some fun, eh?"

The girl struggled free and Allan turned to Jim.

"Daisy there," he nodded towards the older girl, "has a swell little dump up back of the hill. We'll go up there afterward and have a little party!"

The Mexicans then left with a mumbled "So long," and the girls, with jokes and laughter, began to clean up the place for the night. Jim and Allan each had another cup of coffee; then they, too, started to leave.

"See you later," Allan called back to the girls. "Don't take too long."

It was dark when they stepped outside. The rain stopped while they were driving into town. They drove the old truck down to a barn near the Santa Fe tracks where they would pick up the coal in the morning, and parked it inside the yard. The watchman closed the gate after them. On their way back to join the girls they stopped at a service station run by a Hopi Allan knew and they used his toilet and wash basin. At a nearby drugstore Allan made a purchase, remarking as he did so that these white girls were damn particular. He then led the way to a little shack back of Kelly's bootleg liquor place.

"You got some dough, Jim?"

Jim nodded and Allan pushed open the door. They were greeted by a fox-faced Irishman.

"What do you Indians want?"

There was an accent on the "Indians" that Jim did not like. It was as if the Irishman took particular pleasure in reminding them that they were not whites and so had no right to be in a liquor place, even an illegal joint like this one.

Allan said something in reply that Jim did not hear, and the Irishman disappeared into the main room. In a few minutes he returned with two quarts of cheap gin. Jim handed him a ten-dollar bill.

"Six bucks each, buddy."

Allan produced the extra two dollars without protest, while Jim thought how his Navy pals would have handled the matter. The Irishman wrapped the bottles in an old newspaper and put them in a canned milk carton. Before he let the Indians leave he carefully looked up and down the street.

Ever since entering Daisy's place, Jim and Allan had been speaking English, and they continued to speak it as they walked up behind the small bare hill on the outskirts of Holbrook.

"What sort of dump are we going to?" Jim asked.

"It's the only house in town that an Indian can get in. She usually has about six girls, mostly Mexicans. Once in a while she gets a Navajo or a Paiute kid that has run away from her family. It's a neat little place."

"What does it cost?"

"Five bucks."

"Well, look, I put up most of the money for the liquor, but you gotta pay your way here."

Allan laughed. "I've been saving for this!"

They had come to a two-story frame house which sat alone on the side of the hill. Below them they could see the few scattered lights of Holbrook. A Santa Fe locomotive panted and hissed in clouds of white steam made brilliant against the night sky by the electric lights of the railroad station. Allan knocked on the door, which was opened by Daisy. The two waitresses from the hamburger joint were there and a third girl came in from a back room. Allan handed Daisy the box containing the gin and said knowingly, "Let's have a drink."

Daisy took the box and disappeared. Allan, very much at home, flung himself down on the davenport and Jim somewhat diffidently followed suit. The two girls who had served them came over and sat close, with arms about them, placidly waiting for the petting to begin. They hadn't long to wait. Daisy returned with the drinks and sat with Allan between her and the girl called Dolly. She did not seem to expect any petting; she sat upright obviously waiting for someone.

"What's biting you, Daisy? Where's Johnny?" The questions came from Allan.

"I'm looking for him any time now," she replied with a glance at the clock. "He's bringing in a new girl. Two of the girls have gone to Vegas, and Maudie's sick. John's got two new ones lined up, but only one of them's coming with him tonight."

Jim learned that the girl with him was named Lily. He thought her a rather pretty little thing, and she made a great fuss over him as the evening progressed. The drinks went around three or four times. Daisy's uneasiness increased. Allan looked at the clock and suggested it was time to go upstairs, which started an argument between him and Dolly that was interrupted by a knock at the door. Daisy opened the door for a swarthy-looking fellow and the new girl.

The girl, who looked like an Indian, seemed scared to death. As the man led her into the room she hung her head and looked as if she were going to cry.

Daisy tried to reassure her, "You go right to bed now, honey, you don't have to do no work tonight."

As the girl turned to follow the woman upstairs, Jim got a good look at her. He was sure she was a Hopi, and he was amazed to find that this disturbed him deeply. There were lots of Hopi girls – why shouldn't one be in a house? Hopi girls were like all the rest, some were good and some were punks, and the punks came to places like this. Anyway, it was none of his business. As he turned away from the girl his eye caught Allan's. Evidently Allan's thoughts were the same as his. Allan was the first to speak.

"What's a Hopi girl doing in this joint? Who is she? Looks like a girl I saw at Lower Oraibi – one of those Christian Oraibi girls."

No one volunteered an explanation. The Hopi were silent and ignored the girls. Then Lily giggled and suggested another drink, and she and Dolly disappeared into the kitchen.

As Daisy came downstairs Jim demanded, "Is she a Hopi girl?"

Seeing the anger in his face, Daisy countered, "Supposing she is – what's it to you, sailor?"

She gave him a playful push toward the davenport and he fell upon it. Her action infuriated him. Yet why was he getting so mad? Why should this Hopi girl be any concern of his? If she was a Christian Hopi from Lower Oraibi all the more reason why she shouldn't mean anything to him. Those Lower Oraibi people were not real Hopi – *"Kahopi,"* the scornful word came back to him. To hell with her and her snivelling!

Lily returned and sat down on his knee, whispering in his ear, "Let's go upstairs now, honey."

Almost defiantly he followed her up the short flight of stairs. As they went down the hallway he could hear the Hopi girl crying in her room. Again his anger mounted. Even if she was a Christian from Lower Oraibi she still was a Hopi girl. She might even be a relative—his mother's clan had many relationships with the Oraibi people. The thought of her being there suddenly enraged him. He shook off Lily's possessive arm and threw open the door to the room from which the sobbing came.

The Hopi girl jumped up from the bed where she was lying and quickly seized the shawl, which she had discarded earlier, and wrapped it around her cotton dress, as if it would give her some additional protection.

Jim roughly took her by the arm and with a "Come – you don't belong here," he led her downstairs.

Allan was at the foot of the stairs and he watched in amazement as the two came down, the girl following Jim like a puppy. Jim slammed the front door behind them and walked down the hill, holding the girl's hand in a cold, unfeeling grasp.

VIII

NOW WHAT WOULD he do with her? At the first street light he stopped and looked at her. She was very small, even for a Hopi girl. He found himself looking down at her as he would look at a child. She returned his gaze shyly. Her face was still stained with tears, but she had stopped sobbing, and she displayed no fear of him, but only great puzzlement.

"You're no more puzzled than I am, sister," Jim thought to himself.

He found himself thinking in Hopi and he spoke in Hopi as he questioned, "Do you have any relatives here?"

She shook her head.

"Any friends that you could stay with?"

Again she shook her head. What could he do with her? He'd try again. "What's your name?"

"Mary," she replied, looking directly at him for the first time.

A fine name, he thought, for a Christian girl going to work in a whorehouse.

"Mary what?"

"Mary Tomavitu."

"What clan do you belong to? I do not know you. I've just come back to Shongopovi."

"My mother's people were of the Bear Clan, but my father is a Christian and does not follow the Hopi way. It has caused us much trouble."

Sobs interrupted her and it was some minutes before she poured out her story.

"Last week I joined some of my clan sisters in a Buffalo Dance. My father was very angry. He hit me; he called me vile names. I wished to marry a boy at Hotevila, but my father called the Hotevila people many names because they do not become Christians. My father made us live like white people. He tried to make us think like white people. My mother was not listened to in our family."

Jim tried to stem her torrent of bitter talk, but she continued to sob out the rest of the tale.

"I could not be a Christian when I knew the great sadness that had come to us because my father became a Christian. My brothers all left our house as soon as they could do so. The boy at Hotevila married another girl, and —"

Jim was glad that there was no one in the street near them, for now her sobs rose to hysteria. Awkwardly, he patted her shoulder and waited. So she was a Hopi and member of the Bear Clan. She was, then, his clan sister. He must help her.

"How did you meet this white man, this John?"

Once again in control of herself, she gave him her confidence in voluble detail.

"My father took me to a church meeting. He tried to make me stand up and say, 'I accept Jesus as my savior,' but I could not do it. My father was angry. This white man was at the meeting. He told me afterwards he always went to these meetings. He often found girls for his houses there. I left my father, saying I had to go to the toilet. This white man followed me and when I came out of the toilet he spoke to me. I did not want to go back to New Oraibi. I did not care what became of me. I was glad to think how unhappy it would make my father if I did as the white man said. I told the white man I would meet him this morning by the bridge. I knew I was doing what was wrong, but I did not care. All I wanted was to hurt my father and to die!"

Jim halted the threatened sobs by saying, "Come. We must find a place for you to stay. In the morning we will think what you can do."

He started walking and again she followed him like a little dog. They came to a house with a sign that said, "Boarding." With some apprehension Jim rang the bell. A hard-faced woman answered and when she saw them she slammed the door in their faces, her voice cutting the night air.

"Get away from here, you dirty Indians! This is a decent place, not a —"

The slammed door made the last word unintelligible. Jim boiled. He had forgotten for a time that he was a dirty Indian.

As they rounded the corner he found that they were near the yard where the dump truck was parked. He could see a light in the shack of the night watchman, a rather kind-faced old Mexican, he remembered. He knocked on the door. In a few minutes the old man opened it and peered out.

"Oh, it's you. You want to go to the truck? Hey," as he saw the girl, "who's this?"

"This is my sister," Jim replied. "She is to sleep in the truck."

To the old watchman this seemed an entirely reasonable suggestion, and he opened the door that led from his shack into the yard where the truck was parked.

"She might be cold out there," — this as he picked up a worn blanket from the top of a box that had been used as a seat and handed it to Jim. "Do you play checkers?"

Jim nodded a yes.

"Come back and have a game; it helps keep me awake."

Jim led Mary to the truck, and as she climbed in he handed her the blanket. As she took it, she pressed his hand. He closed the door when he saw that she had made herself comfortable on the seat; then he went back to play checkers with the old man.

At midnight the watchman made his rounds of the yard. He had told Jim that he could make a bed for himself in a corner of the shack with some old tarps that were piled there. When he came back, Jim was sound asleep. To while away the long night hours ahead of him he took up a battered magazine of ancient date and began to spell out the words.

It was full daylight when Allan came in and woke Jim. The old watchman barely stirred as the two left the shack. As they went toward the truck they could see the girl sitting up in the cab. She managed a dim smile when she saw Jim.

"Did you get some sleep?" he asked. Then, ""You remember Allan?"

"How about some breakfast?"

This was Allan's suggestion and it broke the embarrassed silence that encompassed them. He knew a place just around the corner, he said, where they could get coffee and doughnuts. With a shy nod of gratitude Mary climbed down from the cab and joined them. The men hurried through breakfast to get back to load the coal, while the girl lingered in the shabby little restaurant, after assuring them she would join them soon.

There was little talk between Jim and Allan as they began shovelling. Allan broke the awkward silence.

"What's her name? Is she Hopi?"

"Mary Tomavitu—from Lower Oraibi."

"She does not belong here."

The compassion in Allan's voice brought from Jim her whole story.

"Bear Clan—her mother? Then we are of her mother's

clan. My mother will look after her. She needs a daughter to help her."

"That will make some trouble, won't it? — between your people and those Christian Hopi, I mean."

"If she's a good girl my mother will adopt her."

Jim could not figure out just what this meant, but Allan seemed very sure, and very eager that the girl should go with them.

At that moment she appeared, still nibbling on a doughnut. She looked quite pretty. Obviously she had tidied up in the restaurant rest room. "Allan here has it all fixed. His mother will look after you. You will go with us to Shongopovi."

For the first time Mary looked at Allan, then dropped her eyes as she murmured, "You are good."

Allan turned back to his shovelling without a word, but Jim noticed that from time to time he glanced at the girl with a decided show of interest, and that she returned these glances with shy smiles.

It was nearly noon when the loading was finished. The boss of the place showed them a dirty washroom in a shed where they could clean up before starting back. Allan went into a small store nearby and bought something to eat on the way, and Jim spent the rest of his money on a box of food to take home: a small sack of flour, coffee, sugar, bacon, canned vegetables and fruit, sweet cookies, and a chunk of beef. Then, with the girl sitting between them, they started back to Shongopovi.

There was a strained silence among them for the first few miles, then Jim and Allan began to speak of Jim's future plans. Their talk of Shongopovi aroused the girl to ask Allan about his house and his mother. Soon the conversation was general, though no mention was made of the events of the previous night. Allan ventured a Hopi song or two in which Jim tried to join. There were jokes and laughter about the quality of Allan's voice and about Jim's garbled Hopi words. By the time they got to Indian Wells the group might have been any party of gay young Hopi, unshadowed by threats of an irate parent and the uncertainty of their reception in the village.

At Indian Wells Allan turned west into an old road.

"Why are we going this way?" Jim asked.

"It is early. It will be fun to go by Rimmy Gus' place near Dilkon."

"Rimmy Gus? Who's he?"

"A white man who came out as a trader about a year ago. I know him 'cause he had me freight out a big white bathtub from Holbrook. He'd bought it at Sears-Roebuck in Phoenix and had it shipped there."

Allan chuckled to himself. Jim thought it strange to end the story there, but suddenly the sight of a juniper reminded him of the wood he had promised his mother.

"Let's stop and eat here, then I can get a few logs of juniper. Got room for them on top of the coal?"

"Sure. This is a good place to stop. We'll cut the wood first and eat afterward. You all right?" Allan turned to Mary with solicitude.

She is a nice little thing, thought Jim — and Allan evidently thinks so, too. Hope he knows what he's talking about when he says his mother will take her in. But mine would, I'm sure, she's a good old girl — all these old Hopi women are. Well, I better get her that wood!

The chopping done, they sat under a juniper tree to eat the bread and meat. Mary asked a few more timid questions about Allan's mother, the questions a child might ask. Allan reassured her that it would all be fine. Jim wondered. Allan's a good guy. All Hopi seem to stick together, he thought. Maybe I'll get on to it all again some day.

"Come on," Allan's voice interrupted his thoughts. "It's getting late, and we got to stop at Rimmy Gus'."

"What's the idea?" Jim protested. Some joke, he supposed. These Hopi always like a laugh — well, he did, too, and he needed one.

An hour or so later they came to Rimmy Gus' trading

post. It was a long, rectangular building built of rock and wood. In front of it a hogan gave shelter to any Navajo who came to trade. A nondescript gas pump stood by the door. The front of the establishment was deserted, but back of it was a group of about a dozen Navajo. They were looking intently at something. The men were solemn-faced under their wide-brimmed, tall-crowned felt hats, but the women, in their wide skirts and velvet blouses, were grinning like mischievous children.

At a gesture from Allan the three Hopi slipped out of the cab and joined the Navajo. As they watched, one of the latter pointed and chuckled. From a bit of two-inch pipe, projecting from the foundation, a stream of absolutely clear water began to pour out over the desert soil. The Navajo covered their laughing mouths with their hands and walked away. Allan, too, covered his mouth and to one Navajo made a broad joke about the white trader's lack of success with the ladies.

At the puzzled faces of Jim and Mary, Allan laughingly said, "Pile in. I'll tell you about it as we go along. . . . Remember the bathtub I mentioned?. . . .Well, this old guy Gus is crazy to get himself a woman. He would give presents to every Hopi girl that came to his trading post and ask her to go with him to his back room. They all thought him very funny, but they would not go with him. Then he tried the Navajo girls, but he said that before he would take a Navajo girl she would have to take a bath in his white man's tub. Now whenever a Navajo girl comes he hopefully turns on the water in the bathtub and coaxes her into the back room. The word gets around and everybody near the post comes to watch the water come out. Just like today, the water always comes out clean!"

Allan's chuckles were echoed by Mary's smile and Jim's hearty laugh. It was the kind of story all Indians liked, with the white man the ridiculous victim of the red man's laughter. Stories about Rimmy Gus and his Navajo girls occupied them until they were in sight of the villages of Second Mesa. As they pulled up the steep road their laughter ceased as all three pondered over what might lie ahead.

"I'll throw the wood off at my place, Allan," Jim said. As he spoke he wondered about Mary—it didn't seem quite right to leave it all to Allan. After all he himself had gotten the girl away from that place. Allan answered his unspoken question.

"O. K. You might as well get off there, too. I'll take care of Mary and see you later."

•

•

IX

JIM LOOKED ABOUT the *kiva* apprehensively. It was the morning of the Buffalo Dance. The sun was just rising as he left home, fully costumed, to come here and join the others for the ceremony. He stood at the foot of the *kiva* ladder feeling alien and somewhat foolish.

His face was blackened, with a blotch of white across his mouth and on his chin. The bulky headdress of brown wooly sheepskin and buffalo horns, decorated with eagle feathers and tufts of down, was heavy and uncomfortable. A woman's bulky white blanket with borders of blue and red formed a kind of kilt. Nervously he fingered a gourd rattle and a stick that symbolized lightning.

He remembered the first time he had put on his Navy "blues." He had been so self-conscious that he had hated to walk outside – but the Navy uniform was nothing like this garb he had on now. Good thing there was no mirror around.

Why had he gotten himself into this, anyway? Whatever made him ask Kathleen to be his partner? He hadn't even seen her at the last rehearsal the night before. Yes, she'd gotten her costume – old Lololomi had seen to that. In fact, the old busybody seemed to tend to everything. Even now he was sending out the first group of dancers, paying particular attention to the girls – they were just little ones, in this act. When would his turn come? How would he ever get through it? Well, it would be the last one – he was sure of that – nothing would get him into this sort of thing again. Not even Kathleen.

His thoughts turned to the night before – he still felt the humiliation of it. First his mother treating him like a small boy as her silence reproved him for being late, then reminding him he must go to the rehearsal – he'd forgotten the Buffalo Dance. Then the hours in the *kiva* the sly looks at him when Kathleen failed to appear, the skill of the little boys, and his own ineptness, the time someone in the choir yelled at him for some unwitting error in the step. He was sure Kathleen was there at the very end – but why was she so late? And where was she this morning? Funny he didn't see Allan anywhere – there hadn't been a chance last night to ask him about Mary – he hoped she was all right.

Was that Kathleen emerging from a group in a corner of the *kiva?* The flowing hair and the bang falling over the face to the tip of the nose made identification difficult. He was sure he recognized the feathers of the headdress and he remembered his mother working on a bodice like that and saying it was a man's dance kilt which she had gotten from some family connection that meant nothing to him. Those were certainly the moccasins and leggings he'd whitened. He hoped it was her father, that old man so intimately fitting the heavy turquoise necklaces. He liked the large fringed belt she wore. Was it a wedding belt? – he remembered something about it. At that moment she turned to speak to someone behind her, and on her back he could see a sun tablet encircled with eagle feathers and white horsehair.

Then she came toward him and smiled. Of course it was Kathleen. For a moment his irritability and depression vanished. Then the voices of the choristers rose in what he knew was the signal for his group to go up the ladder. The man with the drum led, then came the choir, then the dancers. Jim followed the others as they left, man alternating with girl.

He was near the end – that was lucky – he could watch the others and copy their steps when he forgot – after all he'd not had as much practice as the rest. Even as they left the ladder the men began to caper about until they got to the plaza where the girls stood side by side, apparently never lifting their feet from the ground but moving them rhythmically sidewise. Now he lost himself in the long sweeping gestures of this part of the dance as the men moved forward in front of the girls and began to step high, alternately raising one hand to their foreheads and putting one on their hips. He was hardly aware of Kathleen until, on the return to the *kiva,* the men stepped backward in the movement of the dance and faced the girls. She, unlike the rest of the girls, seemed rapt in some secret ecstasy. Again he was aware of the cast of sadness that clouded her face at times. Well, if he was making mistakes she'd not be aware of them. He hoped there'd be time to talk to her later. This wasn't a half bad day – maybe there was something to these dances, though he wasn't sure where the prayers came in.

They had reached the ladder now, and old Lololomi took from each dancer the paraphernalia he carried. Then there was a rush into the *kiva* to make way for the final set of dancers. For the first time Jim looked up and saw that the housesteps were crowded with spectators – Hopi, most of them, from other villages, he figured. In the crowd he saw some Navajo, too, here to feast to the full, no doubt, on the Hopi food which would be freely offered on this ceremonial day. He was glad he'd thought to buy that food for his mother – he felt a bit humble when he recalled how pleased she looked when she found that he had really brought her the wood he promised and a box of food besides. He wondered if some day Kathleen would be a gentle old woman like his mother. In that white nurse's uniform? He almost laughed aloud at the comparison.

It was late afternoon when Jim came out of the *kiva*. It had taken him a long time to get rid of that damn paint. It was all right in the dance, he guessed, but he didn't want Kathleen to see any of it on him afterward. He was aware suddenly that a group of white people had come to see the ceremony.

"Who are they?" He asked the question abruptly of a young Hopi who was standing near him.

"They are from the hospital at Keams Canyon. The white man is the doctor they tease Kathleen about."

Why did he add that? Jim wondered. What did this chap know about him and Kathleen? He looked quickly about to see if she were anywhere near, and he found her at the far end of a line of dancers. So she was still at it. She must be taking someone's place. He watched the white people carefully. The doctor was young and smart-looking. He was observing the dance with serious interest, searching the faces of the girl dancers as they neared — trying to find Kathleen — Jim was certain of that. Kathleen looked embarrassed as the movement of the dance brought her before the whites. Jim was sort of glad of it. This wasn't their affair — they were simply curious — of course she was embarrassed. He'd be glad when it was all over. He wondered how it did end.

As if in answer to his thoughts, Lololomi came along just then.

"Watch," he said. "Now the Buffalo depart. They take with them any sickness of our people. The Buffalo Boys go to the shrine and tell the Buffalo that now they may go to their homes, there to make prayers for the Hopi."

A certain quiet strength in the old man's voice and words touched Jim strangely, although he could make nothing of Lololomi's explanation. He turned away for lack of an adequate answer and found himself facing Kathleen, still in costume.

"Was it not beautiful, Jim? Are we not better Hopi now?"

He could think of no words to say to her. He wanted to take her hand, to ask about the white doctor, to tell her how old Lololomi's words had moved him — but her costume did not leave her hands free, and the doctor was none of his business, and Lololomi was just an old heathen. Buffalo and sickness!

The white people came up at that moment and surrounded her, their loud voices exclaiming over her part in the dance. They seemed so out of place, so out of keeping with the ceremony, that Jim turned away. He hoped they would not ask Kathleen to let them take her picture. But why shouldn't they take her picture? He didn't believe those old superstitions about pictures. Let them take all they wanted to. What was the young doctor saying? He could tell nothing of their relationship from his manner. To hell with all of them!

X

IT WAS GROWING DARK when he returned to his house to find his mother putting away the costume she had borrowed for him. It pleased him to find that Tom and his other uncles had left for him a gift of cotton pants and a velvet shirt. He must have done all right in the dance. It still wasn't altogether dark. He wondered if Kathleen had gone back with the white people. He hoped not. He did want to talk to her — it seemed that he had to.

He was almost at the door when it burst open, all but hitting him in the face. An angry-looking white man, followed by a stern-faced Hopi of middle age, strode into the room.

"You know where this man's daughter is. Tell him. We have come to take her home!"

The white man blurted this out in one breath, and then the Hopi cut in. "My daughter is a Christian — she has no right to be here!"

It took a minute for Jim's mind to adjust itself. Mary, of course! How had they traced her here?

"You are wrong," he said, as quietly as possible, aware

of his mother's questioning look. "Your daughter is not here. She is with Allan Lemtewa's mother." He hoped this was true. "She does not wish to go back to New Oraibi."

"You mind your own business, young fellow!" The white man almost spat the words at him. "Where is this woman's house?"

Jim walked past them and out the door and the two men followed him, his mother looking after them with troubled eyes.

The door of Allan's house was shut against the cold night air, but warm, yellow lamp-light came through the small windows. Jim went ahead and knocked softly, calling out his own Hopi name as he did so.

"Talastewa! Mary's father and a white man are here for Mary!"

The white man brushed him aside and threw open the door. Several Hopi who were sitting on the floor eating jumped up in surprise. Mary fled into the corner of the room and stood there trembling, while Allan and his mother stood protectively in front of her. All looked at the intruders with dark faces. Mary's father tried to drag her with him, and the white man attempted to help him. Mary struggled fiercely and cried out.

"Please help me! I cannot go back. I am a Hopi. I am not a Christian. Please help me!"

Jim closed the door behind him and interrupted the proceedings by seizing the white man and swinging him around.

"Who are you? What right have you to come breaking into people's houses? Why don't *you* mind your own business?"

The man turned on him in fierce anger.

"This is my business! I am Vance Vetch, Christian missionary to heathen Oraibi! This girl is a Christian of a good Christian family. Her father has come to take her home. He has that right. She is only sixteen."

Allan's mother stepped before the missionary and addressed him fearlessly in a torrent of Hopi.

"You are a bad white man for all your fine good words.

You have brought to our people nothing but trouble ever since you came to Oraibi. You have turned children against their parents, husbands against their wives, and brothers and sisters against each other. Your church stands on Oraibi mesa like a bad mark against the sun! I have adopted this girl in our Hopi way. She is no longer the daughter of this man. Since when have fathers owned their daughters in our Hopi country? Where is her mother? She is the one who should lay claim to her!"

There was a mutter of agreement among the Hopi present. Just then Jim was aware of voices outside, and he opened the door to a dozen clan relatives of Allan, attracted by the noise and confusion. Allan tried to explain what had happened, but recognition of Vetch made this unnecessary. The newcomers confronted him and Mary's father in threatening fashion, one man shaking his fist in the white man's face.

"What's going on in here?"

Jim looked toward the doorway and saw framed in it the young white doctor and Kathleen. They entered the room quickly; Kathleen, seeing Jim, came to him at once. The doctor followed her.

"What is the matter here, Jim?"

Before he could reply to her question, the missionary cut in.

"We have come to take this girl home. These heathen have kidnapped her from her people."

Again Kathleen turned to Jim for an explanation. Before he could say a word, Allan blurted out the whole Holbrook story. Jim tried to say something that would make his part clear, but the words would not come. Kathleen did not look at him; her face was set and cold. Jim turned to the doctor.

"This girl does not wish to be a Christian. She has been adopted by this Hopi woman." He indicated Allan's mother. "If she is taken back to New Oraibi she will only go off to Holbrook again."

"That may be true, Jim," — Kathleen must have told him about me, Jim thought. He knows my name — "but still, the fact is that she is this man's daughter, and she is only sixteen."

Jim realized that to the doctor the Hopi way of adoption meant nothing. He ignored it. To him the girl was still the property of her father. He spoke to Kathleen, too low for Jim to hear, and the two of them walked over to Mary, and taking her arms, they led her out of the room. The missionary and Mary's father followed them out. The Hopi men in the room rose in angry protest just as Lololomi appeared in the doorway and blocked their leaving. The old man stood resolute before them.

"Let us not have trouble. This is not our Hopi way. Let us go home now and think about it and make prayers that the girl will have a strong and true heart. I will go to our chiefs and we will go to Keams Canyon to talk to the agent there."

Allan's mother sat down in a corner and sobbed. The sound took the anger out of them. Lololomi turned and walked into the darkness. Slowly all of them drifted out into the night, leaving Jim in the house with Allan and his mother.

"I am sorry to have brought all this trouble to you, Allan."

Allan shook his head. "It was a good thing you did, to take the girl out of Daisy's place. It was a good thing for my mother to adopt her as a daughter. She is a good girl. Why should there be so much anger and so many bad thoughts come from all this that is good? I do not understand. It is not our Hopi way."

There was nothing for Jim to say. He walked out of the house and slowly found his way to the mesa's edge. Away down across the wash he could faintly see the glare of Vetch's automobile headlights pointing towards New Oraibi.

XI

JIM LAY AWAKE a long time that night. After his return home he had discussed the whole affair with his mother and Tom, who had come in to eat with them. They were able to tell him many stories of that missionary at Oraibi who, in his wild-eyed fanaticism, would stop at nothing to make converts of the Hopi there.

Then the talk had turned to his future and what he would do at Shongopovi. They took it very much for granted that he was going to stay, that his life from now on was to be part of the intricate web of Hopi ceremonial and family-clan interrelationships. As he lay in the darkness there came over him a sense of rightness, and he knew that he wanted it that way, too, that his real reason for returning had been to feel one with his people, once again. This desire had ever lain in the back of his mind, blocked out most of the time by the demands and interests of the moment.

Even now he could not give in to the insistent claims of his homeland without protestation. He could not help toying with the idea of staying here for just a few weeks, then re-enlisting. He began to think of the fellows on the ship.

What would they have thought of him if they had seen him dashing out of Daisy's place with the Hopi girl? What would they have thought of him if they had seen him today painted and dressed in ceremonial clothes taking part in a Buffalo Dance? How kind the padre on the ship had been – how different from that ranting Oraibi missionary! No, it hadn't been a bad life at all.

Then he recalled Lololomi standing in the doorway, so strong and dignified. His nobility made one proud of belonging to the Hopi tribe. How quickly his calm but forceful words quieted them all! Even Allan – who was not, some of the time, much of a Hopi – even Allan had gently echoed those words about the Hopi way. He wondered what was happening to the New Oraibi girl. What would her father and the missionary say to her? What would they do to her? Why didn't her own mother help her? Why did she let the father rule their lives? It wasn't the Hopi way. He smiled to himself as the phrase made its way into his thought.

Then the thought of Kathleen and the young white doctor flooded all other considerations from his mind. Of all the Hopi girls he had seen since his return, she interested him the most. She didn't giggle every time he spoke to her as most of the others did. He was sure that she liked him – that a bit of warmth came into her face when he talked with her. He longed to touch her. If he pressed her hand, would she respond? Could he go to her some night the way Hopi boys had always gone to the girls they loved? Would she accept him, or was she so much like a white girl that she would think only savages behaved in that way? If she had become more like a white woman, why, then, did she come back to her village and dance in the Buffalo Dance like any Hopi girl? He must find her sometime when she was not in her uniform. He could not talk to her easily when she wore it. Suddenly he recalled that she had heard all about what happened at Daisy's – what would she think of that? Would she ever let him talk to her now?

All night there warred in his mind the forces of the red man's world and those of the world of the white man. Nor did daylight see the battle joined. Maybe – or so he thought

— he had better take the easy way out and re-enlist. There were fewer decisions to be made in that life — the Navy was a lot simpler than a Hopi village. Well, he'd see —

Allan came in as they were eating breakfast. As he sucked on a cup of coffee he threw out a tentative suggestion.

"Let's go over to New Oraibi and see what's happened to Mary."

Jim was not too eager to go — why get mixed up in all this again? But Allan had helped him out of a tight spot and gotten himself a raw deal as a result.

"O.K. It'll give me a chance to see that silversmith over there that we were talking about the other day."

Allan had his lunch with him, and Nasayungti got together some for Jim.

"Hadn't we better have some water? I don't remember how far it is."

"Just a few miles — forget the water."

They took the foot trail over the mesa down to the washes, Allan leading at a steady dogtrot that ate up the miles. Jim still found it hard to keep up in this sort of travel, and he discovered reasons for frequent stops. Once they halted to take a look at an old shallow coal mine under the mesa's rim, and at another time to view the peach orchards with their stubby, gnarled little trees. He remembered hearing something about Coronado's men having brought in the seeds for them back in the 1500's — not these, he guessed, though they looked old enough to be the originals.

"What's that?" as Allan produced a boomerang-like stick from under his jacket.

"Have you forgotten a rabbit stick? Look!"

He threw it with dexterity and killed a rabbit that Jim had not even seen.

"Here, let's have a try."

But he had lost the skill. Three cottontails ran safely on their way. He couldn't run — he couldn't throw a rabbit stick — well, the Navy wouldn't require either.

"Here, Allan — I give up. I'll watch you."

Before they got down to the deep sweeps of Oraibi wash, Allan had skilfully downed three rabbits.

"Better get in a little practice – they're good food."

Allan did not mean to be patronizing, but Jim found himself resenting the implication.

There was no trouble crossing the wash, for it held only a trickle of water. A few hundred feet beyond the crossing they came to the sandstone buildings of the Oraibi school, surrounded by the ugly clutter of houses, trading post, stores and shacks that disfigured the east side of the mesa. Much of this was new to Jim and he questioned Allan about it.

"They're mostly Vetch's converts that live down here. They quarreled with the old chief on top of the mesa – he couldn't stand Vetch."

"Well, who could? You mean he's been around a long time?"

"Oh, sure. He built the church up there." Allan pointed up to Old Oraibi. "And he still goes up and tries to make them Christians – but he has no luck with that bunch."

"Do they like him down here?"

"There's talk that some of them say they've gotten tired of waiting for Jesus to come and they're going back to being Hopi."

This brought smiles to both their faces.

"Does the old chief still live up in Old Oraibi?"

"Yes, he's still alive. Not many people there now, you'll find. He even has to get help from Moencopi and other villages for the dances."

"Too bad. It's the oldest town in the country, isn't it?"

"They say so. It once was the biggest Hopi village, too. These missionaries can make a lot of trouble."

"They sure can – especially your friend Vetch!"

They were well into the settlement by now. So far nothing had been said about the purpose of their visit.

"I know some people here," remarked Allan. "They probably can tell me about Mary. Want to come with me?"

"Don't believe I will." Jim's voice showed his relief

at not having to join him. "I'll go on up and see about that silver business."

"Well, I'll look you up when I get through – I won't be long. But I would like to know about Mary."

Jim suddenly realized that Allan's feeling for Mary was deep.

"Hope she's all right. I'll see you later then."

Jim took the age-old footpath that winds up among the sandhills and ends finally in a steep stone stairway which leads up over the cliffs to the top of Oraibi mesa. Suddenly facing him was the church of which Allan had spoken. It stood some hundred feet from the closest of the crumbling buildings of Old Oraibi. He was shocked that so many of the houses were in ruins – it looked like a deserted village. Evidently Vetch's attempt to destroy the religion of the villagers had nearly destroyed the village itself.

Jim saw some smoke coming from one chimney of a nearby house. He knocked and inquired where he could find the home of Bill Lanta, the silversmith. The woman who answered sent one of her small children to guide him, and the little girl soon brought him to a neat, well-plastered house which rose three stories above the street. He gave her a dime and she scurried off with a backward smile at him.

The door of the house was open and there were men talking within. He could see three of them at work at heavy tables near the windows of the main room. As he walked in the men looked up from their work and greeted him pleasantly.

"This is Bill Lanta's place?"

In response to his question a middle-aged Hopi came from an inner room. "I am Bill Lanta. You must be Jim Talastewa from Shongopovi. Lololomi sent word to me that you might come here."

Jim liked Lanta at once. He was short and heavy and had a face pitted from smallpox, but his eyes bespoke intelligence and good humor. He introduced each of the men and suggested that they show Jim samples of what they were doing.

"You have come to see our silver?"

Jim found himself answering with enthusiasm.

"Yes – I may want to work in silver. I have just come back to Shongopovi. I do not yet know what I wish to do. Maybe this is it."

Lanta pointed out to Jim the significance of certain designs and explained to him that he and his group were trying to make use of Hopi pottery and basket designs in heavy silver.

"We want to have every piece we make an example of honest workmanship. Already we are finding a good market for all the silver we make. It is a good work. Have you ever done anything like this?"

"No. I did some machine work in the Navy, and before I went away I did some drawing at school. I do not know just why – but I want to do this, even though it is all new to me."

"Come, sit here at this table. See what you can do with this bit of copper. It won't matter if you spoil it." This last as Jim hesitated.

One of the men cleared his work to one side and the others crowded around the table, eager to advise.

"What would you like to try?"

"A plain band bracelet such as yours – maybe that would be best for me this first time."

One showed him how to sketch a design on a piece of paper, another how to cut the heavy sheet of copper. All praised the skill and speed with which he carried out their directions. The tools came easy to his hand, and he found himself transferring his design to the copper as if he had had long practice.

"You will be a good silversmith, Jim."

There was no doubt of Lanta's sincerity. The kindness and patience of the group, their ready acceptance of him, and Lanta's interest and praise kindled Jim's small flame of curiosity about the work into a blaze of enthusiasm. Lanta's next words fell happily on his ears.

"Would you like to work with us here – maybe to learn? We work together, we share each other's tools, we buy our silver together – we are all learning together."

He looked to the other Hopi for confirmation and each in turn nodded.

Jim wondered why they should be so friendly, so ready to be of help to one they did not know. He must remember to thank Lololomi, for he must have spoken well for him. He answered thoughtfully.

"I should like to learn with you. Whether it will be my only work I do not yet know – but I should like to learn."

XII

THE MORNING HAD PASSED quickly. It was already noon and time for lunch.

"Sit with us, Jim," said Lanta, "and eat."

Just as the group finished lunch and the men were having a leisurely smoke, Allan came in, his face serious.

"Mary has gone! She ran away again last night! I have tried to find her. I followed her trail across the mesa and down the cliffs to the west, but it disappeared in the sands. It's that Vetch – and her father – they're to blame!"

Jim explained to the puzzled silversmiths what had happened the night before. Some of them had heard rumors of the affair. Most of them knew Allan, or his family, and they were eager to be of help, particularly if it meant dealing with Vetch.

"That Tomavitu – Christian!"

It was the gentlest of the men who spoke, but the way he spat out the word "Christian" expressed the contempt for their weaker brothers in Lower Oraibi held by all in Old Oraibi who had remained steadfast in their ancient beliefs.

"We must find the girl." Bill Lanta spoke firmly.

"I think she will kill herself. Or she will get that old Navajo Klishanni to kill her!"

The words were blurted out by Myron Mansa, the oldest man in the group. An exclamation of horror broke from Allan's lips. Jim looked at him and then at the others.

"Can't we do something? Allan and I —"

He was interrupted by Myron.

"Come — I have horses. We'll go after her."

They followed him to his corral near the foot of the ancient trail to the mesa top. Myron signalled to Jim and Allan to mount two of the horses there and he took the third. They circled the end of the mesa to try to pick up the trail where Allan had lost it in the sandhills. From time to time they separated and rode in great circles. It was Allan who finally found tracks he was sure were hers — between two corn fields away to the west, in the direction of the isolated hogan of Klishanni. They followed them together.

"I do not understand this Klishanni business," said Jim.

"You tell him, Myron." Allan spoke as if he feared to do so.

In short sentences, with many pauses between them, Myron told how Klishanni, born badly crippled and so unable to ride or work, had become a healer, a medicine man, among the Navajo. He was feared by the Hopi because they were sure he practiced witchcraft.

While Myron was telling all this, Bill Lanta came riding up. He had no news to bring them but felt they might need his help. He listened for a time to Myron and then he continued the story.

"You may not know, Jim, but it has long been the custom for a Hopi to seek death when disgrace makes it no longer possible for him to face life with honor. In the old days men would purposely seek death in battle, making no attempt to escape or to protect themselves. Men — and women — would sometimes hire someone to kill them. Many a Hopi during our history has hired some man of another tribe to kill him. Three times in his long, long life Klishanni has been hired by Hopi to do this — two men and one woman, all of Old Oraibi, have chosen to die in this way rather than face a future that seemed hopeless to them."

"I have heard my father tell this," said Allan, "but I did not believe it. Even now I cannot believe that Mary – she is so little."

His voice broke and Jim reached over and patted his arm.

"We will find her – you'll see."

Myron again began to speak, almost as if to himself, and his words added to their fears.

"He hates women, even Navajo ones, because he is ugly and crippled. For even a small present he will shoot her with that old rifle. But, look!"

In the moist earth at the bottom of the ravine the prints of a woman's moccasins were clearly defined. Now the men were sure they were on the right trail and they urged the horses to their utmost speed. Jim was no more used to riding bareback that he was to running, and he was soon very sore and weary and he barely managed to keep riding very close to Allan.

The latter spoke little for a long time. Then he turned slightly towards Jim and, as if the words were a surprise to himself, exclaimed, "I know now that I want Mary for my wife!"

Why at this moment do I think of Kathleen? The question stirred in Jim's mind. To Allan his only comment was, "Let us ride faster."

After several miles of breakneck speed the horses needed rest. The men pulled up by a low cottonwood that marked a spring and briefly rested by the tree, now bare of leaves. The government had erected a windmill at the spot and furnished a watering trough for sheep and cattle. The horses were allowed a short drink and the Hopi also drank before they rode on. They slowed down from time to time only to check to be sure that they were following the right track.

About a mile from the spring the trail wound up over a low saddle between two long, broken brick-red mesas. As they crested the ridge they could see smoke issuing from a hogan directly ahead.

"Klishanni!" The terse identification came from Bill Lanta.

After a few moments of careful watching they could make out two figures beyond the hogan. Even as they watched a shot rang out and one figure dropped to the ground.

Klishanni suddenly seemed aware of the horsemen, for he hobbled toward his hogan and managed to get inside the doorway just as the men rode up. He greeted them with a threatening gesture of his gun. Jim could not remember any Navajo, but the old man's actions needed no words. Myron yelled to him in Navajo, while Allan rode furiously to where the shooting had taken place. Jim heard him call frantically and, jumping off his horse, he ran to where Allan was leaning over Mary, who was bleeding badly.

There were no words between the men. The girl was alive, but an ugly wound in her chest was revealed when Allan pulled away her dress to find the source of the blood. Jim tore off a piece of his shirt—the first aid of his Navy days was now proving its value—and with it stanched the bleeding as well as he could, all the while directing Allan how to help him.

It was cruel to put her on a horse, but there was no alternative. They must get her out of here. Allan mounted quickly, and Jim and Myron, with all the gentleness they could summon, handed Mary up to him. Jim, with surprising command, showed Allan how best to carry her so as to cause her as little jostling as possible.

Mary was barely conscious. She sobbed uncontrollably and seemed unable to open her eyes. She clung desperately to Allan as they started the ride back toward Oraibi. Jim and Myron followed closely. Lanta had turned back after the brief meeting with Klishanni. As they passed the hogan the Navajo came to the door and screamed abuse at them. They were too concerned about the girl to give him any attention. As they crossed the divide between the mesas they saw a car bumping and pitching on the road that runs south of the red mesas from Oraibi to the Sunshine Crossing of the Little Colorado.

"I'll ride ahead fast and tell them to stop for us," and

with the words Myron put his heels into the horse's sides and almost flew across the desert. Soon he waved back to them, and they could see that the car had stopped.

The car was a small truck and its owner a Hopi who worked at the Oraibi trading post. As they loaded Mary into the back of the truck he told them that the nurse from Oraibi had gone into Flagstaff that day and that there was no doctor there. To take Mary back to her father was out of the question.

"Can you drive us all the way to Keams Canyon?"

The driver hesitated just a moment in replying to Jim's question.

"I —"

"The girl will die unless we get help quickly," put in Myron, and there was decision in his voice. "It is a terrible wound and she still bleeds too much."

The driver nodded. Allan got into the back to hold Mary and save her as much as he could from the rough jolting. Jim and Myron rode off, leading Allan's horse.

"I'll come to Keams Canyon tomorrow, Allan," Jim called as the truck pulled away for its trip over the treacherous desert road.

Jim left Myron with the horses on the outskirts of New Oraibi. He somehow did not want to have to talk with anyone about what had happened. He would walk back to Shongopovi. In the morning he would find some way of getting to Keams Canyon.

XIII

IT WAS ALMOST NOON the following day when Jim rode up to the hospital at Keams Canyon. He had managed to borrow a horse and had left Shongopovi as early as he could see the trail. He had ridden fast and again he was feeling the weariness of one unaccustomed to the saddle.

He almost dreaded facing Allan. Had Mary lived? If so, would she have courage enough to face life again? How did she feel about Allan? Would he, Jim, have a chance to see Kathleen, to talk to her? Maybe here he could tell how things stood between her and the doctor.

He looked up, and there was Allan standing in a patch of sun against the stone wall of the small hospital.

His smile of greeting told Jim that Mary was alive.

"She was dead when we got here, but Dr. Cummings gave her life back to her."

Unconscious, he must mean, thought Jim. Aloud he asked, "Will she –"

"Yes, she will live. Kathleen just told me."

The name stirred Jim's pulse.

"Kathleen is here now?"

There was not time to answer the question. A car lurched to a stop in front of them and from it stepped Vetch, Mary's father, and a middle-aged Hopi woman wrapped in a large shawl, who was obviously Mary's mother. There were looks of contempt from the two men, but the woman did not glance at the young Hopi, as they strode into the hospital.

In a minute they could hear loud talking going on in the reception room. It was Kathleen's voice speaking.

"You must not talk so loud or I shall have to ask you to wait outside. I am sure Dr. Cummings will not allow you to see Mary."

Her commanding tone seemed to have its effect. Jim and Allan could hear no more of the conversation. They could tell when Dr. Cummings came into the room. He seemed to be talking to Vetch very firmly. They wondered what they should do. Then they were startled by a whisper.

"Allan! Jim!"

They turned to see Kathleen beckoning to them to follow her. She led them around back of the hospital into a small building which served as quarters for the nurses.

"I am not supposed to bring anyone here, but Dr. Cummings has told me that I may talk to you here."

They sat down in the small bare living room, as Kathleen continued.

"Mary is very ill. She is not yet out of danger, but she will live – we are sure of that. But what shall we do with her when she is better?"

She turned to Jim as if he were the one to answer, but it was Allan who spoke at once.

"I wish to marry her."

Jim wondered if he were right in thinking that there was just the slightest hint of gladness in Kathleen's face, as she turned to Allan.

"This may help everything. But," – this to Jim – "I thought she was your sweetheart."

"That place in Holbrook!" It was difficult for Jim to explain, but he felt a sense of relief as the words came. "I took her out of there because it seemed bad to me that a Hopi girl should be in such a place. She might even be my clan sister, I thought, so I took her away. I did not know how Allan felt about her until yesterday, when we went to find her at Klishanni's."

He hoped she would not ask him any more questions about Holbrook.

Kathleen seemed almost to ignore what he said as she again turned to Allan.

"Have you told her yet that you want to marry her?"

"There has been little time. Yes, I told her as we drove here – but her eyes were shut. I do not know if she heard me."

Kathleen's smile implied that she was sure Mary knew what he had said.

"She will have to be here at least a week. We can keep her from seeing her parents for several days. I do not quite know the law – how soon you can marry. Do you?"

Both Allan and Jim shook their heads.

"We'll find out soon. Would you marry as white people or as the Hopi do?"

Allan hesitated only a moment.

"I am a Hopi and Mary wants to stay a Hopi, too. But it takes a long time to have a Hopi wedding. Her parents might make much trouble if we wait for that."

"Why not marry both ways?"

The question came from Jim. He was warmed by the answering light in Kathleen's eyes, as Allan replied, "Good! We do it both ways; the white way first and the Hopi way later."

Dr. Cummings joined them at this point. Allan tried to explain the situation but halted in embarrassment, so Kathleen told him all that they had talked about. She wondered if the reservation superintendent might help them.

"No." Dr. Cummings spoke thoughtfully. "No, I don't think we should get Lyons involved. No matter what we do to help – and we must help Allan and Mary in this – we'll get into trouble with her father and old Vetch. I have been talking to them; she can not go back to them. The next time she will succeed in getting herself killed! Her mother, I think, is still a Hopi at heart and, if necessary, I believe she will do what she can."

There followed a rapid exchange of questions and answers between him and Kathleen, so fast that Allan and Jim could not keep up. Then the doctor turned to Allan.

"This is likely to get us all into a lot of trouble, but I see no other way out. Why don't you go into town and get a license? It does not take long."

This caused Jim to wonder. Was there an exchange of glances between the doctor and Kathleen, or did he simply imagine it?

The doctor continued his remarks to Allan.

"I am not only a doctor but I can act as a minister, too. I can marry you here as soon as Mary is well enough. She is willing, you say?"

Allan turned to Kathleen for help and she did not fail him.

"I am very sure of that," she said quietly.

Again the doctor spoke.

"You'll have to take care of the Hopi end of it yourself. I don't presume to know anything about that, and Kathleen here tells me it's a very involved affair."

The laughter in his voice broke the tension. He extended his hand to Allan and Allan's smile indicated the things he could not say. The doctor patted him on the back and pressed some money into his hand. "I don't know what a marriage license costs but, if there's anything left over, use it to start a bank account for the first baby!"

Allan, in deep embarrassment, tried to return the money, but Dr. Cummings laughingly pushed him out the door.

"Call it my wedding present."

They watched as Allan almost ran down the path. Then the doctor's face became serious and he turned to the other two.

"Kathleen has told me about you, Jim. You can help us in this. Mary will make your friend a good wife. I must go to the ward," and he left them almost abruptly.

Jim did not know what to say to Kathleen now that they were alone. He wasn't sure what he wanted to say. He stood there feeling very foolish. Her gentle voice broke the silence.

"You asked me the other day why I wanted to come back to the reservation. I tried to tell you. I asked you the same question, but you did not give me much of an answer. I wonder if you can tell me now. I want to know."

His words came haltingly at first.

"I guess I am like you. I now feel that only here would I ever truly belong. Again and again I have felt that if I came back and participated in the ceremonies, I –"

His voice trailed off. The words were hard to find. There was another period of embarrassed silence. The doctor might return any moment. He just had to know.

"Kathleen, are you going to marry Dr. Cummings?"

She was unprepared for his abrupt question. She gave a startled laugh and was about to make a flippant reply when she saw the seriousness of his expression.

"Don't answer like a white girl, I don't want jokes. I must know." There was worriment and pain in his voice.

"No, Jim, I will not joke like a white girl." She looked at him directly as she spoke. "I will answer you like a Hopi. He has asked me; he is kind, he is a good doctor, he is a good man. But I have said no." She paused. "I will marry a Hopi and have Hopi children."

Her final words were spoken as if she had just made the decision and was replying to some question within her own heart.

"I hoped you would talk like that." Then, in a surge of relaxed gaiety, he blurted out, "I think I will marry you!"

She could not help laughing at him, although she sensed that laughter might hurt him at this point.

"It's not as easy as that!"

He started to turn away. She came to him and took him by the shoulders.

"I have been back for only a few months, and you for only a few days. We must wait and see. I don't yet know how it is going to work out for me, and I know it will be hard for you. Maybe we can help each other."

Her hands dropped to her sides and they both stood for a moment in silence.

She was right, of course. And she did give him hope. She was the girl for him, he knew it now for sure. And he *was* a Hopi, he knew that, too.

"But Mary and Allan are our problem now!" Her voice had lost some of its sternness. "Do you think Allan's family will let him take her to Shongopovi after all this?"

"Allan's mother has been good to her. She likes her, I know. She talked to my mother about her."

"Even if they are not yet married in the Hopi way?"

That phrase again, he thought. There is much to this "Hopi way."

"Yes, I am sure," he said, though why he was so sure he did not know.

"Let's go in and tell her." There was eagerness in Kathleen's voice as she led him toward the door.

As she opened it, Jim's hand fell upon hers. She did not withdraw it, but returned the pressure of his fingers. No word passed between them as for a moment they looked deeply into each other's eyes. Then he gravely followed her into the hospital.

Mary was in a corner bed. She smiled sadly at him as he went to her. Kathleen put her fingers on her lips as a sign to Mary not to try to speak. In a few words they told her what was planned. Her eyes lighted up and the sadness went from her smile as they finished.

"Now I will live," she murmured as she closed her eyes and settled down into the covers.

XIV

"MY MOTHER, I AM GOING to marry Kathleen Lensa."

Jim's mother stopped her corn grinding and looked up at him.

"You must wait a while before you do that, my son."

Jim almost laughed aloud as he said, "You women stick together — that's what she told me yesterday!"

He had had no idea what his mother's reaction might be. He already had had evidence of the intricacies of Hopi clan relationships, and he knew that the innumerable taboos regarding marriage might place all kinds of obstacles in his way. He had thought about it most of the night and decided that the only way to find out where he stood was to discuss it with his mother; the clan mothers were the ones who held these things in their hands. Then he had a moment of panic. What a fool he was! Kathleen hadn't said she'd marry him — why on earth should she? — she probably was stalling like all the rest with her "we must wait."

His mother did not get up from her kneeling position before the *metates,* but she did not go on with the grinding.

Apparently she was turning the whole affair over in her mind. Jim thought she would never speak. When she did it was as if she were thinking aloud.

"A marriage between the Lensa clan and ours would be a good marriage, my son. But Kathleen is almost like a white girl to us. She has been away from her people a long time, she has made much money. She is used to lots of fine clothes, such as white girls wear, she –"

She fell silent again. Jim waited for the question he felt sure would come either now or later. It came at once.

"Will you live here like Hopi, or like white people? Maybe you will go away!"

"We have not discussed that, my mother."

How little we have discussed, he thought; nothing, really. Yet, strangely – perhaps because his mother did not say no – hope rose within him. Women seem to know these things; maybe she knows more about how Kathleen really feels than I do. One thing I know. This is my life. For the first time there was no indecision in his voice as he spoke of his future.

"I know now that my life is here."

His mother rose and came to him, her face aglow.

"Now you are indeed my son, a true Hopi son!" Then, "What will you do?"

"I think I will have cattle and sheep, and I am going to work with Bill Lanta in Old Oraibi and learn how to make silver."

"It is good, good!"

His mother's joy in his decision touched Jim deeply, and he felt sure of her understanding in whatever venture he might undertake – even marriage. Her quiet strength he felt would ever be a source of vigor for his work; he would be worthy of it, he determined that now.

"I'd like to go into Flagstaff soon to see about buying stock. I'll need a car, too. Oh, yes," as she looked at him questioningly, "I've money enough."

"Good, good! You must see Lololomi before you buy. Few Hopi have cattle. You must talk with him. He is wise and he is also one of your fathers."

She returned to her grinding while Jim busied himself with checking over the clothes and gear he had brought back from the Navy. These past days had granted little leisure for such things.

"I'll see if Allan is around," he said a few minutes later.

His mother nodded her approval. There was no one at the Lemtewa house, so he returned to his own to be met by young Sequa-Honau.

"Lololomi has told me to ask you to go to his *kiva,*" the boy announced.

Jim wondered how his mother had gotten word to the old man so quickly, for he did not doubt that Lololomi knew what he had decided. He wished that it would not be necessary to continue discussing it, but the old man already had proved his kindness and thought for him.

"I'll go at once," he told the youngster, and he added, "I may be needing a sheepherder soon."

The youngster beamed and dashed off.

When Jim climbed down the ladder into the *kiva* he was surprised to find assembled all the leading older men of the village. For the first few minutes nothing was said, then Nemtaka, the village chief, handed him a small sack of tobacco. He rolled a cigarette and joined the old men in their smoking. They sat on the long seat extending around the *kiva* walls and on small boxes that served as stools. The tobacco, papers, and box of matches were placed on the floor within reach of all. Nemtaka was the first to speak.

"It has been told to us, my son, that you plan to stay at Shongopovi, that you will marry and have a home here and work with us."

Jim nodded as the chief continued.

"You have been away from us for a long time, a long time. You are almost like a white man who has come to live with us. We hope it is your desire to live as a Hopi, that you wish to live the Hopi way of life."

Again Jim nodded his reply. There was silence for several minutes, then Nemtaka looked directly at him.

"We wish you to speak to us now, to tell us your plans for your life here."

Jim finished his cigarette before he began to speak. How could he say what he had to say so that they would accept him? He could be fairly sure of Lololomi, but what of the others? Should he speak of Kathleen? No, that must wait. He began somewhat diffidently.

"I want to live the Hopi way as best I can."

He looked about for approval, but the faces of the men were noncommittal. "I have been away a very long time, I know. I must learn our customs and our religion all over again. I can do it; I know this, too."

His speech began to take on something of the deliberateness of theirs.

"When I first came I could hardly speak our language, but now it has come back to me. I think the Hopi way of life will come back to me, too."

Lololomi gave him a nod, and he could sense that the others were now listening with greater interest.

"I plan to buy sheep and cattle; I have money for them and for a car."

"Cattle and automobiles are things the white men have brought to us."

Jim did not know the speaker, but he listened respectfully as the old man continued. "It is true that now many Hopi have cars, and many Hopi have cattle. It is also true that some Hopi too often use their cars to go to Holbrook," — Jim winced — "to Flagstaff, to Winslow. There they get drunk and go to places where good Hopi should not go."

Jim fidgeted. He supposed they'd all heard of his going to Daisy's house in Holbrook. Would they hold that against him? Would they decide they did not want him here? Well, there were other places to go. He found himself bristling as the speaker went on.

"When a car is used for purposes like these it is a very bad thing for a Hopi to have."

The old windbag, thought Jim; bet he likes to get drunk now and then himself! But a different man now took up the comments.

"But some Hopi have cars for bringing in coal, for

doing hauling for the white traders and the government people; these are good uses."

"It is the same with cattle."

Jim perceived that the general tone had changed. Their talk now definitely included him. They were a fine lot, really — except that one.

"Some Hopi have cows and they do not care about us who have plantings of corn. They do not care how much damage their cows do to our corn. Other Hopi keep their cattle out on the range where they cannot hurt our corn. Some Hopi who have cattle sell them and spend all the money on foolish things in Flagstaff, while others use their money for good things for their families."

There was much talk of all the problems that had arisen after cattle were introduced on the reservation, of the many farmers who had lost almost all their crops because of strays. Jim was amazed by the practical wisdom of their words. These old fellows knew what they were talking about. Lololomi again turned to him.

"You see the many things that you must know about?"

"I do indeed see that I know very little. I ask your help and advice, and I shall always be glad of it."

It was the man who had annoyed Jim earlier who spoke next.

"Washington has sent a white man to Keams Canyon to help us with our grazing problems. He is a good man. He will tell you about buying and where to graze your cattle."

"Good," Jim said gratefully. "I will go to see him. What is his name?"

"John Vadas. He is a *Mo'rmoni*. He likes Hopi. He will be of good help to you."

The meeting seemed to be at an end and the men stood up, when Lololomi spoke gravely.

"My son, we all know about the thing that happened in Holbrook. We are very glad that you took the Hopi girl from that house, but we do not think it was a good house for you to go to."

Now he was in for it, and just as everything seemed

O.K. Well, might as well get it over with. The old man left little unsaid, but as he concluded his voice was gentle.

"Many white people think our Hopi way of life is sinful because we do not think it wrong for a Hopi boy and girl who love each other to spend the night together before they are married. They think our divorce is wrong, too, because it is so easy. A woman has only to roll up her husband's things when he is away and place them for him at the door, and he is divorced. We have great freedom in these things, my son, yet we are not an immoral people.

"When you were a little boy I adopted you to cure you of a sickness. I shall continue to be a father to you, but I want a good son, not a bad son. I want a real Hopi, not a *Kahopi*."

The old man was silent after his long speech. The others nodded agreement and looked at Jim to see how he would reply. He waited only a moment and then, encouraged by Lololomi, he said, "In every way I will try to be a good son to you, my father."

XV

JIM WAS JUST LEAVING his house the following morning to look up Allan and learn what news there was of Mary, and of Kathleen, when he met young Sequa-Honau in company with a pleasant-looking white man.

"Nemtaka says you want to see him," the boy said, pointing to the man with him.

Seeing Jim's puzzled look. the stranger introduced himself.

"I'm John Vadas, and I came to talk with Nemtaka about the sheep that some of the people here own. I understand you are interested in getting some cattle. You are Jim Talastewa, aren't you?"

He spoke with such disarming friendliness that Jim found it easy to shake his extended hand.

"Yes, I'm Jim, and I am interested in cattle; but not many here seem to think much of the idea."

"That's true, I know. Still there is nothing against it that I can see. Maybe I can help you get started."

They squatted by the door for over an hour and talked of what cattle to buy, about the range, and about many other matters of related importance. The boy listened eagerly. He interrupted only once when sheep were mentioned.

"You will let me herd them for you, won't you, Jim?"

Vadas laughed, and when Jim nodded to Sequa-Honau he ran off happily.

"I'm going into Flag tomorrow, I'll be glad to have you go with me. Can you meet me down at Toreva about eight?"

"Thanks, I'll be there," was Jim's ready reply.

John Vadas had just left when Allan came by.

He looked after the departing Vadas and remarked, "He's a good man."

"I think so, too," Jim replied.

"All the Mormons treat us right," Allan added.

Jim waited for Allan to continue and when he did not, asked, "Mary – how is she? Could you get the license all right?"

"Yes, here it is. Kathleen said to tell you Mary is better and that we can marry soon."

"You do not sound too happy about it. Anything wrong?"

"It's my mother. She wants us to marry first in the Hopi way and then go to town and get married in the other way."

"Did you explain why you have to hurry and do it the other way around?"

"Well, I started to and then someone came in and I did not want to talk about it before others."

"Is your mother alone now?"

"I guess so; I've been gone for about an hour."

"I'll go home with you. Maybe, we can talk to her together."

When they got there Allan's mother was busy at the stove. She stopped her stirring and looked up as they entered.

"This is Jim."

"I know. Your mother tells me you will stay at Shongopovi."

'Yes, I will stay." Then, as if he had to get it over with, "We wish to tell you of Mary."

Her face darkened slightly, but her words belied the look. "Mary is a good girl. Allan is a good son."

Reassured, Jim told her of all that had happened, concluding with Dr. Cummings' willingness to perform the marriage and of how it seemed the best way to protect Mary. The mother turned to Allan who nodded his agreement with all that Jim had said.

"I see," the mother's voice was gentle. "You will marry the Hopi way, too?"

"Mary and I are both Hopi; we will be married the Hopi way."

"Good. Dr. Cummings' way is right. We will find a clan mother for Mary when there is time for the Hopi way."

Allan's elation showed in his face. Jim in turn found in the mother's unquestioning acceptance of his right to speak, assurance that the village was ready to regard him as one of them.

"I'll go back with you," said Allan as his mother turned back to the stove.

The two walked along in silence for several minutes. Even then nothing was said of what had transpired at Allan's.

"I'm going with Vadas tomorrow. I may buy some cattle in Flagstaff."

"Tomorrow? There is a dance. You should take part."

"Another dance so soon? I did not know they were rehearsing for another one."

"It's a dance everyone knows. They will rehearse it just tonight, and that's all."

"I guess I won't, this time. I want to get started. This is a good chance for me to see about the cattle. I better go with Vadas."

"O.K. I'll see you when you get back."

They parted at Jim's door. The day was nearly over. He had not realized how long they had talked at Allan's. But it was worth it. It looked as if it would be O.K. for Mary and Allan now. He heard a hint of the tom-tom in the kiva. Practicing for the dance. No, he couldn't do it this time. He must get started. Cattle, a few sheep — he couldn't disappoint the youngster — a car, yes, he'd need a car, he'd get to Keams Canyon oftener if he had one. He smiled as he thought of taking his mother for her first ride; he'd take her to see Kathleen. Well, his mother would be waiting supper for him, and he must turn in early; he'd have to be up at daybreak so as to be sure to meet Vadas.

The insistent beat of the kiva drum awoke him at dawn. He guessed he'd take a look at the dance before he left. Breakfast was a hurried affair; he knew his mother had been up long before he was awake in order to prepare it. She had a lunch for him, too, and she patted him and smiled up at him as she gave it to him.

"I don't know when I'll be back, but it's O.K. this time."

The quick light in her eyes showed that she understood what he meant. He walked towards the plaza to look on for a few minutes before starting down the trail. He had gone but a few steps when his ear caught a strange sound mixed with the chant of the ceremony. What could it be? He hastened to the scene of the dance, and there, to one side of the participants, a white woman was playing revival hymns at a small portable organ. As she played, Vance Vetch and a group of Hopi converts shouted out the words, defiantly trying to break up the Indian ceremony.

A surprising number of onlookers had assembled — Hopi, Navajo, and a scattering of other tribes — and they were watching with amusement the added drama that was taking place. Only Lololomi, who was directing the dance, showed any distress. The dancers went on as if there had been no interruption. When they retired for rest and prayer Vetch began to harangue the audience in a loud and strident voice.

"I have come to bring you salvation! I have come to bring Jesus Christ into your hearts! I have come to wash all sinners in the blood of the lamb! I have come to save you from the great burning!"

A long scriptural reading was followed by an equally long prayer, during which all of Vetch's followers knelt and murmured "Amen," from time to time. The Indians listened gravely, but Jim noted that an occasional young Hopi steadily held his hand over his mouth. Vetch was still on his knees when old Lololomi strode up to him and took him by the shoulder.

"Go from here! We are not *Kahopi* here in Shongopovi. We are true Hopi. We do not want you here. Go!"

His face contorted by fury, Vetch jerked to his feet and threw off the old man's hand and shoved him backwards. Lololomi stumbled and fell back upon the bare rock of the street, his head hitting a loose rock, causing a scalp wound from which the blood ran freely.

As he lay unconscious, the crowd surged forward and surrounded the intruders in an angry, muttering mob, scolding them and arguing with them and demanding of them that they leave at once. A group of Hopi women rushed to the assistance of Lololomi and, with the help of a few of the older men present, they managed to carry him to a nearby house. Apparently the wound was slight, for Jim could see that he was already regaining consciousness.

Intimidated by the angry looks and gestures of the Indians, Vetch and his followers beat a hasty retreat down the street and through a covered passageway to where their two cars were parked, their movements somewhat hampered by the portable organ. The crowd followed them, and some small boys began to pick up rocks, but the older Hopi saw to it that these were not thrown. As the cars started off, someone in the crowd made a ribald remark which changed the anger of the Hopi to laughter. It did not miss the ear of Vetch, but he did not think it prudent to ask his Hopi converts to translate it for the benefit of himself and his wife.

In a few minutes the dance was being resumed and Jim continued his walk to the trail. He was rather glad that no one had noticed him – he didn't want to seem to shirk – he certainly would have pitched in if there had been any more trouble. But these old men knew how to handle things – people of peace – after all, that was what Hopi meant.

XVI

"GLAD TO SEE YOU made it." Vadas' greeting was hearty. "I forgot to tell you yesterday that we'd be in town overnight."

"That's O.K. I told my mother I didn't know when I'd be back."

"Your mother's a fine woman, Jim. Everybody thinks a lot of her."

The drive was proving a pleasant experience for Jim—he'd rather dreaded it in some ways—he didn't want to have to answer a lot of questions. But Vadas knew a lot about the Hopi and seemed to understand their way of life and to respect it. He did not speak of them as if they were merely picturesque, colorful characters. To him they were hard-working, intelligent human beings. Jim became aware that he was learning a lot about his own people. He found himself telling freely the story of Mary and Allan and of the trouble Vetch was causing, and he sensed that the white man's sympathies were with the Hopi.

"Frankly, Jim, I share your feeling about Vetch. He's a fanatic and fanatics always bother me. There's something unbalanced about him; he'll go off the deep end some day. There are a lot, though, who aren't like Vetch. Look at Doc Cummings, for example."

Somehow Jim hadn't thought of the latter as a missionary.

"The Hopi have a real friend in him," continued Vadas, "and there have been lots of good teachers and doctors on other reservations who really tried to help the people."

"Allan says you are a Mormon," said Jim after a lull in the conversation.

"Yes, I am," Vadas replied.

"Why is it the missionaries you Mormons send out here don't behave the way Vetch does?"

"Well," laughed Vadas, "we saints –"

"Saints?" questioned Jim.

"We don't usually call ourselves Mormons," Vadas explained. "Our church is called the Church of Jesus Christ of Latter Day Saints."

"You're Christians, then, too?"

"Why, of course, Jim. What did you think we were?" There was no offense in Vadas' voice, and he laughed off Jim's embarrassment at his brash question. "About our missionaries – our church teaches that when a Mormon goes on a mission he must live and act in such a way as to win the respect of the people he's working among."

They reached the transcontinental highway at this point and traffic made further conversation difficult.

When they arrived in Flagstaff they drove at once to a small hotel in a grove of pine trees on the outskirts of the town. The proprietor expressed his pleasure at seeing Vadas, and then he shook hands with Jim.

"We're always glad to have Hopi here."

This was something different – a decently clean place where they took in Indians – the fellow sounded as if he really was glad to see a Hopi. Well!

As they put their things in the room assigned to them, Vadas asked, "Did you bring much money with you, Jim?"

"Oh, about four thousand dollars."

"My God, man, where on earth did you get that amount of money?"

"Well, I made good money in the Navy and there weren't too many chances to spend it. And my mother didn't spend any of what I sent her. Last night she made me take it all back, insisted I'd need it on this trip."

"Look, boy, you're going right over to the bank and put that into an account. I'm not going around the country with you carrying all that dough!"

The bank was across the street from Babbitt Brothers Trading Company. Vadas introduced Jim to an officer of the bank who took care of him. Soon all Jim had for his neat bundles of twenty-, fifty-, and hundred-dollar bills was a small passbook and a pocket checkbook. John Vadas was the one who seemed the more at ease when the money had been deposited in the Coconino National Bank.

They lunched in a small restaurant where again Vadas was welcomed, and again the owners were people who seemed not to mind having a Hopi as a customer. This white man's world wasn't half bad; more like on the ship. It hadn't mattered there that his skin was red. Fellows in the Army had had a rougher time of it, he'd heard; he certainly couldn't complain. A hearty voice greeting Vadas interrupted his musing, and he looked up to see a calm-faced young man approaching their table.

"Hello, Vadas. Glad to see you in town. Who's this?"

"Jim, this is the very man we came into town to see. Ted Livingstone, this is Jim Talastewa of Shongopovi."

"Good enough – fine people, the Hopi. How much wool will we be getting from them this year?" He directed the question at Vadas.

All his life Jim had known of the Livingstone Trading Company. It had stores, ranches, and all sorts of commercial interests throughout northern Arizona, as well as trading posts through the Indian country. It was one of the oldest firms in the Southwest. It would be something to tell his mother when he got back home, that he'd eaten with Ted Livingstone.

Livingstone joined them at their table and ordered lunch. Both the place and the talk were friendly. Jim found that though he said little he had no feeling of being excluded. Again, in listening, he learned much about this land from which he had been away so long, and more about the Hopi and their problems.

"Jim here wants to buy some sheep and cattle." Vadas made the statement as they were rising from their meal.

"I'll be glad to help." Livingstone's reply was hearty and genuine. "With Vadas on hand we'll probably lose some of our best stock to you, Jim. But we'll make up for it when you come back to sell us the wool. I warn you we Livingstones drive a shrewd bargain."

John Vadas laughed as he rejoined, "Ted's a tough man to deal with, all right, but he won't cheat you."

"Don't you be too sure of that!" But there was no hint of dishonesty in the tone of his voice. "Well, I'll be looking for you later."

Left to themselves once more, Vadas suggested that on the morrow Jim go with him to make the rounds of the nearby ranches that the Livingstones owned.

"Ted's in charge of the family's sheep business. He does drive a hard bargain, but he can be trusted. He's a good friend to have, a good friend to the Indians. You can go to him for advice, Jim, any time you're in Flagstaff. Don't hesitate to do it. I wish we had more like him in business in northern Arizona."

"I've heard of the Livingstones all my life, but I never thought I'd be doing business with one of them. Thanks for lunch; this is a nice place."

"Well, I've some things to do that wouldn't interest you. You spoke of getting a car. Why don't you look around and meet me here for dinner about six?"

"O.K. Thanks again."

The first automobile dealer Jim encountered took him at once to the firm's second-hand lot and tried to rush him off his feet with a brightly painted roadster that he assured Jim was just the thing for the Hopi country. Jim said little but agreed to ride in it for a trial. He took the wheel from the salesman and drove up a fairly steep grade near the Lowell Observatory.

"The rear end of this crate is gone, you know it is. And

I noticed that you've doped up a crack in the engine block. Good for the Hopi country? This car's been dynamited and you know it. Now, will you or I drive back to town?"

Jim's astonishment at his own vehemence was matched by the salesman's amazement. This was no gullible young Indian on whom he could unload a car that was a lemon on the lot. And he had felt so sure of wangling a good fat bonus!

"How in hell do you know so much about cars?"

"I was a machinist in the Navy for seven years; you learn something about engines there."

The salesman said nothing as he drove Jim back to town.

Jim made the rounds of the agencies, and he finally found a new pickup truck that suited him. He could have delivery in about a week. He was about to write the check for it when Vadas came in.

"Thought you might be here. Got one you like? Good! Let's have a look at the contract before you write the check."

They pored over the document together.

"It looks all right to me," said Jim.

"It *is* all right. Finish your check and we'll go get some dinner."

Jim had a sense of pride in consummating a deal quite on his own. Here was another firm not out to rob the Indian. And what a really swell friend John Vadas was turning out to be.

Dinner at the little restaurant was another pleasant meal. Jim noted that when some Navajo came in they were treated just the same as white customers – and they had no John Vadas with them. Red man, white man, maybe they weren't so different after all.

Dinner over, they walked about the town. It was Saturday night and the streets were crowded with shoppers – Indians and whites. Tall, lanky Navajo men in wide black hats sat on drugstore fountain stools alongside Navajo women in velvet blouses and wide swishy skirts, both soberly sucking ice cream sodas. Short, wide-faced, smiling Hopi jostled each other as they went in and out of Penney's.

Vadas suggested that they see a movie, and Jim readily agreed. It was a long time since he had seen one. They used to have them on the ship every night, and he never thought of missing them.

Tom Mix was the star of the only picture available. On this occasion the great Mix was portraying a ranger in the Park Service at Grand Canyon. There were shots of Bright Angel Trail, of El Tovar Hotel and of the Hopi House, the curio store on the South Rim where so many Hopi were employed. The climax of the evening, so far as the audience was concerned, came when Mix, to rescue the heroine from a fate worse than death, rode desperately into Williams; a Williams that was depicted as a sleepy, adobe town with strings of peppers hanging on the walls and lazy burros dozing in the streets.

At this scene the Indians, cowpunchers, sheepherders, loggers, Santa Fe workers and lumber mill employees that comprised the audience joined in a roar of laughter that rocked the theater. Jim turned to Vadas.

"I don't see what's so funny about it."

"It has nothing to do with the story really," laughed Vadas. "But right now Williams and Flagstaff are rival towns and the people here get a great kick out of what Hollywood has done to Williams in this movie. It's been shown here three Saturday nights, as a matter of fact."

For the better part of the reel, Mix rode with dashing skill through what seemed endlessly long streets for such a small village, while the laughter and the yelling of spectators mounted higher and higher.

"I still don't find it so funny," said Jim as they were leaving the theater.

"Oh, it's as good a way as any to spend an evening in this town."

"What happens when they show it in Williams?"

"We'll have to go and see for ourselves some time," Vadas laughed.

XVII

"WHEN THE GRASS has dried a bit, along about May, will be the time to get these cattle, Jim." The speaker was John Vadas.

"Good! I'll be here then, Mr. Livingstone," and Jim turned and put out his hand.

That made the bargain so far as Jim was concerned, but Ted Livingstone, as a matter of course, replied, "Swell! When I get back to town I'll drop you a letter confirming the deal, then there will be no misunderstanding if I'm not around when you come for them."

The three men were standing in front of the old Hashknife ranch house among the cinder cones that run out from the San Francisco Peaks toward the Little Colorado River. From where they stood they could look through the juniper and the piñon pines to the great sweep of the Painted Desert fringing the wide valley of the river. Out of sight beyond the painted cliffs to the east were the Hopi mesas.

"These cattle have been born and raised in this country, so there shouldn't be much trouble in getting them used to the food and water of their new range."

Vadas' words were reassuring to Jim, who was not yet feeling too sure of what he was getting himself in for. Neither Livingstone nor Vadas, though, had seemed to question his ability to handle cattle and here at the Hashknife was the finest lot of them he had ever seen. It hadn't taken him long to decide on a dozen head of bred yearling Herefords. John Vadas had been so enthusiastic about his choice that Ted Livingstone had threatened to raise the price on the quotation he had given them.

"These cattle really belong to my brother; he handles that end of our business. But he's in Los Angeles for a while. I'm sure the deal will be O.K. with him. In fact, if he's back when I get home I'll have him write you the letter of confirmation."

The cattle purchase made, they drove down on the desert towards Winslow to look at some sheep that Livingstone had said were available. Jim felt on more familiar ground here, for often as a small boy he had herded sheep for his clan uncles and had listened in on their talk regarding them. They looked at three different flocks before Vadas felt sure of their selection. Twenty-four ewes and a ram were finally chosen, animals with fleece that was heavy and of good quality. Back in Livingstone's car, Jim sat on the front seat and with Vadas' fountain pen he wrote out a check covering the transaction. Livingstone took the check, and when he saw the amount in full, he exclaimed in amazement.

"Golly, Jim, I didn't expect the whole thing in cash! I tell you what — I'll throw in a couple of ewes for good measure, then you won't have to worry if you lose a few during the year."

All the way back to Flagstaff they talked and laughed and joked with the freedom of men who felt sure of themselves and of each other. It was four when they arrived; early enough, Vadas suggested, to make it home that day. Home — it was really that now, Jim thought; possessions, work, maybe, even — a wife — home —

They took the old road out from Flagstaff, the one through the cinder cones. As they drove eastward the yellow pine trees became smaller and smaller and finally, around one bend in the road, they were replaced by large piñon pines and junipers. These in turn became smaller and smaller as Vadas and Jim dropped lower and lower into the desert stretches of the valley of the Little Colorado. The lava and cinder cones were left far behind and soon they were among the eroded flat red rocks near the river itself. A few hundred feet back of the scattering of giant cottonwoods on the bank they could see the stone square of Sunshine Trading Post.

They stopped for a word or two with the trader, who assured them that the river was low enough for them to ford it safely. As they drove down to try it he followed them in his old truck to be sure that they could make it. The two deep ruts of the road ran right into the water and, a hundred feet on the other side, emerged again upon the sandy banks. John threw the car into low and gave it a good run as it plunged into the water. The trick was to keep moving and not let the flowing water have a chance to eat the sand out from under the tires.

"There's always a possibility of quicksand here, then down we'd go!"

Jim admired the skill with which Vadas kept the car moving. One had to know this country to get around in it.

"I remember," he said, "hearing that, during Snake Dance time, many a tourist car disappeared here, and in other washes, too."

"Yes, it's tricky to get through them all right, but one soon learns when he can make it and when he can't."

"What happens if you can't make it here?"

"Oh, you try the Tolchaco Crossing, or else go round to the new bridge at Cameron. But that's too far."

They hit one or two holes as the car roared through the muddy water, but they were not stopped by it. When they had gained hard ground on the opposite bank they stopped and waved to the trader who returned their signal before they started up the long sandy grade that took them out of the valley.

A lull in the conversation was broken by Vadas.

"You know, Jim, the more I see of this Hopi country

the more I realize how wise your old chiefs have been in resisting attempts to cut up the reservation into individual allotments."

Jim did not reply at once. His mind went back to a talk he had had with Lololomi a few days before as they nooned under a tree near the corn plantings. The old man had reached down and taken up a handful of the light sandy soil and rotated it between the fingers and palm of his hand. He had spoken slowly, whether for Jim's benefit or just in the contemplative way of the Hopi, Jim could not be sure.

"These are good fields where we are working. They must remain ours. A man dies, a woman dies, but the Hopi people remain. Our land must not belong to this woman or to that man, it must belong to the people. White men come from Washington and tell us we must divide up the Hopi land. But they do not understand our way."

"I've been wondering about this land business, John," and Jim told him what Lololomi had said.

"The old man's absolutely right. The allotment system is no good for your people. Their security lies in the land, and don't let anybody ever tell you it doesn't. Once the tribal ownership of Hopi lands is broken down, the Hopi tribe is finished."

"Well, is there much talk of doing this?"

"Too much to suit me. Sometimes the way your old men stick to your traditional ways of doing things drives me nearly crazy. But in this I go along with old Lololomi one hundred percent. Don't get me started on this subject; I'll be talking all the rest of the way."

As they bounced along the uneven dirt road, Jim found his spirits soaring, and now and then he sang snatches of the Buffalo Dance songs. To his amazement John Vadas knew them, too, and joined him, bellowing them out in full voice and pounding the floorboards with his free foot, as they jolted on through New Oraibi and across the Oraibi Wash, now dry as a bone.

It was night as they drove over the bare rocks of the mesa top into Shongopovi.

"Why don't you have supper with us, Mr. Vadas?—"

and, catching himself at a look from the other man, "John?"

"Be glad to if your mother won't mind – I'd like to see her again."

There was no mistaking his sincerity.

"She won't mind, but it won't be white man's food."

"All the better for that!"

Vadas' laughter as they entered the house brought a shy smile to the face of Nasayungti.

"You are welcome," she said in Hopi, and his thanks were expressed in the same tongue.

Jim doubted that a white man had ever eaten in his mother's house before, and he knew her over-eagerness to please would but add to her diffidence. But the zeal with which Vadas waded into the mutton stew brought a wide smile to her usually passive face and, although she did not understand all that was being said, she joined in the laughter when John joked Jim about being a big sheep and cattle man now.

John did not linger long when the meal was over.

"I've got to be on my way to Keams," he said. "Let me know if you need any help. Goodnight."

Nasayungti listened carefully to Jim's account of all that he had done, occasionally interrupting him with "Good! Good!" Then she said in her quiet way, "Allan was here. He says he goes to Keams Canyon tomorrow. He will get married there. He wants you to go with him."

He could not exactly tell whether she approved, but he'd have to really talk to her about it all some other time. It had been a long two days and he was suddenly tired. Keams Canyon tomorrow; that meant he'd see Kathleen. He'd be able to tell her about the car, the sheep, the cattle; he'd show her the bankbook. The stock had made a big hole in the amount, but there was still a good deal left, more than most Hopi made in a year. Maybe she'd realize that he was no ordinary Hopi farmer; Allan and Mary – well, maybe his own time wouldn't be too far off.

XVIII

SUPPORTED BY ALLAN and Dr. Cummings, Mary was able to walk down the corridor to the large, sunny room of the hospital in which she and Allan were to be married. She looked attractive in a dress loaned by Kathleen. The excitement of the occasion had given her a sparkle that had not been evident in the trying days through which she had passed. Allan wasn't making any mistake, Jim felt sure of that, and he felt doubly sure when Kathleen looked from one to the other in smiling approval.

Dr. Cummings made the ceremony as brief and simple as possible, using a silver ring which an Oraibi friend had given Allan for the event. Mary insisted on standing throughout. She had seen one white man's wedding; she was determined that she would stand, as had the white girl on that occasion. Allan's first sense of possession came as he held her arm through the short ritual. Only Jim and Kathleen were witnesses and they talked briefly with the bride and groom while Dr. Cummings completed the necessary papers. They left Mary and Allan sitting in the sunlight to plan for the day when Mary could leave the hospital.

"I'll see you when you come on duty at three, Kathleen," Dr. Cummings said.

It was only eleven by the office clock at the hospital entrance. Kathleen and Jim looked up at it almost the same moment.

"Let's go for a walk, Kathleen; I want to talk to you."

"Give me a minute to change my clothes."

A little distance from the settlement of Keams Canyon they found an old wagon road that gradually led up over a mesa edge. They walked along, hand in hand. Neither spoke for a long time.

It was Kathleen who finally commented, "They did look happy, didn't they? I just hope that old missionary won't make any more trouble for them."

"I hope he doesn't make any trouble for you or Dr. Cummings. Maybe he'll go to the superintendent and complain."

"Yes, I think he will, and Dr. Cummings expects it, too. The superintendent is not too friendly with us just now, either. He thinks we're too soft with the patients. And he never did like the idea of an Indian girl as a nurse in a hospital – that's a white girl's job, he says. I am sure, though, that the church will back us up."

"You're not a Christian, are you, Kathleen?"

"No; not if you mean am I a member of the church. Real Christianity isn't so far away from the Hopi idea. Christ was a peaceful man, too. But I never could feel at home in any of their churches. No, I guess I'm not a Christian."

"Dr. Cummings doesn't seem like a missionary. Does he try to make all the sick people become Christians?"

"Of course not, Jim! He'd never think of doing that; he's a doctor. He says if people's bodies and minds are all right it isn't so hard for them to be good Christians, or good Hopi. It is his church, though, that really helps here. It built the hospital, it pays us, it buys all the supplies."

They lapsed into silence again and walked on for another mile or so until they emerged upon the southern tip of the mesa. Here they sat down in a patch of sunlight with a low-spreading juniper at their backs. Before them and below them stretched an ever-widening canyon that twisted and turned until in the far distance it joined a wide desert valley. They could see Navajo children herding sheep, and the soft breeze now and then brought to them faint snatches of song. Jim continued to hold Kathleen's hand and she pressed closer to him.

"I now own twelve cows, all bred yearlings, two dozen ewes, and a fine ram – and I'll have a new truck next week." Jim made the unvarnished factual statement, looking straight out over the canyon.

"Oh, I'm glad, Jim, I'm glad! I was so afraid you'd waste your money."

"When can we get married?" He put the question abruptly. Then he looked at her thoughtfully, sitting so trim and clean beside him. "How can you ever be married in the Hopi way? Think of that mud the women will rub all over you. It's a horrible thing to do!"

"I don't think I'd mind it too much – one can always go through with a custom – I'll wash it all off and be none the worse for it."

Jim did not know whether this was an answer to his question or not.

"How will we name our children if we marry in the Hopi way? Will we give them Hopi names or white names?"

"Jim, Jim, here we've known each other only a few weeks and you are beginning to worry about what we'll name our children! I don't even remember promising to marry you!"

Something in her voice gave him the answer he wanted and he pulled her to him and kissed her almost fiercely. She did not resist and when she made a little move to hug him to her he kissed her again, more gently but nevertheless firmly.

"Now who's behaving like a white man? You are *Kahopi*. Hopi don't kiss each other – like that! What white girl has been teaching you?"

Her raillery was what they needed, and they found themselves laughing together; their first laugh, they suddenly realized, for none of the occasions on which they had been together had warranted gaiety.

"Can it be soon, Kathleen? We can make a go of it, I know."

"I don't know. Don't ask when, just yet."

They sat on the edge of the cliff, dreaming of the future, and from time to time gave voice to their desires.

"We'll have a Hopi house, but we'll have bigger windows; we'll have things that white people have, too. We can place them so they won't spoil the house, we'll have a bathroom like the one at the hospital."

"These things cost a lot of money, Kathleen."

"I know they do, but I'm going on being a nurse after I'm married."

She saw his face cloud.

"I know that's not the Hopi way, but I want it to be our way."

As he protested she defended her position passionately.

"It's wrong for me to have taken all this training and then not put it to use. The Hopi people need trained nurses. Maybe I won't work in the hospital; I'd like to get into the field service helping mothers with their babies. Don't look so serious, Jim, we'll manage."

She went on in great detail about how high the infant mortality rate was among the Hopi and just what a good nurse could do to help lower it.

Of course, she's right, he thought, I feel a little that way about my Navy training, but I won't let all of that be lost, either. He smiled as he remembered the first car salesman, but . . .

"But you'll be making more money than I will, and that doesn't seem right."

"Well, if we both work hard at our jobs it will be right. Growing corn, looking after cattle and sheep, and doing silver work on the side – all this means you'll be working harder than I am. If you took an easy job and I had to work hard, or if I was a lazy housekeeper and you had to work hard then it would be wrong. As it is, it will be right."

There was a note of finality in her voice as if this were

a matter to which she had given much thought.

"The old men will have things to say about it."

"Of course, they will; that's what old men are for," she laughed. "The women will, too. But sensible people will see it the way we do; I am sure it will be all right."

She looked at her watch.

"It's almost two o'clock; I'll be late for duty if I don't run!"

They lingered for a long embrace and then walked quickly down the road to the hospital door where they said good-bye. Allan was waiting at the office, joking with a Navajo girl. The two started the long trip back to Shongopovi.

No one was driving their way, but the trail seemed smooth and easy as they trotted along together. Soon there was much talk of what the future held for both of them. They stopped to eat with some friends of Allan at Polacca, below the great precipice of Walpi. After a smoke and a bit of talk they continued under the stars to their own village.

XIX

A POST CARD from the dealer in Flagstaff informed Jim that his truck was ready. Jim had already arranged with Tom Nesviki to drive him into town and to bring back one load of sheep. Tom offered to share the services of two reliable boys he had as sheepherders, and Jim said he'd like to use young Sequa-Honau, too.

They left Shongopovi at dawn. The road was in good condition and all went easily, so they were on their way back by early afternoon. Tom and his boys went on ahead with one load of sheep. Jim with the happy Sequa-Honau and their load of sheep drove the new truck slowly. He and the boy sang song after song on the leisurely drive out the level, smooth road toward Leupp, on the great mud flats of the Little Colorado.

Tom had said that his sheep were grazing near Burro Springs, across the wash a few miles east of Oraibi, and that Jim should watch for the turn-off. They had agreed that, for the present, Jim could use the same range. As he followed Tom's ruts across the desert he hoped his spick-and-span new car would not get too muddy – he'd like Kathleen to have a look at it when it was brand new.

Tom had halted almost at the edge of the wash. There they unloaded the sheep, and Tom's boys demonstrated their herding skill by driving the animals down the slopes and across the wash to join Tom's small flock on the other side. Two youngsters with Tom's group on the other side called out a greeting, for they had driven the flock close to their side of the wash. Although he said nothing, Jim noted with satisfaction that his solid, healthy-looking animals were far superior to Tom's rather bony beasts.

"Keep them looking as well as they do now and I'll give you all good presents."

"And while you're at it, see if you can't get a little fat on the bones of mine," added Tom. Then he turned to Jim, "I heard they are having one of the dances of *Po-a-mu-ya* at Old Oraibi, the Bean Dance. We're in time to see some of it."

"I'd like to," replied Jim, "and it will give me a chance to see about some silver work I'm interested in doing. I hate to take my new truck up through those sand dunes. I'll park it in the peach orchards above New Oraibi and meet you on top later."

Tom nodded in agreement and drove off, while Jim went on through the collection of houses at Hubbell's Trading Post and parked his shiny new car on the solid earth at the foot of the mesa. Most of the people were up on top watching the ceremony, but a few had stayed behind and they came to their doors, broad smiles expressing their admiration of the new pickup.

Jim had soon left behind the steep hills of fine sand, which clogged his steps like soft snow, and he began to climb the almost ladder-like steps that were cut in the solid rock of Oraibi mesa, now rounded and smooth from much use. Even the hand-holes, cut to enable one to steady himself on the steeper parts of the trail, were worn into deep cups by the hands of generations of Hopi who had lived on the mesa top through a procession of centuries.

Jim was almost at the top when a young Hopi came leaping down the trail.

"There is trouble up there," he said tersely. "I go for the superintendent."

He dashed down the trail with no further word, and in a moment was running through the sandhills in the direction of the school.

Jim hurried to the mesa top. He ran quickly to the center of the village, for in that direction he could hear people shouting. As he rounded a corner of one of the crumbling houses he stopped in consternation. The dance plaza was a milling crowd of angry Hopi, many of them in the colorful costumes donned for the ceremony. Here and there were elderly men in cotton trousers, the directing priests of the *Po-a-mu-ya.* Rising above the tumult came the whine of a small organ and snatches of Christian hymns. Dominating the scene was a great pillar of smoke and flame.

Jim saw Tom over to one side and ran over to him with a question. "What has happened? The fire? What is it from?"

Sullen with anger, Tom explained, the words coming from him bitterly.

"There is great trouble here. The ceremony was almost over when Vetch . . ."

"Vetch again!" Jim burst forth angrily.

"Yes, he and the *Kahopi* from down below came with their organ and began to play and sing so as to break up the ceremony. At a pause in the ceremony he called the people here bad names. He accused the chief of helping to steal Mary. He grew angry. The people would not listen and went on with the ceremony. They sang louder than his hymn-singers. This made him still more furious and they left the woman at the organ and went off."

"There must be some way of stopping him, of making him let us alone!"

Jim saw that this was not the end of the story and he listened thoughtfully as Tom continued.

"The people here laughed at him and went on with the ceremony. But in a few minutes he came back. Some of those hymn-singing *Kahopi,*" he fairly spat out the word, "they knew where the ceremonial things were kept. They broke into the houses and brought here masks, prayer sticks, costumes — everything they could carry. They dumped them in a pile and Vetch yelled threats at us as they poured gasoline on them and set them on fire!"

"No! They wouldn't do such a thing as that! Surely they wouldn't!"

"You see — the smoke — it is still there." Tom's voice was filled with grief as he added sadly, "Some of the things they burned were as old as the Hopi — they can never be replaced. There will be great trouble because of this."

At that moment, in a voice that all could hear, the chief of Oraibi called out, "My people, you must listen to me. Much damage has been done to our sacred things. My heart and your hearts are filled with great sadness. I feel now that I would like to kill this white man. You all know that I stood with the white man against Yokeoma and his people. Now this white man stands against me. I would rather be shot down by the white soldiers than give up our ceremonies as this white man would force us to do. My heart is too angry now for me to tell you what we must do to him. But we will finish our ceremony, no matter what he says or does!"

The dancers silently took their places and the ceremony was resumed. Vetch's wife played the organ as loudly as she could. The Hopi converts and Vetch fairly yelled out their hymns. The villagers and visitors who were not participants at one moment watched the ceremony in respectful silence, and at the next moment broke that silence to jeer at the intruders.

The ceremony was finished within a short time. A few minutes later the Hopi disappeared from the plaza, leaving it to Vetch and his followers. The latter closed the organ and went to their cars. Vetch was white with anger and frustration. There was an ominous silence over the old village.

Jim walked over to Tom's truck and they drove down to where the pickup was parked. They were too heavy-hearted for conversation.

"I am afraid, Tom, that this means trouble."

Tom's set face was answer enough.

"Thanks for the help with the sheep. I'll see you back at Shongopovi."

XX

SOME OF JIM'S WORRY of the night before had worn away with sleep. At breakfast he announced to his mother that she was to have her first automobile ride as soon as the meal was over. Her face lighted up with pleasure and she bustled about her morning tasks with great energy. By some sort of "moccasin telegraph," that Jim had not yet learned to comprehend, the whole village seemed to be on hand for the event, and his clan aunts decidedly counted themselves in on the expedition.

One of these aunts sat between him and his mother, and into the back piled the others and every youngster who could climb in or hang on. The women began to giggle with excitement and, finally, as the assembled crowd began to joke them, they laughed aloud, hurriedly covering their mouths with their hands as they did so. Jim looked behind him to be sure that none of the children would fall off, and then he slowly started the car. Nasayungti and his aunt were obviously somewhat frightened, but their delight and pride in Jim and in the car allayed their qualms.

He drove out the mesa road and down the steep, narrow

stretch that led to the wash which separated the two arms of the mesa, then across to Shipolovi and Mishongnovi, the other two villages of Second Mesa. There, friends and relatives of his mother came out to see the car and to gossip. It was without doubt a great day for his mother. She explained to everyone what a fine son he had always been, that now he was home again, that he had saved his money and was a wealthy man. Jim thought she spread it on a bit thick.

Upon their return to Shongopovi, Jim helped them all out of the car and had just lifted the hood to show them the engine when Jack Palakvi and his old father came toward them, leading a boy of about ten years. He was a straight, fine-looking youngster, his face alight with intelligence; but, as they came closer, Jim realized that he was blind.

Old Palakvi spoke.

"We wish you to do us a great favor. This, my grandson, can not see with his eyes, they are dead; he sees with his fingers. He touches everything and his fingers tell him what it is. He has heard us talk about automobiles, but he has never been able to see one with his fingers. We wish he could put his fingers all over your automobile so that in his mind he will know what it is."

"Sure, let him go ahead."

Jim felt somewhat ill at ease in the presence of this child who was not like others – rotten luck not to be able to see. Old Palakvi was one of those in the *kiva* whom he had liked.

The old man lifted the boy up on his shoulders, and, as they moved along, the father directed the small hands to all parts of the car, all the time trying to explain to him in Hopi what his fingers were touching. But the puzzled look on the child's face indicated that he could not "see" the truck as a whole.

"Let's take him for a ride," Jim suggested.

Jim shooed off the youngsters who were still clinging to the back hopefully.

"We're just going a little way; I'll take you all some other time."

The Palakvis got in, the boy next to Jim, who started the

motor and let it run for a while so that the boy would get accustomed to the vibration. The child grasped Jim's arm but as Jim let in the clutch and started slowly forward he relaxed and smiled and soon was gaily inquiring as to what he was "seeing" and what kept the car moving. They had driven out on the village road about half a mile and were just about to turn back at the junction where the Shongopovi road intercepts the main road between Oraibi and Walpi, when they saw a car coming in their direction. It was Dr. Cummings' car, Jim was sure, and as it came closer he saw that Kathleen was driving and that she was alone. She came up to them and stopped.

"So you got your car, Jim. It's a beauty. But I must talk to you. Can you wait a minute?"

She pulled into a turn-out, and Jim walked over to her.

"I just heard about the trouble at Oraibi. Vetch came to see the superintendent early this morning and the superintendent told him that he'd see to it that all our ceremonies are stopped. He's almost as mad as Vetch, and he'll be madder than ever when he finds out about Mary. Dr. Cummings and all of us will be in for it then. What can we do about it?"

Jim had not expected things to come to a head so soon.

"Let's go to the village; we can talk at my mother's house."

His heart was heavy with worry as he drove back to Shongopovi and he scarcely heard the thanks of the small blind boy as he walked off between Jack and old Palakvi. Kathleen followed and joined him at the house. Jim's heart lifted as he saw that his mother received Kathleen pleasantly and put out a little stool for her to sit on. Jim explained briefly to his mother the problem facing them, and asked if it would not be wise to have some of the older people of the village come in and talk with them about it.

"Let me tell them," Nasayungti said simply, and left Jim and Kathleen to themselves.

"Somehow I was never here before, although my mother and yours are friends."

"My mother seems to have been much alone," Jim admitted, a bit regretful of his own neglect over the years, "but she never complains. Lololomi and the others are all very good to her."

"And now you're home again!"

There was no time for further conversation between them, for the house began to fill with the old chiefs and the leading clan women. Tom Nesviki, too, came in.

"The sheep are fine, I was just down that way. Your herder is going to be all right, too; he's your boy Sequa-Honau, Kathleen."

"He's a good youngster, Jim. I'm glad you're using him."

Nasayungti made coffee, and the inevitable tobacco was passed among the men. From the comments, it was evident that news of the trouble at Old Oraibi was already known in the village and that many of those assembled were sure that they were facing a crisis in Hopi life. When they learned that Tom and Jim had witnessed much of the affair, Lololomi asked each of them to give an account of what he had seen happen.

The men sat in the middle of the room, and the women ranged themselves around the walls with their backs to the men. That the women were alert to everything that was said was obvious. Tom was just finishing his story when someone came to the door. It was opened to admit the village chief and two others from Old Oraibi who had come to discuss the matter with the leaders of the Second Mesa villages. They were pleased to find that the situation was already known and that they could count on help.

Kathleen then volunteered the news of what she had heard at Keams Canyon that morning, whereupon the Oraibi chief jumped up and dramatically asserted, "I will go on with our ceremonies as long as I live. We Hopi cannot live without our dances; they are part of our way of life. Let the superintendent bring his soldiers just as he did when they rode into our village and tore the children from their mothers' arms to send them away to school where so many died; let him call his soldiers in again; let them shoot me down! I will still do my ceremonies!"

The old man's passion stirred them all, and there was a

chorus of approbation. The words of defiance were echoed by Lololomi, by Nemtaka, by the representatives of all the societies responsible for the important ceremonial dances of the villages of Second Mesa. At this point another Hopi entered the room breathless, as if he had run a great way. He stammered out, "The superintendent is down at the school. He is coming here to see the village chief."

All looked at Nemtaka. A slight smile came to the latter's face, but it passed in an instant. As he stood up he looked impassive and poised to meet any situation.

"Remain here. I will go to my own house. The superintendent can find me there."

There was only desultory talk after Nemtaka left. The women scattered to their homes with promises of additional coffee for the talks that would follow. Tobacco and paper and matches were thrown to a spot in the middle of the room where anyone could help himself to the makings for a cigarette. The men sat at seeming ease, drank coffee, smoked lazily, ventured an occasional comment, and waited for Nemtaka's return.

Nearly an hour passed before he rejoined them, and his face was grave as he stood before them.

"The superintendent has gone. He has left very bad words with us. He says that he knows all Hopi like him and that to show this to Washington we are to adopt him and give him a Hopi name! He says if we do not do this at once he will make great trouble for us. His words were crooked to me, but I think he means that if we will do this he will allow us to continue with our religion and our ceremonies. I told him I must talk with the other old men of our village. I would say no more, so he went away."

The tension that followed Nemtaka's remarks was lessened by the joking suggestion of one of the younger men in the room.

"Let us initiate him as one of the boys in the *Po-a-mu-ya*."

There was a laugh at this, for the speaker always officiated as one of the Whipping Kachinas, in the initiation ceremonies. It was easy to see that he longed for an opportunity to thrash the superintendent with his handful of yucca whips.

Silence settled over the room once more, a silence that lasted several minutes. It was finally broken by the laughter of old Lololomi.

"This superintendent – he knows nothing of our ceremonies, he knows nothing of our language. I am an old man. There is nothing he can do to hurt me. I will adopt him as my son in the way we adopt a sick child. I will adopt him, and I will say that I will cure him as we cure a child who is sick in the head."

Laughter swept the room. It halted as Lololomi held up his hand.

"I will give him the name *Chee-va-to!"*

The laughter that greeted his final sentence was uncontrollable. Jim listened and looked on in complete bewilderment. Then he recalled a ceremony in which a clown pointed at a Hopi who was dirty and disgusting in appearance and said, *"Chee-va-to!"* Just a day or two before, Nemtaka used the same word about a young man who was being criticized for his gross habits. *"Chee-va-to"* – "billy-goat" that's what it meant, as nasty a word as the gentle Hopi ever use.

The evening then was given over to the consideration of a multitude of suggestions about the staging of the adoption ceremonies, although wise old Lololomi had little need of them, it seemed to Jim. The serious events which had provoked all this apparently were quite forgotten. As there appeared to be nothing he could do, Jim looked about for an easy way to leave the group just as Kathleen signalled from the doorway that he should follow her.

"That Lololomi is a smart old man; if he can manage this adoption it will make the superintendent so ridiculous among our people that he'll have to go."

"Well, let's hope it works!"

They walked together to the house of Kathleen's mother. Jim hesitated to enter, but Kathleen insisted.

"They know," she said, and the words were all Jim

needed to make the happenings of the evening seem completely unimportant.

Kathleen's mother herself brought him food and coffee while other family and clan members came in to talk of the news from Old Oraibi. All were warmly hospitable to him and seemed to take it for granted that he would one day become Kathleen's husband. Allan Lemtewa, who was some vague clan connection – Jim wondered if he'd ever get all this sort of thing straightened out – Allan reported on Mary's good progress and listened with some embarrassment to many broad remarks about his marriage. More food and coffee appeared and were consumed while Vetch and the Oraibi affair were thoroughly aired. Jim mentioned Lololomi's scheme and this group too rocked with laughter.

"Superintendent Lyons may have some other trouble, too."

It was Allan who spoke, and they all turned to him for an explanation.

"Well, it is being said that he and Buck Skinner, the trader at Keams Canyon, are brothers in evil. Skinner used to be a partner of Denham, the big Gallup trader; he supplied Buck with all his goods. You remember the trading post burned down the other week. Buck told Denham that everything in the place was burned up, but some Navajo claim that the night before the fire Buck moved all his stuff to a barn behind the superintendent's house. Yesterday a white man came and asked a lot of questions. The barn is empty now, but this white man wants to find out what became of the goods that were in it. Skinner and the superintendent had a long talk after the man went away and the Navajo that works in the office said they locked the door while they talked and they looked mad when they came out. Maybe the superintendent gets a bad name and other trouble, too."

It was a long speech for the usually silent Allan, and he looked up in apology as he finished. Those listening heard his gossip with satisfaction. They were not surprised. It was Kathleen's mother who voiced the general sentiments.

"It is what one expects from a man whose heart has

been so bad toward us. It is good that Lololomi will give him a bad name. Maybe then he will let us alone. We have done no wrong to him."

During the friendly talk of the rest of the evening Kathleen and Jim leaned against each other near the fireplace, in the corner of the room. They had reached the point of understanding where few words are necessary.

"Some day we will have a house like this, warm and comfortable, and with all trouble far away."

"This is a clean house; our house must always be clean."

Jim wished he could rid himself of this obsession with cleanliness. The Hopi are clean, he insisted to himself, but this is desert country, water is scarce . . .

As if reading his thought, Kathleen interrupted him, snuggling closer to him as she spoke.

"Maybe we can show them how to make a cleaner village. Maybe we can find a way to get more water here. They will follow us if we are good Hopi. That is why I must go on with my work, I want to help our people to keep well and strong. The white people can help us much in this."

"The old men are stubborn, Kathleen. It will be hard to convince them that any of the white man's ways will be right for them."

"That is because they have been tricked so often, and sometimes they have not understood. Language is a barrier. When I was at school my feelings would often be hurt by things that were said to me in a joking way; I would take them seriously and think they were making fun of me because I was an Indian."

"Me, too. I never did know when some of the boys on the ship were kidding. When one of the Chief Petty Officers called one of us a 'son-of-a-bitch' it meant he really liked the guy! When another called us that, it meant he was mad at us. The words were the same, but the tone of voice was different."

It was almost midnight when Kathleen sent him home. He stepped outside to find everything covered with a light layer of dry, fluffy snow. As he walked along the deserted street the ruddy glow of lamplight and fireplace against the already drifting snow accented the warm security of the village community. In spite of men like Vetch and Lyons, Hopi life could be richly satisfying, he was sure. He was beginning to understand why he had come back. He belonged here. The wrongs of these people were his wrongs, and their peace and contentment would be his, too.

XXI

As usual, the *PO-A-MU-YA* ceremony was celebrated at Shongopovi, in February. The beans that had been sprouted in the *kiva* to portend the harvest were weak and gave little promise of successful crops. The old men were worried, for other signs as well indicated a year of drought and threatened famine for the Hopi. There must be many prayers for good rains. The kick-ball races which were to take place within a few days would be the next public occasion on which appeals could be made to winds and to sun to bring moisture and warmth to their fields after the seed was planted.

Lololomi sought out Jim and told him he was invited to join the men in the races. Soon, he hoped, Jim would be initiated into the men's societies and be able to take part in all the major ceremonies. Until then he must await the invitation each time. Gradually Jim was absorbing some of the long and complicated procedures attendant upon each ceremony. Even the most casual encounters with the old men added to his knowledge. He wondered when he would be completely part of it all. Well, he'd accept each invitation as it came and do what he could; he still did not believe all this rigmarole, but if it helped the village to have him participate — well, what had he to lose?

The balls to be kicked by the racers were made in the *kiva* by Lololomi. The old man jokingly went about the village collecting one or two hairs from the tops of the toes of the fastest runners, and from Allan he got some of the fur of a very swift rabbit killed in a hunt. With these items, and hair from horses noted for speed, and pine pitch to hold the mass together, he molded the balls skillfully.

The races were begun with prayers, the racers joining the old men in the *kiva* for the purpose and rejoining them there when the races were ended.

The first race was held over a short course and Jim had no trouble keeping up, but his bare feet were cut and sore, for his lack of skill caused him to bruise them as he kicked at the small ball. With each race the course was extended, until on the final day the racers had to cover eight to ten miles. Jim returned home that last night to nurse aching leg muscles and toes that were black and blue and bloody. His mother had a special meal waiting for him, and she patted him in silent approval of his having taken part as a member of the community.

He was resting on his pile of sheepskins and blankets in a corner of the house, when Lololomi came in. The old man sat near him and offered some tobacco and papers. For a long time they smoked in silence.

"My son," said Lololomi, "my heart is happy that you have been in the wind races and that your prayers have joined ours. This is good. I am glad that you plan to marry. Last night I talked with your uncles. They wish to know if you will marry in the Hopi way or like a white man."

Because he knew that his question might embarrass Jim, the old man did not look at him but kept his eyes on the floor and seemed in no hurry for Jim to reply. He even produced more tobacco and they each smoked again before Jim replied.

"My father, my heart is happy that I was allowed to make the prayers to the winds that bring us rain and to join the men in the races. As you know, it is Kathleen Lensa I plan to marry. We have both been away from our people for a long time. We have lived and have thought like white people, but now we know that our hearts were always with our people here. That is why we have come back. When we are married we may do some things the way white people do them." He could see Lololomi's face darken. "But we will marry as the Hopi do and we will live as the Hopi live."

Jim could tell nothing from the old man's face as he continued to smoke. Minutes passed before Lololomi turned to Jim and spoke directly to him.

"Your uncles and I have watched you carefully since your return. We believe that you seek the truth, and we believe your heart is good. When you were a small boy you were whipped by the Kachinas in the *Po-a-mu-ya,* and in this way your feet were first set upon the Hopi way. After our corn is harvested and our wood and coal have been gathered for the winter, we will prepare for the *Wu-wu-che-ma* ceremony. This year we have the initiation for the young men who wish to enter our men's societies. Your uncles have asked me to prepare you for this, that you may be a true Hopi."

He stood up to go, but turned back to Jim for a final word.

"I will be your ceremonial father. I will make your ceremonial sash. You will be my son."

Jim knew that now there must be no turning back; this elaborate initiation was both the end and the beginning. What was it Kathleen had said once? "No, I don't believe any of these things, but somehow I think it is right for us to have these ceremonies." She had said that, that and something about unity. Well, he'd decided this was where he belonged, there was no way to be a half Hopi. He'd go through with it all. He stood up and faced the stern old man.

"Thank you, my father."

"It is good, my son," and a smile spread over the wrinkled face.

From an adjoining room where she had been sorting her corn supply, Nasayungti came to Jim, put one arm around him, and rested her head against his chest. He looked down at her, patted her, then gently put her to one side and walked out into the night.

XXII

THE DAYS THAT FOLLOWED were busy ones for Jim. The sheep demanded more of his time than he had thought they would. More and more often he was halted in the village by one of the old men and long conversations ate away the hours. Word had gotten about that he was to be one of the initiates in the *Wu-wu-che-ma* and young men of the nearby villages as well as his own came to congratulate him. There was work to be done in his mother's fields and that, too, was time-consuming.

At least every other day he tried to go to Old Oraibi to join the silversmiths. He found that it was work he thoroughly enjoyed and that the men engaged in it were fine companions. That old village seemed peaceful enough these days. No one had seen anything of Vetch. Superintendent Lyons' adoption had been carried out with due ceremony. Mary would be out of the hospital any day now, and Kathleen was spending all her free days with her mother and aunts at Shongopovi. This last was a thought he liked to dwell on; it must mean she was getting ready for their marriage. He was learning to let the pattern of events fall into place.

It was late one afternoon when he set out for Old Oraibi. On the trail he met Bill Lanta, who held up a fine rabbit for Jim to admire. "I am about ready to go back to the village. This one's enough for today."

Until now Jim had been working only in copper, for silver was too expensive for practice. He knew that he was daily gaining skill, and so he sounded out Lanta on a project to which he had given much thought.

"You have heard that I am to be married?"

The silversmith nodded his head.

"I – I would like to make a ring for my wife."

Lanta looked at him questioningly.

"I know," Jim went on, "that it is not the Hopi custom to use a ring, but it is a white man's way that seems good to me. And if I could make it myself . . ."

"I will think about it," Lanta answered gravely. "I will try to get you a good design, a very old one that I know. It will bring you good children and contentment in your marriage."

He did not even smile as he said this, nor did he again refer to it that day, although Jim worked with him until well into the evening.

A few days later Bill Lanta appeared at Jim's house, all smiles this time.

"I have found for you the design I spoke of; see!"

The two men pored over the sketches Lanta had brought, the latter explaining the intricate symbolism of the designs. The complete design was too elaborate for one small ring, so Jim finally chose a pattern involving male and female fertility symbols.

"If the ring is to bring us many children, they must be both boys and girls."

"It is a good choice. When will you come? This will be your first silver. It may take longer than you think. But you can do it well, I know."

Jim was pleased by Lanta's praise.

"I will come tomorrow as early as I can. Thank you for your help; you have gone to much trouble for me."

The work that he began the next day took many hours to complete. When he had the design drawn, Lanta found some bits of turquoise for him and showed him how to use them to accent the design. It all required exacting work, but Lanta praised him highly for the result and Jim, too, thought that perhaps it was worthy even of Kathleen. He hoped that it would be a surprise to her, but he still failed to realize how little escaped the watchful eyes and ears of his people.

"I hear that you are a very successful silversmith," was Kathleen's greeting when next they met.

Her enigmatical smile told him that she knew about the ring.

"I'm only making a silver ring for a sweetheart of mine – a white girl in San Francisco."

He hoped to tease her, but her mood had changed.

"Don't show it to me, Jim, until we are married. In this, I will be like a white girl."

He reached toward her, but she pulled back. They had just chanced to meet near the Shongopovi plaza and she had no wish to feed the gossip and speculation already rife in the village.

"I hoped to see you today. There is a vacant house in my mother's section of the village. Maybe we could look at it."

"I thought – that I would have to move in with your family."

Jim spoke hesitantly. He had learned that this was the custom, but it was one of the many things about Hopi marriage that he dreaded.

"I would not want that any more than you." He was warmed by her understanding. "But it does not have to be that way."

"I do not understand."

"We can have our own house if it is in the part of the

village controlled by my mother's clan; that is why I think we should see this house I speak of."

"I can go now if you want to."

"That is exactly what I want," and this time she quite unashamedly tucked her arm in his.

As they walked to the door of the unoccupied house an aunt of Kathleen joined them for the inspection. The place consisted of one large room the width of the entire block of houses, so that its doors and windows opened upon two different streets. In one corner there was a small fireplace, made in the old Hopi way, with a hood of small sticks protected from the fire by a coating of adobe. Along the two long walls were narrow seats of stone and adobe. At one end a low doorway opened into a small dark storeroom which also had a small fireplace complete with a slab of black stone on which to make the tissue-thin corn bread of the Hopi.

As they looked at the stone griddle the aunt smiled at Kathleen and said, "Think of the burned fingers you're going to have the first time you use that!"

"You'll have to give me a lesson; this afternoon, maybe?"

"Oh, you'll have practice enough, you'll see!"

They discovered that there was an underground storeroom, too, and outside a steep stone stairway led to the roof, which would be a cool and airy sleeping place for the hot nights of summer.

Certainly the house was the best they could hope for and with the conveniences they would add it could develop into a really attractive home. He could tell by the look on Kathleen's face that she was already planning how she would furnish it.

"Don't you think it's all right, Jim?"

"Yes; yes, I do. It does need plastering, though, and the roof looks as if it might leak."

"We'll take care of that, won't we?" she asked, turning to her aunt.

The pleasant little woman nodded happily and almost ran out of the house—to spread the news, no doubt.

"It all begins to look real now. When will it be?"

"Soon now my aunts will talk with yours and then we will know."

"The waiting is hard; is it for you?"

"Yes, for me, too."

She pulled his head on a level with hers and kissed him with more passion than she had yet shown. He would have seized her, but she pulled away.

"No; if I know my aunt she'll have the women getting ready to plaster any minute! We'd better go!"

As they were leaving, Tom Nesviki came by.

"How do you like our house?" they asked almost in one breath.

"Good, good! I'll bring you a load of wood for it the next time I go into Winslow."

As the three of them stood chaffing each other, a group of small children ran past them, laughing and yelling. As they looked after the youngsters they saw two white men enter the plaza and walk over to the house of Nemtaka. They recognized Superintendent Lyons and one of his assistants.

"I'd like to see what's going to happen," said Kathleen, "but I promised to meet one of the visiting nurses at the day school and I've just time to make it."

Jim and Tom walked slowly toward the house of the chief who stood in his doorway talking with the white visitors. As they approached they could hear the superintendent saying, "— — — — —good for the Hopi people. Now that I am *Chee-va-to,* the son of Lololomi, more than ever I want to be friends with you."

Nemtaka covered his mouth with his hand to hide his smile, and the listening children laughed and scampered away. The superintendent flared with anger and turned upon Jim, who himself could not keep from smiling at the offensive name.

"What's so damn funny?"

Jim could think of nothing to say and he tried to turn away, but the furious white man would not let him go. He grabbed him by the arm and swung him around.

"Look here, you! You speak English. What's so damn funny about my being adopted?"

To that question Jim could give a straight answer.

"There's nothing funny about being adopted by the Hopi. The way you pronounce *'Chee-va-to'* just sounds funny to us here on Second Mesa."

The two white men stamped off, the superintendent muttering, "These goddamn Hopi!"

That evening the people of Shongopovi listened with special delight to the news sung out across the night by the Crier Chief. In cutting satire he recounted how Lyons had told the people of Old Oraibi that he had been adopted and that his name was *Chee-va-to*. The Crier Chief paused for effect. Then he continued with the story of how Lyons sensed that something was wrong, and of how one of the teachers told him what the word really meant, and explained all of its connotations. The Crier Chief then imitated Lyons cursing out Lololomi for playing such a trick upon him.

Old Lololomi smiled softly to himself as he heard the words of the Crier Chief. He went over to a corner of his house and, smiling mysteriously at his wife, he picked up a drum and, sitting with it between his knees, he began to beat out softly a gentle rhythm. Then with words and a tune of his own making he began to sing.

His song told of a man who in his proud arrogance was cruel to the people in his charge, and how a simple old man with no pride gave to the proud man a silly name that clung to him like a drag rope, until that man's eyes no longer looked down upon the simple old man but were on a level with the old man's eyes. The song had many verses and many of the words had two meanings. The first meaning even a child could understand, but the second was clear only to the wise old men and women. There were many such who listened that night to old Lololomi's song, and they laughed aloud, and they did not put their hands over their mouths.

By the end of the week every *kiva* in every village knew the song. Superintendent Lyons suddenly found that office work kept him so busy at Keams Canyon that he had no time to visit the villages.

Old Lololomi made a new verse to his song. This told how bad it was for a man to stay inside his house all day. What could a man do in a house all day? Would he grind corn all day – like a woman?

•

XXIII

KATHLEEN NOW SPENT every free hour at her home in the village in preparation for the wedding. She could always get a ride there as soon as her work was done, and early the following morning Jim would drive her back to the hospital at Keams Canyon. This was about the only time they had together, and every precious minute of the drive was spent in making plans for the future.

Almost two weeks had passed since the visit of Superintendent Lyons, and nothing untoward had happened as a result of it. Mary had been discharged from the hospital and she and Allan had settled happily into the routine of village life. The strenuous ordeal of their Hopi wedding might be long delayed, however, because Mary was far from strong. Vetch had made no further trouble for them and Lyons had made no complaint to Dr. Cummings. Yet Jim could not shake off a feeling of apprehension. There was something ominous in the silence of these two white men. The Hopi had outsmarted both of them, but it seemed to Jim unlikely that they would let such incidents pass without retaliation. The marriage of Mary and Allan, the adoption of the superintendent, the song of old Lololomi – these had settled nothing. Indeed, Jim felt, they would be looked upon as aggressive acts and inevitably would provoke equally aggressive acts in return.

As he drove Kathleen back to the hospital some days later, he voiced these fears to her.

"I'm afraid I feel the same way, and Dr. Cummings does, too. I hope that if trouble is coming we can get it over with before we are married. I sometimes think my aunts feel it, too, and that's why they don't set the date."

"And my uncles," Jim said. "They already have the cotton for your wedding clothes, but they take hours every day just picking the seeds and dirt out of it. They act as if they really didn't want to start the spinning and weaving."

"Yet, they do want us to marry, don't they?"

"I'm sure of that. I sometimes think I am still more like a white man than a Hopi. I get so impatient about the whole thing."

"Did I tell you we have to let our hair grow long?"

"Hair – long?"

Distaste for the idea was evident in his voice.

"I knew you wouldn't like it; I guess I didn't tell you. But in the ceremony it has to be woven together to show that we will have a long married life."

"We've really let ourselves in for something, haven't we?"

Jim looked at Kathleen gravely as he spoke.

"Are you sorry? Want to get out of it?"

Kathleen, half laughing, half serious, turned toward him. Jim put one arm around her.

"I guess I'm sort of scared for both of us. I have such a hazy idea of the whole ceremony, and it seems to me that the girl gets the really rough end of the deal. How do you find out how it all goes? If it was only all down in writing –"

"But it isn't," said Kathleen, "and we have both been away so much that there's been no chance to learn by watching others."

"Girls always know more about these things."

"Oh, they do? Well, this is my first experience and –"

"And the last; you do believe that, don't you?"

Jim pulled the car to the side of the road and turned off the engine.

"Yes," said Kathleen thoughtfully. "It just has to be for good. Last night," she went on after a pause, "my mother and my aunts and I talked for a long time. For the first time I really got the whole ceremony sort of straightened out. It's not so bad, really."

"Lololomi talks to me about it, too, from time to time, but he takes it for granted that I know so much more than I do about Hopi customs, and I hate to show my ignorance."

"There are really four days that are important," Kathleen started to explain.

"Only one, as far as I am concerned!"

Kathleen reached for his hand and went on. "First, I have to grind a lot of corn meal in my house. Then I send for you to take me to your house where I grind more."

"What will we ever do with all the stuff?"

"We won't have much to say about it."

"It seems to me that everybody has more to say about this wedding than we do."

"Well, it is a clan and village affair – that we have to accept."

Jim said nothing, and Kathleen continued her explanation of the ceremony they would have to go through.

"The day I grind corn in your house is the first day of the four I spoke of. I stay there and grind for a second day, and that evening the 'mud war' is announced. It takes place on the third day."

"Ugh!" Jim said in disgust.

"Let me finish, Jim. The real wedding ceremony is on the fourth day. The hair-weaving takes place then. From that time on I am Mrs. Jim Talastewa!"

Jim was staring straight ahead as she finished. Finally he spoke. "I don't know."

"Don't know what? Whether you want to marry me?"

"That is the only thing I do want. But all this – this – monkey business – I hate it!"

"Don't, Jim!"

"I'm sorry, but it is for you I hate it all."

"I don't mind really. It is not nearly so complicated as it was in the old days. It used to take weeks, and the girl would have to grind as much as a thousand pounds of corn meal!"

"I guess the war – the boys and girls going so far away to school – have changed many things. I know how it changed things for me. Do you know about some rabbit hunt I'm supposed to take part in?"

"Oh, yes, my mother talked of it, too, last night. The old men must decide the time. I think, from what my mother said, that it will be soon."

"Have I no say about it?"

"Oh, Jim, do try to let things fall into place of themselves. That is the Hopi way."

That phrase again, he thought. I wonder if I can ever completely accept it. He started the car and in silence they drove toward the hospital.

"About those wedding clothes –" he began.

"Don't worry about them. Lololomi will see to them, I am sure. Often they are not even started until after the marriage. They really are ceremonial clothes for the bride rather than her wedding dress. I am supposed to stay in your mother's house until they are presented to me, though. Then we go back to my mother's house."

"Do we have to live there? What about our own house, the one your aunts have been fixing up?"

"I have not yet talked with my mother about this. It used to be the custom for the man to move right into his mother-in-law's house for good. To even have a house of our very own is something we should be thankful for."

"Well, I'll be glad when we are settled in it – if we ever are!"

Jim reached over with his free hand and drew her close to him and kissed her. The car swerved wildly on the dirt road.

"I still think that's a white custom that isn't half bad."

Kathleen laughed nervously and, as he skillfully righted the car, she chided him, "You better watch out what you're doing or we'll both have a burial ceremony to go through instead of a marriage one!"

•

XXIV

A FEW MORNINGS later Jim came to drive Kathleen to the hospital as usual.

"You forget," she said. "This is my free day. I am going to use it to practice making *piki*. I ground a lot of corn meal last night. Look!"

She held up her fingers, full of bruises from the rough *metate* stone.

"Oh, Kathleen –"

"They are not as sore as they look. I certainly need practice in all of this; I've not done any of it since I was a child. I thought it would be fun to make my first *piki* in our own house."

"How is the house coming along? You and your aunts are always so secretive about it."

"We are supposed to be; that is the Hopi way," she teased.

"Well, I need to take a look at my sheep; I'll leave you to your *piki*. I really rather like the stuff!"

"It will taste pretty good with your mutton," she laughed as he turned away.

Kathleen's aunts were already in the little storeroom of their house when she got there. They praised the softness of her corn meal, although they laughed at her sore hands and said they were like those of a white woman.

Kathleen carefully built a fire, under the *piki* stone, in the corner fireplace. The slab of stone was about eighteen inches long, twelve wide, and about an inch thick, and was mounted on small stones six inches above the bed of the fireplace. By the time the fire burned down to a bed of coals the stone was hot enough to use. In a pottery bowl she made a thin batter of blue corn meal which she placed to one side as she knelt in front of the stone to begin her first attempt at *piki* making.

With a piece of cotton cloth she wiped clean the surface of the stone. Then she dipped her fingers in the batter and tried to spread a thin layer of it over the hot stone without burning her fingers. But she got the batter on too thickly. A barrage of laughter from her aunts beset her as she tried to lift off what looked more like a white man's pancake – slightly blue-tinted – than a thin piece of Hopi *piki*. There was nothing for it but to try again, for Kathleen knew that to her onlookers all this was a test of temper as well as of domestic skill.

The next time, in her attempt to spread a really thin layer, she pressed upon it too hard and burned her fingers. If only her aunts would go and let her practice by herself. This time it really did look more as it should, and she managed to peel it from the stone with greater dexterity. It did not satisfy her critics, however, so one of the aunts came and sat beside her and demonstrated the swift, skimming motion necessary to spread the batter thinly, but evenly. Her sheet of *piki* was cooked almost by the time she had finished spreading it. She peeled it off quickly and hurriedly brushed on another sheet of batter, over which she held the already cooked sheet so that the rising steam would soften it and make it possible to fold it into a short parchment-like roll.

The aunt proved an able instructor. By following her directions carefully, Kathleen soon had a half dozen pieces properly cooked and rolled. It was going better now. She stopped and wiped her face with her handkerchief. It was hot in the crowded little room. She'd be glad when this ordeal was over; she hated to admit the doubts that crossed her mind. She hoped it tasted halfway palatable.

One aunt reached over for one of the rolls of *piki* and shared it with the others. They ate with varying expressions, most of them of distaste. One pretended that she could not bite through it, another said that it tasted like mud, a third claimed that she had broken a tooth on it. The smiles that followed were proof to Kathleen that these were but crude jokes and that she was succeeding. She finished up the batter and looked with some pride at the rolls of evenly thin *piki*. She would take some to Jim's mother and some back to the hospital. Dr. Cummings and the nurses there were still doubtful that she'd prove a true Hopi after all her nurse's training; she'd show them!

XXV

TWO DAYS LATER the news spread across all the mesas that Superintendent Lyons had gone to Holbrook, there to take the train to Washington. Jim and Kathleen pondered what this move might mean as they drove to the hospital early in the morning.

"I hope it is a good sign; maybe he'll never come back!"

"I wish I felt sure of that, but I still don't trust him."

Jim's comment reflected the insecure feeling he had not yet been able to shake off. But why waste this fine morning on thoughts of the superintendent? He and Kathleen had more important things to discuss, and their time together was limited.

"My mother has asked me when we are to marry in the white man's way." Jim made the statement a bit timidly, for they had not yet talked of this.

"She is a surprising woman, Jim. Even though she does not approve of it, she knows it must be done — and it must. When do you think?"

"I talked with Allan yesterday and he says it is not hard to get the license. I could do that today."

"Would you mind if I asked Dr. Cummings to marry us as he did Allan and Mary?"

"If — if he would not mind."

"Mind?"

"Well, he — and — you —"

"He understands all that, he knows how Hopi I am. He likes you. Oh, he'll want to do it, I know. I'll ask him today."

Jim halted the car out of sight of the hospital and leaned over and kissed her.

"The sooner we're married one way or another the better for me, and for you, I hope."

"The Hopi way is the real one for us, Jim. I'll walk from here," and she had opened the door of the car and was on her way.

"Kathleen! I didn't mean —"

She turned and waved.

"Will you be back at the village tonight?"

He could not tell whether or not she had heard him. Well, he had a busy day ahead; he wanted to take another look at his sheep. Sequa-Honau certainly was learning how to look after them; he'd go to Oraibi, too, and get the ring he'd asked Bill Lanta to keep for him; then to Flagstaff for the marriage license.

It was late evening when he got back to Shongopovi and he was just in time to hear one of the leaders of the village call out that there would be a rabbit hunt the following day in which all the unmarried men and women were to participate.

He approached Kathleen's house slowly and found her with her hand on the door, just about to enter. She turned when she heard his footsteps, and a quick smile came to her face.

"You heard the announcement?"

"Yes, I heard — I had stopped at my aunt's; my mother was there. She tells me it is in a way the beginning of our ceremonies."

She motioned him to enter and he saw laid out on the table piles of blue corn meal and of corn husks.

"See," Kathleen pointed to them, "my mother has these all ready for me to begin making the *someviki* tomorrow."

At his questioning look she explained, "*Someviki* are little cornmeal cakes tied and wrapped in husks; girls use them in the rabbit hunt. You'll see! I'll have to start on them early in the morning."

Allan and Mary had come in, and soon women of Kathleen's clan began to arrive. As the latter busied themselves with matters that had no meaning for Jim, he and Allan stepped outside to talk of the rabbit hunt. They were soon joined by Mary, and there was no opportunity for more than a hurried good night between Kathleen and Jim.

"I'll be at the rabbit hunt – it's lucky it's my free day. I – I – was not angry this morning. For me, too, it can not be too soon."

She lingered a moment in the doorway until he turned the corner out of her sight. He had not kissed her, but the quick pressure of his hand and the light in his face when she spoke told her that all was well between them. With a hint of a smile on her lips she turned to join the chattering women inside.

•

XXVI

IT WAS NOT YET DAYLIGHT when Kathleen awoke the next morning, but some of the women were already there to help her make the *someviki* for the day's rabbit hunt. They set to work at once to make a thick sweetened dough of blue corn meal. This dough was rolled into cakes which were tied in corn husks and boiled. The work was finished by breakfast time. As soon as the meal was over they all went to the plaza where the young people were assembling. Jim was already there and he hurried to Kathleen's side. They were soon joined by Mary and Allan.

There was great merriment when Robert Tewataka appeared with his rabbit stick. For ten years he had been taking part in these hunts, but, despite his prowess as a hunter, he had not yet succeeded in capturing a bride. Smallpox had left its scars on his seamed face, and among the women it was gossiped that he was sterile — so he remained a bachelor.

"You'll get many rabbits this year, Tewataka, and here comes a bride for you!"

This joking remark by one of the young men of the

village caused Tewataka and everyone else to look toward the main street into the plaza. Down it came a middle-aged woman as broad as she was tall. Her great, round moon-face was wreathed in grins as she joined the bantering group, carrying her *someviki.* When someone in the crowd jostled her towards Tewataka, she hung her head in calculated maidenly modesty as a chorus of jokes and decidedly ribald insinuations deluged the two of them.

At this point some of the old men arrived, and the jesting stopped as they made prayers for a successful hunt. These concluded, the same old men led the party down the steep, mesa-side trail and out across the desert toward Burro Springs, skirting the edge of Oraibi Wash for two or three miles. Tewataka and his panting partner arrived just as the group was spreading out — and the hunt was on.

Within a few minutes a rabbit was spotted. A stick whirled through the air, and Tewataka announced the first kill; his fat companion ran and seized the still kicking rabbit and held it high for all to see. Amid shouts of congratulation she presented him with some of her *someviki.* He accepted it with a broad smile and called to the men near him to share it with him.

Another shout, another stick whirling through the air, another soft thud announced another kill. Four girls rushed forward and there was an argument as two got to it at the same time. One succeeded in yanking it out of the other's hands and ran with it to the man who had killed it and gave him her *someviki* as a reward.

More than an hour passed before Jim killed his first rabbit. Kathleen joined three other girls in searching for it. They had about decided that he must have missed, when Kathleen found both it and the throwing stick, and she held them up exultantly. When she presented to Jim some of her *someviki* several of the nearby men did not wait for an invitation to taste it with him; they were more than curious to find out how good a cook this Hopi nurse might be. Jim was a bit proud how quickly the cakes disappeared; he did not mind at all that there were few left for him.

It was late afternoon when the hunt ended and the party

met to compare results. Allan proved to be the winner with twelve rabbits to his credit, Jim was second with eight; every man had at least one, and Robert Tewataka boasted three. He and the fat woman walked off together happily, and there seemed to be no doubt that Robert had at last got himself a wife. The two were again subjected to a barrage of jocular remarks, most of them suggesting that it was high time they were getting married as it was plain from her size that children were already on their way.

The sun was setting as they climbed up the mesa trail, the desert orange-brown and gold in its last rays. The whole village was at the top to greet them and to sprinkle the dead rabbits with sacred corn meal before the young people scattered to their homes.

As Kathleen and Jim neared her house, Kathleen pointed to the rabbits he had killed and said, "My mother will be proud to have these; they are proof that you can support me well." This with a mischievous smile. "Take them in to her now."

Jim hesitated a moment. The door opened and Kathleen's mother greeted them.

"Good evening, my children. Has the hunt gone well?"

Kathleen held up one of the rabbits which her *someviki* had claimed from Jim, and he laughingly held up the rest of them.

"You are a good hunter," said the mother as she accepted them. "You will be a good husband to my daughter."

They followed her into the house and there she laid out the rabbits in traditional fashion and sprinkled them with sacred corn meal.

Jim was not used to the solemnity with which all these little rituals were carried out. It still seemed a bit of hocus-pocus to him. But Kathleen never seemed to question them, and he guessed he'd come to accept them too, in time.

Kathleen interrupted his musing by handing him some of the husk-wrapped *someviki*.

"These are for your mother and your clan relatives," she said. "They better accept them – they must not object to me now!"

She smiled up at him and put her arm through his. They walked together out of the house to a long covered passage that led to the block of houses where Jim's clan lived. In its shadow they embraced tenderly.

"It won't be long now," Kathleen whispered. "Dr. Cummings said to come any time."

"Tomorrow? I got the license."

"Tomorrow? Well, why not?"

"I'll come for you as usual."

"I will be ready."

She broke away from him and he heard her faint "Good night!" as she disappeared in the direction of her house.

XXVII

As JIM AND KATHLEEN drew up at the hospital the next morning one of the girls from the office ran out.

"Oh, Kathleen, I'm glad you are here. There has been an accident. Dr. Cummings wants you in the operating room at once. Hurry and change."

"Wait around, Jim. I'll see you as soon as I can," Kathleen called as she ran into the building.

"Anything really serious?" Jim asked the girl.

"A Navajo; a compound fracture of the leg. He was felling some trees on Black Mountain when it happened. The leg was so badly infected by the time he got here that the doctor wasn't sure he could save it. He and Kathleen can probably do it, though!"

Jim was warmed by the praise, but he found that he resented a little the coupling of names.

"Anything I can do for you while you're waiting?" the girl asked.

"No, I'll make out. Guess it will take some time, won't it?"

"A good while, I imagine. Well, see you later."

Jim had been told that there were papers in the superintendent's office that Dr. Cummings would have to sign when he performed their marriage, and he might as well get them now. Good thing the superintendent had gone. He wasn't anxious to run into Lyons again; not now, anyway.

The Hopi girls in the office joked him a bit when he asked for the papers. When would the wedding be? Could they come? He was pretty lucky, they hoped he knew it. Would Kathleen go on being a nurse?

He was glad to get away from their prying questions to which he had given only mumbling answers. He drove the truck under a cottonwood tree, to whose branches a few brown leaves still clung tenaciously. He waited. An hour had passed when he heard Dr. Cummings calling to him. He walked to meet him.

"You have brought me and the Navajo boy luck, Jim. I'm sure we've saved his leg for him. Kathleen will be busy for a while, but I'm free until after lunch."

As he spoke he turned back toward the entrance to the hospital and Jim walked alongside.

"Kathleen tells me you'd like to have the ceremony today."

Jim nodded in assent and the doctor continued.

"Why not stay for lunch and we'll have it afterward?"

"No, it's no trouble," – for Jim had started to protest. "I've been wanting to know you a little better, now's a good chance. Let me show you over the place. You'd probably like to see where Kathleen puts in her time. I hope she'll be staying on after you're married. I don't know what we'd do without her."

There was little need for Jim to say much as they made the rounds of the hospital. He liked the way the doctor accepted him and treated him as if he were capable of understanding the professional aspects of the building. He had feared that he'd be condescending and that, despite what Kathleen had said, he'd try to preach about things. He began to understand why Kathleen admired him.

They entered the ward where Kathleen was still busy

with the injured Navajo, who was just beginning to shake off the effects of the anesthetic.

"I've persuaded your Jim to have lunch here," the doctor said, "and afterward we'll see to it that you have that little ceremony we talked about!"

She smiled at them both.

"Thanks, Don. Have you seen the hospital, Jim? Isn't it wonderful?"

"It reminds me of the ship – so clean and orderly."

It was the first time in many days that he had even thought of the ship; the words came almost without thinking.

"That's a real compliment, Jim. We like to think we're pretty shipshape, don't we, Kathleen?"

The doctor put everyone at ease. The men were about to leave the ward when the Navajo suddenly called out in terror and anger.

"My leg, my leg, you have taken away my leg from me!"

Jim sensed what the man was saying, but he really could not make out the Navajo words. To his surprise, Dr. Cummings seemed to understand completely. He went to the bed at once and in the patient's own tongue reassured him that his leg was all right, that it was still asleep and therefore he could not feel it. At a signal from him Kathleen drew back the cover and revealed the bandaged leg in its plaster cast. A look of relief flooded over the victim's face and he relaxed back upon the pillows. Jim was deeply impressed by the doctor's knowledge of Navajo and by his kindness on this occasion. With him there certainly was no difference between the white man and the red.

As they walked along the hall Jim timidly explained about the papers he had gotten at the superintendent's office.

"Good! Let's have a look at them. Here's my office. Please go on in."

Jim laid the papers on the table and the doctor read them thoughtfully.

"These seem to be all right. I'll fill them in after the ceremony. Sit down – I'd like to talk to you."

Jim offered him a cigarette.

"No, I don't smoke. But I like the way your old men go at it; such ceremony!"

They sat facing each other across the doctor's desk.

"You're marrying a wonderful girl, Jim, but I guess you know that. Did she ever tell you that I once asked her to marry me?"

Jim nodded, wondering what was coming.

"I wish she had said yes, but I think you'll be very happy together. I want you to know that if I can ever do anything to help you I'll always be very glad to do it."

"Thank you," Jim heard himself say.

"While you're here I want to talk about this difficulty with Vetch. I'm afraid we are in for trouble in that quarter."

"And so am I." Jim found himself speaking freely. "I don't know why I think something is going to happen, but I do. I've talked to Kathleen about it."

"This superintendent we have now is a cruel man and a vindictive one, and he and Vetch are great friends. He's furious over the trick old Lololomi played on him, and together they'll find some way of getting back at your village, of that I'm sure."

"But he has gone to Washington; maybe he won't come back."

"I wish I could think that; but no such luck! They'll probably try to make trouble for me because I married Mary and Allan, but I've made a report about that to my superiors in Philadelphia and they have approved of my action. My church takes a very different attitude to missionary work from that of our friend Vetch."

"Yes, John Vadas told me that."

"Good for Vadas! I'm glad he's a friend of yours. Now I'm going to tell you something that is just between the two of us."

Jim glanced up to find the doctor looking at him very directly.

"I have asked my church to do what it can to secure the dismissal, or at least the transfer, of Lyons."

"Won't that be hard to do?"

"Well, maybe. I understand, though, that the district attorney of Navajo County is just about to bring charges of fraud against him and that crooked trader here; that'll help."

"You mean about the burning of the trading post?"

"So you've heard it, too? He'll be madder than ever when he learns this has gotten about. You and your people better keep your eyes open, Jim."

Martha Honani, one of the nurses, came in just then and smiled at Dr. Cummings.

"Everything is all ready, doctor."

Dr. Cummings laughed as he turned to Jim. "We have a little surprise for you and Kathleen," he said. "Come, we'll go to the dining room."

There they found Kathleen at the door, the picture of astonishment and delight. The small room was decorated with long, twisted streamers of colored paper. A large wedding cake adorned the main table. A small piano had been rolled into one corner and, as Dr. Cummings led Jim and Kathleen into the room, one of the teachers from the day school struck up the Wedding March. It was all done so simply and so joyously that Jim felt but little embarrassment. He did wonder whether he should have brought the ring he had made, but he rather wanted to keep that for after they were married in the Hopi way. It was too late now, anyhow.

The doctor read through the formal little ceremony and, very much as a matter of course, handed Jim a small gold ring as he guided him through the repetition of the vows. Kathleen's hand trembled a bit as he took it in his. Then it was all over, and the nurses and staff members crowded around them with congratulations. Jim was amazed at how completely they all accepted Kathleen, and at how easily she moved among them. There were good things in this white man's world, and good people, people like these.

Suddenly their hands and arms were full of gifts, and Dr. Cummings was making a presentation speech on behalf of the hospital as he handed them a complete set of cooking utensils.

"We'll all be over to sample your *piki* one of these days—or whatever you are likely to make in these pots and pans."

"Don't forget, I'm not married yet in the Hopi way. You better come over first and help me grind the corn meal."

Just then the cook came in to apologize for the cake. It was a bit difficult to make much of a wedding cake in just a couple of hours' time.

"I think it was wonderful to do it at all!" exclaimed Kathleen. "How did you know it was to be today?"

"We didn't know—that was the trouble. But yesterday Dr. Cummings told us it might be soon, and so we got ready."

The explanation came from Martha Honani, who, as she spoke, looked at Kathleen with worshipping eyes.

Lunch was a wonderful meal. Everybody was friendly and gay. Jim and Kathleen were called on for speeches. Jim tried to thank them, but felt he did not do a very good job. Kathleen's eyes danced with happiness as she concluded, "I mean that about the corn meal. You better come up and see how we do it the Hopi way."

Then she turned to Jim, "I've got to get back to work now or Dr. Cummings will fire me."

She looked up at him. The sudden realization that she expected a kiss before all that group gave him acute embarrassment. He looked about him and caught a hint of understanding in Dr. Cummings' eye. Quickly he bent and kissed her cheek. Amid a burst of laughter Kathleen fled from the room. Gradually all dispersed to their various duties. Dr. Cummings walked with him to the pickup.

"Jim, you and Kathleen can do a great deal for your people. You can live in a way that will be a splendid example for them to follow. I hope you will. You can convince them that sanitation, good health habits, and proper infant care

are not incompatible with the fine Hopi way of life. You can do much to overcome the suspicion that the old men have. Good luck!"

He held out his hand and Jim took it in gratitude, in admiration, in the understanding that here was a true friend. Two Indian helpers brought the boxes with the wedding presents and stowed them in the back of the car. Jim waved to them all and drove off, a song in his heart and on his lips – a Hopi *Kachina* song.

•

•

XXVIII

"LET'S PUT ALL THESE GIFTS in our own house," said Kathleen. "My aunts say that they have it all ready for us."

"Does that mean that our Hopi wedding can be soon?"

"I think so," said Kathleen, "but you know how slow our people are to decide these things."

"Does your mother know about today?"

"Why, of course. Like your mother, she does not quite approve of our going through a white man's ceremony, but she knows it has to be."

"Married – but not married – it seems sort of silly to me."

"Now, Jim, please! I know these days will be hard, but I feel sure we shall not have to wait long."

They had reached the village by this time, and Jim drove as close as he could to the house in which they would some day live. As they were unloading the gifts, they found themselves surrounded by villagers, eager to help. Jim could hardly manage a look at the house, so filled was it with Hopi of all ages. Every article was examined with great curiosity, and Jim and Kathleen were subjected to all kinds of jokes.

"Let's get out of here," said Jim at last.

"We'll go to my mother's house," whispered Kathleen. "Maybe there will be time to talk with her about when the Hopi ceremony can be."

They had difficulty getting rid of the crowd. After what seemed hours they found themselves in the house of Kathleen's mother where, as if by pre-arrangement, were assembled many of her aunts, and Jim's mother and aunts, as well. The two mothers smiled at their children to put them at ease, and the talk began.

Kathleen told of the day's ceremony, and her listeners hung on every detail. Then she turned to her mother.

"My mother," she said, "Jim and I are eager that our Hopi marriage be soon. When can it be, do you think?"

"You must find time to grind much corn meal for the *piki* that will be needed," said one of the aunts.

"I am sure that Dr. Cummings will give me the time I need," said Kathleen. "Don't you think he will, Jim?"

Before Jim had time to reply another aunt remarked, "Lololomi and the others are already at work on the wedding garments."

"Aren't they beginning work on them early?"

"Yes, it is earlier than is the custom. But they say the time is short. In the old days it would have taken many weeks, but sometimes one must make changes even in customs that are very old."

Kathleen remembered that once Dr. Cummings had said to her, when they were talking of the stubbornness of the Hopi, "Your people are more flexible than you think. Give them time."

He was a good man – Don – an understanding one, but with Jim she was making no mistake. She looked over to where he was sitting, quietly listening to the women talk. She motioned him outside.

They clung to each other in the darkness, then abruptly she turned from him and went inside. He stood for some time looking up at the stars. Soon, soon, it must be soon.

In the week that followed Kathleen and Jim avoided each other by tacit consent. Fortunately her duties at the hospital were demanding, and his sheep were at the stage where they required a great deal of his time.

There was a report that strange Indians were prowling around the range, so early one morning Jim and Tom Nesviki rode out to see that their flocks were safe. They took with them two boys to relieve Sequa-Honau and Tom's herder.

"Yes," said Sequa-Honau, in answer to a question from Jim, "we did see some strange men about and —"

"But our sheep are safe," interrupted Tom's herder, "and some of them are getting fat!"

At that, the men smiled at each other.

"Drive the flocks closer to the village," suggested Tom, "then you can take turns herding and see the wedding ceremonies, too."

"Who is to marry?" asked one of the boys.

"Why — Jim here and Kathleen."

"Kathleen?" Sequa-Honau's eyes lighted up. "Will Dr. Cummings be there?"

"He has already married us in his way," said Jim, smiling at the boy's eagerness. "I am sure he will come to our Hopi wedding if he can, but we do not yet know the time of the ceremonies and he is a busy man."

"With sick boys," was Sequa-Honau's quick remark.

"After you have brought the sheep near to the village we will plan how you will take turns herding them," Tom explained. "We'll see you soon again."

The two men started the drive home, happy because the sheep were safe and well and the lamb crop on its way. They stopped only at the trading post for some cotton yarn Jim had ordered a few days before.

"I am glad that you are to marry soon," said Tom. "Are the old men working on the garments for Kathleen?"

"Yes," replied Jim. "That is why I am getting this yarn. Lololomi said I better order some in case they did not have enough."

"Good!" Tom said.

That night Jim joined his clan uncles in the *kiva* and took his turn at weaving. Two white cotton robes must be made, one for Kathleen to wear and a larger one for her to carry in a reed mat, together with her wedding belt.

"There are many things to know about these robes," Lololomi explained. "The one Kathleen will wear is the one she will use at her death. When her soul arrives at the edge of the Great Canyon she will spread out this white wedding garment and upon it float down to the Underworld."

Jim did not care to think of death. He was just beginning to live. I could not ask, he thought, for a better father than Lololomi. The old man continued his explanation.

"After the naming of your first child the other robe may be given to her relatives to be used in many ways."

As he seemed to pause Jim remembered that he had brought tobacco and paper and matches for the smoking, without which no occasion was complete. He threw them into the central area. There was the usual deliberation as the men rolled and lighted up. Then one of the men remarked, "You must get the reeds for the case. We will show you how it is made."

It pleased him that he was to have a real part in the preparation of the things that Kathleen would wear or carry as part of the ceremony. Up to now he had felt that the men were patronizing him just a little bit—they were so much wiser than he—he knew that, really. Tonight, though, they were different; they acted as if he were really one of them. Lololomi interrupted his musings.

"The belt is important, I will weave it myself. It must be braided just so and the fringe must be made with care. Kathleen will use it in many dances in the years to come."

The group worked until late into the night, lightening their tasks with jests, much smoking and many songs, and with the telling of long stories of the Hopi past.

"We shall work here tomorrow and for many days until all is done." So spoke one uncle as the group was breaking up. "You will have the reeds soon?"

"Yes, tomorrow, if one of you will go with me and show me what to get."

There were many volunteers, for they seemed to like his humility, and Jim asked one of the youngest to come to his house at dawn. He so wanted everything to be just right for Kathleen, and it made him glad that all these men seemed to want that, too. None of this was as bad as he had feared. He hoped it was going all right with Kathleen; there was no chance to talk with her these days.

The men were talking now of other garments, something he hadn't known about. Lololomi again decided the matter.

"It will take too long to make these now." As he spoke he turned to Jim. "There is a wool dress and a white shawl with a blue border that we wish to make so that Kathleen's costume is complete. But these are not needed now; we shall make them at a later time."

"Thank you, my father. You are kind to explain all these things to me."

On each of the following days the men worked in the *kiva* fashioning the robes and the enormous buckskin boots that looked like accordioned white stovepipes. Jim found the proper reeds for the case and was instructed in the making of it; all approved the result. Old Lololomi was still working faithfully and with painstaking care on the wedding belt. It looked as if the garments could be ready within another week.

Jim wondered if Kathleen had talked with Dr. Cummings, if he would give her time free. With the corn grinding and all, she would need a week or more.

Just then a shadow fell across the entrance to the *kiva*. Jim looked up to see Sequa-Honau beckoning to him. The others seemed not to notice. He climbed the ladder.

"Is there something wrong with the sheep?" he asked the boy.

"Oh, no. This is my day in the village. Kathleen just told me to tell you she is at Nasayungti's house."

Jim stopped to hear nothing more and in minutes he had seized Kathleen in his arms.

"Oh, Jim! Jim! Dr. Cummings has given me ten days holiday – another wedding present, he says."

"Ten days is not long for a Hopi wedding," Nasayungti reminded them gently. "We must get busy at once." In mock anger she turned to Kathleen. "Go away from here – trying to steal my son! Go to your own house and grind corn meal and make *piki,* you lazy girl!"

XXIX

KATHLEEN HAD REASON to be thankful that her mother's clan was a large one with many aunts to help with the grinding of the corn meal. Even distantly related women came to help her. And in the houses of her mother's clan other women gathered and took turns on the *metates,* gossiping and singing as they worked. For two days they all toiled from dawn to dusk, and the piles of finely-ground meal rose higher and higher.

Late in the evening of the second day Kathleen's mother said there was enough and that the following day would be spent in making the meal into *piki.* Kathleen smiled to herself as she remembered Jim's wondering what they would do with it all, and she looked somewhat ruefully at her sore hands.

The *piki* making went easily, the work lightened by many hands; by nightfall one of the aunts announced there was now *piki* enough for the days to come. With smiles and sighs of relief the women scattered to their homes, leaving only her mother and two clan aunts to advise Kathleen of what the next days would require of her.

"Now you must send word to Jim to come take you to his mother's house," one aunt explained. "There you will remain until you have finished the wedding ceremony and have been presented with your bridal garments. Only then will you return here to your mother's house."

"Lololomi is passing now," said the other aunt. "He will take your message to Jim."

The women were by turns gay and serious as they helped Kathleen prepare to go to the house of Nasayungti. Her rather short hair must somehow be arranged in butterfly whorls. A great basket plaque must be piled high with the newly-made *piki*. Endless instructions must be given.

"Until you return here you will have no name," said her mother.

"No name?" questioned Kathleen.

"Only *meu-wi,*" explained an aunt.

"Meu-wi?"

Much as Kathleen had wanted to do all this in the Hopi way, she now began to doubt that she should have attempted it. Even the language of the ceremonies had gone from her. Her second question received a ready answer.

"Yes, for a time you are just a female in-law, which is all the word means."

"Your father would be proud of you, I think."

Her mother spoke the word sadly. Kathleen's thoughts turned to her father for the first time in months. She had scarcely known him. She could recall a time when he gave her a *kachina* doll which he had fashioned, she remembered that he was always kind. But she had been only about five when the word came to the village that he had been killed by a stroke of lightning while working in his fields. She remembered well her mother's sorrow; she, too, must have married one she loved. Strange, she thought, that both she and Jim should be fatherless – but the mothers were the important ones among the Hopi. She reached toward her mother and patted her gently, using the Hopi gesture of deep affection.

Jim and Nasayungti were eating supper when Lololomi knocked. Jim wondered why his mother smiled so knowingly as she let the old man in. Lololomi spoke deliberately.

"Kathleen is ready to grind corn in your mother's house. She asks that you come for her tonight. There are but four days now." Then, as if he sensed the one remaining dread in Jim's mind, he added, "Do not worry about the war with the mud. It will soon be over. Go now, my son."

"You heard?" said Jim to his mother.

This time he understood her answering smile. Jim found Kathleen dressed Hopi style in a dark red print dress with black circles and stars.

"As close," she explained to him, "as I could get to Hopi designs for sun and stars."

He would have lingered to admire and talk with her, but her clan aunts urged her departure. Her mother handed her a large basket plaque piled high with rolls of blue *piki,* and the two young people set off for his house. They had to walk slowly and steadily to keep the food from falling off the plaque. Kathleen's eyes never left it as Jim guided her down the street, across the plaza, through the covered passageway, and in front of the houses of his mother's clan. As they walked along people called out to them, congratulating them, wishing them a long life filled with contentment and many fine children. They arrived to find the house crowded with relatives.

"You are welcome, *meu-wi,*" said Nasayungti, as she took the plaque from Kathleen.

Jim wished he could manage Kathleen's poise — he wondered if she felt as uncertain about all this as he did; he hoped she did. He was glad to note that Lololomi had come in; he felt more secure with the old man around. He hadn't yet gotten used to so many women managing things; the Hopi way again, he guessed.

He realized his mother was pressing some of Kathleen's *piki* upon him.

"You must eat it, my son," explained Lololomi in his soft voice. "It will show that you accept her as your bride."

As if there was any doubt about that, Jim thought.

Now his mother was making sure that every man of his clan got at least one piece of *piki* and by eating it acknowledged his acceptance of Kathleen as a relative. In all it was a gathering of high good humor with a great deal of teasing directed at the bride and groom.

As Jim saw how radiantly happy Kathleen was over her complete acceptance by the people of his mother's clan, a wave of complex emotion swept over him. She looked so modest, so pure, so trusting that only with difficulty did he keep from taking her in his arms before them all. There came to him, too, a sense of the great responsibility he was assuming. Could he ever secure for her here at Shongopovi the sort of life she had come to know?

As she stood there saying good night to the last of his relatives, he suddenly felt again as he had when he first saw her in her nurse's uniform, and later in the bulky costume of the Buffalo Dance. He felt he could never be worthy of her.

"*Meu-wi* and I have much to talk about," hinted Nasayungti.

Of course, he would leave them together. He liked to think of Kathleen there in his mother's house. He'd spend these four nights in the *kiva* – it would be easier for all of them.

With his hand on the door he turned back toward Kathleen.

"Good night," she breathed softly but made no motion towards him.

"Good night, my son. Sleep well."

There was blessing in his mother's soft voice.

Before going to the *kiva* he walked over to the edge of the mesa which faced the west. Among the great square-faced blocks of rock he found a place that was protected against the wind. The rocks were still warm from the last rays of the setting sun, and he sat with his back against them as he watched the pageant of the winter sunset. Its beauty was lost on him because of the gloom which enveloped him.

He heard the soft scuff of moccasins and looked up to find Lololomi coming to a seat beside him. The old man did not look at him. He sensed Jim's feelings and refrained from the discourtesy of looking him in the face when he was so torn with emotion. The old man slowly rolled a cigarette and then passed the makings to Jim. The calm presence of his ceremonial father was already bringing comfort to him. Back in the village the whispered pulse of one of the big drums began to beat. Someone began to sing. The drum-beat gained in strength as the song progressed, and as the rising sound quavered in the evening air the great stars began to appear.

"My father — I — I — I feel most unworthy. I have done so much that is not right for a Hopi to do. I —"

Lololomi did not let him say more.

"Tomorrow at dawn, my son, you will run to our Sun Spring. There you must bathe and sprinkle corn meal" — he handed him a small leather pouch of it — "and make prayers. It is right that you should feel this way. You now see ahead of you the great journey of a man's life. The way is long and dark and difficult. It is always so even if a man's heart is right. As you pray tomorrow, strength will come to you."

They smoked together in long silence. When Jim finally looked over to where the old man had been sitting there was no one there. He walked back to the *kiva* slowly and thoughtfully, his depression somewhat lifted by the promise of Lololomi's words. The *kiva* was deserted and he was deeply satisfied to find it so. He made a bed of some sheepskins and blankets that were lying to one side. What was it Lololomi had said? Four days? Three more nights after this . . . It was hours later when he finally fell asleep.

He arose at the first hint of dawn. He wrapped a blanket tightly around him and, taking a gourd dipper, he slipped out of the *kiva.* The morning was bitterly cold and the icy air stabbed through the folds of his blanket like knife blades of the coldest steel. He ran swiftly across the mesa and down the trail. There was some protection from the wind as the trail twisted and turned through the blocks of rock, but once he was away from the talus slopes and out on the desert it cut into him again. He ran as fast as he could, his bare feet numb against the cold earth. It was a good mile from the foot of the mesa to the Sun Spring. He thought he would freeze to death before he could reach it.

As he gained the top of the low rocky ridge above the spring, he looked down to find Allan there. He, too, must be torn by doubts – this was rather comforting knowledge. Allan looked up as Jim approached, but they exchanged no words. In silence they threw off their blankets and with gourd dippers began to splash water over themselves and each other. In contrast with the icy air the water of the spring seemed warm and soothing. Alternately they rubbed themselves with it and splashed it over each other. Ordinarily such a bath would have been a scene of hilarity, but not on this occasion. Solemnly they wrapped their blankets around their shivering bodies and moved apart, each sprinkling corn meal around the spring and upon the ground on which he stood as he made a silent prayer for strength and vigor of mind and body.

They stood in supplication as the sun rose and flooded its warmth upon them, physical assurance to match the spiritual confidence afforded by their prayers. They continued to stand in silence as the sun rose higher and higher; then, purged of their uncertainties, strengthened to face the future, they turned and in the bright sunlight ran separately back to the mesa top.

•

XXX

WHEN HE RETURNED to his house early that morning he found that Kathleen already had ground a great pile of corn meal. He wondered how she could bear to look at any more of it. His mother explained that this corn meal was for Kathleen's clan and that the meal already ground at Kathleen's would later be given to their clan in payment for him. She and Kathleen seemed to find this idea rather amusing; in spite of himself, he found himself joining in their gentle laughter.

As soon as word got around the village that Kathleen was grinding corn meal in Jim's home, all the women relatives of his clan came crowding around his house. Each in turn laid claim to him, telling in embarrassing detail how he had made love to her and insisting that he must marry her. One woman, old enough to be his grandmother, seized him by the arm and loudly proclaimed that he was the father of all her children. The noisy group laughed and mocked him; mixed with their raillery were threats to kill Kathleen for stealing him from them.

Throughout the day the shrill cries of the women followed him wherever he went. He wondered if they would ever weary of their foolish jokes. Kathleen, too, was the target of some of them, he knew. The Hopi idea that teasing strengthens the character was all right, but there were limits to what one could take. Once during the day he encountered Lololomi and he protested that no one could keep his temper through this sort of thing, but this time the old man failed him, only smiling at his protests.

Nor was there any solace from Kathleen, who scarcely looked up from her grinding all day. It was late afternoon before he managed to elude the bantering women and take the trail to the Sun Spring. It was deserted. With a sigh of relief he sat down and bowed his head in his hands. He drowsed off; when he awoke it was dark. He wondered if he could stand another two days of this. Why was Kathleen so sure they must go through with all this?

He made his way back to the village and to the *kiva*. The men were again at work on the wedding garments. They nodded greetings to him. Lololomi made a place for him.

"See, the belt is almost done. You did well today, my son. The time will pass."

It was later than Jim had realized, and shortly the men left for their homes and again he was alone in the *kiva*. The bed he had made the night before was where he had left it. He slid into it slowly; two more nights after this. Tomorrow he would leave early and spend the day on the range. It seemed like desertion of Kathleen, but women seemed not to mind these things so much. That mud fight was still to come, and he hated to think of it. Those wedding garments were beautiful, though; Kathleen would look swell in them, even in the big boots.

When he returned to the village the following evening he was aware of unusual activity. Quantities of sticky clay were soaking in tubs and pans of every available size. At a corner near his house two large empty oil drums were being filled with muddy water. He feared the worst as he went into his house. His mother and Kathleen and several members of his clan were just starting supper. Kathleen looked at him happily, but she seemed tired, he thought. His mother patted him gently as she made a place for him. Suddenly the hoot of an owl was repeated several times. It was an ominous sound, he thought, but it brought only smiles to the faces of his relatives.

"That means the mud war is on tomorrow," said one of them.

Jim's distress was evident in his face. It was Kathleen who tried to allay his fears.

"It is all right. I do not mind." Then in a whisper, "But get all the clean water you can and put it in the storeroom. This will soon be over." She gave his hand a quick squeeze. "Good night — think of me!"

He rose and said he would go to the *kiva*.

"We are not working there tonight," said one of the men present. "We can finish easily tomorrow or the next day."

That's a break, thought Jim, I'll be alone again. I need that; but I don't want it for long! One night after this —

When he returned early the next morning the house was crowded with uncles and aunts of all ages who were on hand for breakfast and the fun that would shortly begin. He was amazed to find Kathleen gay and apparently quite eager for the muddy fray. Jim wondered if he could manage to keep his temper under control when they began to throw mud at her — she was always — so neat and clean — like the ship, he thought. And those remarks the women made — he hated them worse than the mud.

They had scarcely finished eating when the attacking party arrived. They were all women of his father's clan, many of them strangers, led by one of the village women that he liked least. He had not realized that his father had so many relatives. Surely many were trading on the slimmest of relationships as an excuse to be in on the fun. Their gaiety was that of children. Superintendent Lyons and Keams Canyon seemed far away. Vance Vetch and his fanatic followers were completely forgotten. The blanket of depression and apprehension that for many weeks had weighted down the spirits of the village seemed to have lifted entirely at the prospect of the traditional mud fight.

Jim's mother and old Lololomi hurried Kathleen into the small storeroom where they had her lie down with two small box stools on either side of her. Over her and the boxes they threw sheep skins and blankets so as to hide her completely, and then Nasayungti took her place before the *piki* stone. She signalled Jim to start a fire; as he was doing so an aunt hurried in with a bowl of *piki* batter. Nasayungti composed herself, and the men who had been breakfast guests gestured to Jim to come and help them hold the door shut against the invaders, whose voices could now be heard directly outside.

Almost at once the attacking party began to bang on the door, their voices rising in yells and screams. Jim knew it would not be long before they would be able to force in the door, but it was necessary to hold out against them as long as possible. The men were so intent on this purpose that they did not notice that one small girl had found a loose window and succeeded in prying it open. Before they realized it, she had slipped inside and wormed her way up under Jim and the other men and managed to draw the door latch. The door began to give.

Jim knew there was no hope now of keeping out the "Warriors." He hated to think of the abuse the house would take in the melee that was to follow. He had been assured, though, that any damage would be taken care of by the attackers. He wished now that he hadn't provided his mother with such a good woodpile – there'd probably not be a stick of it left.

There was a great yell from the crowd and then a tremendous heave broke the door free. The men at the head of the line catapulted into the room. Jim and his group were hardly able to rise before the women and girls in the party raced over them, their hands filled with sloppy masses of mud, and scattered through the house in their search for the bride. All of Jim's people made a great show of innocence, but the "War Party" knew she was somewhere. They surged finally into the storeroom. Seeing the great bundle back of Nasayungti, they pushed her over, spilling the *piki* batter as they did so. Kathleen could not get to her feet before they were upon her. Into her hair, over her face, upon every part of her body they rubbed fistfuls of the cold mud. She finally managed to throw them off and dash outdoors, but two women had crawled up on the roof and were waiting for her with a tub filled with dirty water, and they emptied its contents upon her as she tried to escape from the house. She gasped for breath and, blinded by the cascade of muddy water, she slipped and fell, this time to be the victim of small girls with pails of sticky clay.

Kathleen gave no outward sign of her affront at these proceedings, though she could not help but wonder why she had felt she must go through with it. She was glad that Dr. Cummings and the girls at the hospital were not here for this — she almost wished that Jim would step in and protest. But the worst was over now surely. She could not remember having witnessed one of these "wars." Her aunts had told her that at the end they would turn upon whoever was father of the groom, for it was by his consent that his son was marrying and thus leaving the clan. Since Jim had no father, it was Lololomi whom they would turn upon and whose hair knot they would cut.

All this went through her mind as she managed to seize the youngsters who were responsible for the latest indignity to which she was subjected. Shouts of laughter were directed toward her; the remarks made her blush. Now the supplies of mud and water were running low and invective became the chief weapon. When they found that Kathleen stood her ground and could not be moved to anger they called for Lololomi. The old man did not wait to be dragged from a hiding-place but presented himself to them almost proudly. In an instant they were upon him, threatening to scalp him but contenting themselves with cutting off the knot of hair at the back of his head and smearing him with the last of the mud.

As Jim feared it would be, the woodpile was next attacked. The marauders carried off every stick of it, remarking that they could put it to better use than the bride could

– by using it for fuel, they could make better *piki* than she could make.

The tumult ended as abruptly as it had begun. Jim and Kathleen found themselves in the house facing each other, with Lololomi at their side.

"I look like a schoolboy," Lololomi said, referring to the loss of his hair and his dirty face.

His remark loosened the tensions.

"Oh, Jim, this is horrible!"

Little trickles of muddy water ran from Kathleen's hair over her bare shoulders, for the ruthless women had all but torn her clothes from her.

"Can we ever get this house clean? And all that wood you brought! It is all gone!"

Her voice trailed off in tears.

He drew her to him, and the old man looked away.

"It is over now, and even the mud doesn't spoil you!"

He gave her a quick kiss. Just then his mother came into the room. The voices outside were dying into the distance.

"Come," she said, "we must make ready for tonight."

"Tonight?"

"Yes, they come back tonight."

"Oh, no!" Jim interrupted.

"Oh, *yes,* but with *piki,* to show that they will make peace."

The speed with which the house was put in order amazed Jim. He had thought it never could be made livable again. Even a few of the "enemy" came in to see what repairs were needed and they put their efficient hands to work at once. Merriment mounted as the women bathed and put on clean clothes, and the men did the same. By the time of the evening meal the house was orderly once more. A few of the small children still had specks of mud behind their ears and in their hair, which occasioned further laughter. But as the sun went down and the stars came out the serious aspects of the morrow's ceremony began to overshadow the day's hilarity, and from the few words spoken by the older people it was evident that the religious significance of the wedding was now predominant in their thinking.

Almost with solemnity the attacking clan members came bearing their *piki* and begging for peace. Later came Kathleen's mother and relatives with the quantities of corn meal which she had ground before coming here. This they presented to Jim's mother in "payment" for her son. Jim wondered if he were worth such a tremendous quantity of the stuff.

As the last visitor left the house, his mother turned to the two of them and took their hands in hers.

"I am happy to have you marry my boy, and," as she turned to Jim, "you are getting a good wife; you must be a good husband to her. Now we must all get to sleep."

Her simplicity and sincerity moved them both; these were the qualities that made him glad to be a Hopi. And this would be his last night alone!

XXXI

THIS WAS THE DAY which, in the eyes of the Hopi, would truly make them husband and wife; more *piki* making, he understood, a lot of funny business about washing their hair — funny idea! Funny? He must stop questioning all these things; he was a Hopi, wasn't he? Yes, he'd decided that; it was important to Kathleen. The white man had some funny ideas about marriage, too. He remembered a fellow in the Navy who talked about the kind of celebration they often had in Oklahoma — a shivaree, he called it — sounded pretty rough; and all that rice throwing. No the Hopi way had something, it was just that he was getting tired of waiting. He must talk with old Lololomi, who always made him feel right about things.

The stars were still out as he walked to his house, which he found flooded with light and filled with the women of his clan. Kathleen's mother was there, too. They all seemed very busy. He couldn't find Kathleen at first. Suddenly she appeared in the doorway of the storeroom, her hands full of the things that would be needed for the feasting later in the day. She quickly put these down and came to him.

"Isn't it a wonderful day?"

"Day? The stars are still out! Did you get any sleep?"

"Not too much, but I'm fine. It's nearly over, Jim. This is the important day. I'm glad, aren't you?"

"Glad! What do you think?"

Further talk between them was impossible, for both mothers approached them with great bowls of suds – of soap-weed, yucca roots, they said. The two lots were then poured into one large bowl and mixed thoroughly before being divided again into the two bowls. Kathleen's mother signalled Jim to kneel in front of her bowl of suds which she had just placed on the floor. Jim's mother had put down her bowl of suds right next to the other one, and she motioned to Kathleen to kneel by it so as to face Jim. They were directed to bow their heads into the bowls, and then the hair of both was thoroughly washed and briefly intertwined. All of this was done in utter silence and with great solemnity.

"You are now my daughter," Nasayungti said softly.

"And you are my son," pronounced Kathleen's mother.

And all these days of waiting ended only in this, Jim thought. *Only* in this? Why, Kathleen was now his wife, his wife! He wanted to shout it from the mesa top!

There was time for only a shy glance at each other before they were subjected to a thorough rubbing so as to dry the hair. Then Kathleen spoke.

"Come – we go now to the mesa's edge – to the east, to pray to the Sun."

"How do you know all these things?" Jim asked when once outside.

She put her finger on her lips for silence and with her other hand grasped his. Without further word they walked toward the rising sun. At the edge of the mesa they stood in its light, hands still clasped. After a moment they turned to each other and were lost in a tight embrace.

"What did you pray for?" he asked after a long interval.

"For you," she said, "for us. But we must go back. Breakfast must be served before the sun is high, and I have more *piki* to make."

Even as they approached the house the women were calling to her that *piki* stone was hot and she must be the first to use it that day. They had scarcely gotten inside before guests began arriving. Everybody in the village, it seemed, would be there to sample the bride's *piki* and eat the mutton stew that was simmering away in enormous quantity. All the men and boys brought gifts, the traditional cotton and beans in most cases, although some of the younger ones came with pots and pans and other household articles.

It was well into the afternoon before the last one departed. Those who had brought gifts took home with them trays of corn meal. Jim was a bit relieved to note that very little was left. But one of the aunts reminded them that if some were left over it would mean good luck for the bride – for the groom, too, he hoped. It had been a gay day, full of jesting and praise for the feast. The women, Kathleen among them, were busy throughout the long hours serving the many who came. It might just as well not be their wedding day, for all he saw of her. He looked up often to find her smiling at him; she was beautiful – and good – these were all good people. They joked him because he had so little to say, but there was warmth in their words; he felt truly one of them.

For Kathleen the hair ceremony was not yet complete. Late in the day Jim's mother arranged it for her in the style of the married woman; parted in the middle, a bang on either side, and the long part arranged on either side of her head in twists wrapped with cotton cord. The twists formed loops on the ends which were turned up and bound so that they lay away from her face. Jim pulled one loop playfully.

"I don't believe it would go with a nurse's uniform, but I like it."

"I wear it this way until I go home in my wedding clothes. When will they be done?"

"They may be finished now. Lololomi is seeing to it that the work is being done fast."

"Maybe we can be all through in the ten days Don gave me."

"It will be something of a record, I guess."

Nasayungti was busy at the stove.

"I must help her; I am supposed to make the supper tonight. And we'll have my wedding cake!"

"Wedding cake! Hopi?"

"Yes, I learned how – little crescents of blue meal wrapped in corn leaves and boiled. Maybe we can sleep on them and they'll bring us luck. The white girls tell me that's what they do with their wedding cake!"

"I don't like crumbs in bed."

"Silly!" And she left him to join Nasayungti, who had watched their byplay with a gentle smile.

He went to the door and stood looking out. It was good to have all of them gone. He guessed some of them would be back after a while, though. He would like to talk with Lololomi; maybe he was in the kiva. He called to the women that he would not be long and started off.

He walked in leisurely fashion, his mind filled with the week's events. They all *did* seem to wish him well, and to want him here. They had all come: Tom, old chief Nemtaka, Bill Lanta and the others from Old Oraibi. The ring! He'd forgotten to give Kathleen the ring! He turned back and then checked himself. No, he'd give it to her tonight, that would be his own ceremony. It would make it all easier – tonight – He'd missed Allan; his mother said Mary wasn't very well – the rabbit hunt was too much for her. She wanted to have their Hopi wedding soon, but she wasn't up to it yet. That was a foolish thing, to forget about the ring – but tonight . . .

He had just put his hand on the *kiva* ladder when he heard his name.

"Jim! Jim! Come quick!" And Sequa-Honau dashed up to him. "There is trouble – at Allan's!"

Jim could hear angry voices as they hurried toward the house, and the voices were unmistakably those of Vetch and some of his converts. The group had assembled in front of Allan's house and Mary's father was fairly shouting.

"My daughter must come with me. She is living in sin

here with a heathen. I have heard she is even talking of a Hopi marriage. I have come to end all this!"

As he raged he kept pulling Mary toward him, and Vetch moved around to take Mary's other arm. Jim was about to intervene when Allan, his face dark with anger, rushed out of his house brandishing a huge axe.

"Wait, Allan, wait! Have you told this fool that you have been married in the white man's way?"

"No, there's been no time," Allan panted.

Suddenly from the roof a torrent of mud and water descended upon Vetch. Jim looked up to see Allan's younger brother dumping the contents of a large bucket, left from the mud war. Vetch had dropped Mary's arm and, fierce with anger, he lunged toward Allan. Jim seized him and spun him around.

"You have no right to come here this way. Your daughter and Allan have been married by Dr. Cummings; there is nothing wrong in what they do. Let them alone!"

"But we heard they were being married here, in the heathen way," Mary's father burst in.

"My marriage is the only one taking place today – in the 'heathen way,' as you call it."

One of the villagers signalled to Allan and he quickly took Mary by the arm and ducked into the house and through the rear door into a side street. It was the run of but a few seconds to the edge of the mesa. Under there they managed to hide, protected by a block of sandstone that formed a small cave-like pocket near the place where the ceremonial eagles were buried.

Convinced that Mary's wedding was not taking place as they claimed, Vetch, to cover his chagrin, announced grandiosely, "Our main purpose in coming here today is to sanctify ground for a church, a church which is to rise on the mesa top back of the village. A church such as I have built at Oraibi!"

There was a gasp of consternation, of unbelief, even of horror.

This was a black day for them. The joy of the wedding ceremonies faded. Anger turned into sullen resentment against these *Kahopi* who would force their belief upon the faithful Hopi of Shongopovi.

Nemtaka came forward, thrusting to one side the converts from New Oraibi. He confronted Vetch.

"You and your followers, go from here. Every time you come to our village there is trouble. You will build no church upon our land. Go!"

He took a defiant step forward so that his face was only a few inches away from that of the startled missionary. Vetch fell back. The crowd muttered its approval of the chief's stand. Vetch and his group knew they must retreat. As they turned to leave, Mary's father shouted ugly threats and Vetch turned to Nemtaka with a final menacing statement.

"You will regret this, you and your people. I shall go to Keams Canyon as soon as the superintendent returns, and then we shall see if you can stop me from building my church upon this rock!"

He stamped his boot upon the mesa rock and left, his small flock following in evident confusion.

•

XXXII

JIM WAITED until the last of the villagers had gone to their homes. He was glad that Allan's house was far from his own. He didn't want the day spoiled for Kathleen, too. Spoiled? Nothing could spoil it. He called to Allan's mother, who had timidly appeared in the doorway, that he'd be around to see Allan later in the week; he was just starting off when he saw the two of them coming from the edge of the mesa. As he hurried toward them he saw that Mary was very frail and that only Allan's supporting arm enabled her to walk.

"Thanks, Jim. I'm sorry we did not get to your house today. My mother says she told you."

"It's all my fault." Mary was close to tears. "I wonder if I'll ever get well. We wanted to marry here when you did. Now we have even spoiled your wedding day."

"Don't worry about that, things will be all right. Kathleen and I will come soon to talk to you. You better get inside now. Don't worry about those *Kahopi*."

He found he enjoyed using the word. They better not try to make trouble; they'd be up against a lot of young fellows, now — he and Allan and Tom — and Vadas would be on his side, too, he felt sure. As he neared the kiva Lololomi was just emerging from it. I am glad Lololomi was out of this fracas; he's getting too old for this sort of thing, he thought. The old man waved to him to hurry.

"We are nearly through down there; maybe tomorrow you can come and see that all is ready. Tonight you will want to be at home, eh?"

He smiled a bit mischievously as he patted Jim's hand.

"I will see you tomorrow, my father. There is much I would like to talk about with you."

Supper was ready when he got to the house. Kathleen greeted him. "See, I have prepared the corn meal with beans just as a Hopi bride should."

His mother nodded her approval.

"You were gone a long time. Is my wedding dress finished?"

"Just about," he said. "Lololomi says one more day."

"You must tell me the names of all who have done the work so that I may repay them!"

The arrival of more well-wishers broke up their talk. There were food and "wedding cake" for all who came and the evening passed quickly. No one mentioned the trouble at Allan's; Jim was thankful for that. All were pleased that the wedding garments were nearly done and they promised to be at the feast on the day that Kathleen would return to her home wearing them. When the good nights were said Nasayungti pointed to herself and to the storeroom. That would be her room tonight. Jim found himself a bit embarrassed, but Kathleen smiled at the gentle woman, patted her and lightly touched her lips to the wrinkled cheek.

"I like the idea of being in your house this first night — don't ask me why!"

She went to the door and looked out.

"It's a wonderful night. Can't we walk a bit?"

"Good. I'd like to."

They made their way to the edge of the mesa and sat down at the spot where he had looked up to find her standing above him in her stiff nurse's uniform. How long ago that seemed!

"I'm glad you're not a sailor any more."

"And so am I; I'd rather be your husband."

"Thanks, sailor!"

They were silent for a time watching the gigantic clouds pile up over the San Francisco peaks. Suddenly Jim reached into his pocket and pulled out the ring.

"Oh, it's beautiful, Jim. I've been so anxious to see it."

Teasing, he held it away from her.

"I don't believe you really want it."

"Want it? Of course I do. Let me see it."

As she reached for it he pulled her to him.

"Oh, Kathleen!"

She pulled away as she took the ring and held it up so that the moonlight caught it.

"It's lovely, Jim," and she raised it to her lips and then to his. "Put it on my finger the last thing tonight."

They fell silent and in a few minutes they rose and walked back to the house.

The storeroom door was shut. One dim lamp and the dying fire in the wood stove gave the room its only light. The bed of sheepskins and blankets was ready.

"If you have a Hopi wedding you have to be satisfied with a Hopi bed!" He found he was able to laugh freely.

"Nothing wrong with it that I can see," she countered, "but I am not sure this hair-do will be very comfortable."

They lingered over the preparations for the night, talking lightly and laughing easily. Then they were ready. Jim blew out the lamp. They slid into the bed almost with one movement.

"The ring," he said. "Here it is."

She held up her left hand.

"Do you know where it belongs?"

With his right hand he slid it slowly on her third finger.

Far off the Crier Chief sounded his all's-well . . . "Another day has passed, never to return. Lolomi! Lolomi!"

XXXIII

THEY WERE SLEEPING SOUNDLY when Nasayungti slipped in at dawn to start the fire. Kathleen awoke with a start. Then she looked about and smiled. She reached over and pulled Jim's hair. He opened his eyes slowly.

"And what are you doing here?"

"I'm Mrs. Jim; remember?" And she held up her left hand.

Nasayungti returned when she heard them talking. After greeting her they got up and seized their clothes and made for the storeroom from which they soon emerged arm in arm.

"There will be another rabbit hunt today," Jim's mother announced. "There must be meat for feasting tomorrow."

"And I must get white corn meal mush ready to bake, and you must go to the *kiva* to see that the weaving is done."

He had never seen Kathleen so gay, so young. He hoped that nothing would go wrong on these last days. The women still seemed to have plenty to do, and not to want him around too much, either. To his surprise he found most of the older men already at the *kiva* and all the wedding robes spread out. He joined the group silently, for the way in which they were smoking indicated that they were making prayers. Lololomi emerged from the shadow.

"We have put the prayer plumes on the robes," he whispered. "They will bring happiness to Kathleen and to the souls of her children. Tomorrow we will bring the garments to your house."

He held up the belt proudly and Jim looked at it carefully. He marvelled at the skill in the old man's gnarled hands.

"Kathleen will be proud of this."

The men were apparently leaving shortly. Some were going on the rabbit hunt, he supposed. One of them gave him what was left of the cotton yarn.

"This," he said, "is to hang on Kathleen's ears as earrings. She will wear them until they drop off."

"Yes, it is an old custom," Lololomi explaimed. "Other women may want some of it, too. Come. We will walk together and talk, as you wished."

They turned toward the trail to the Sun Spring. Jim found that he did all the talking. He poured out his thoughts – the doubt he still felt at times that he could be a true Hopi, his great ignorance of all their ways and customs, the way his mind too often questioned his actions, the fear that Vetch would yet bring trouble to them all.

"Do not fret about these things, my son. That you think about them is good. All will be well. I have things I must do. We will finish the wedding garments today." And Lololomi turned back toward the village.

Jim stood there, looking out over the eye-stretching view. The rabbit hunters made their way down the trail – he wasn't expected to join them today. He decided he better see how his sheep were. He went back for the pickup. As he drove over the rough roads he was aware that his cares were falling away; maybe it was Lololomi – or Kathleen!

He was gone most of the afternoon. He had parked the car before his house when he heard a familiar voice. He looked up at the powerful figure of John Vadas.

"Congratulations, Jim! How's the old married man?"

He handed Jim a small box. "Here's a sort of wedding present. They're government publications on sheep and cattle and they're the real McCoy. They're by men who know what they're talking about."

They squatted by the doorway and leafed over the pamphlets. Kathleen came out with some *piki,* thinking the visitor was one of the weavers.

"I'd be glad to have some, I sure like it!" Vadas' voice was hearty and sincere. "I sure wish all the best to both of you. This country needs young folks like you."

"And we're probably going to need you," Kathleen replied.

"Any time," boomed Vadas. "By the way, have you heard what happened up at Old Oraibi?"

"No, what? When?"

"Well, that thunderstorm last night—I don't think you got any of the storm, but it really rained over there. And at Old Oraibi a really queer thing happened. That church of Vetch's was struck by lightning and burned to a shell."

"Really?" The exclamation came from them both.

"Yes, and, as if that wasn't enough, the same bolt of lightning seemed to fork and it tore a corner out of the wall of an old abandoned house near there. You won't believe this, but in a little pocket in the wall, where some darned son-of-a-gun had hidden them, were the two big prayer sticks that disappeared from the old Hopi shrine when Vetch began building."

"What does everyone think about it? Aren't they excited?" Kathleen's voice evidenced her delight.

"They sure are at Old Oraibi. The poor converts at New Oraibi don't know what to think. Old Vetch never prepared them for a miracle that would work in favor of the heathen!" He laughed heartily and with a happy, "Good luck, kids!" he was on his way.

"I didn't tell you about something that happened yesterday," began Jim diffidently, "because I didn't want to spoil things."

Kathleen's face was troubled as he recounted what had taken place at Allan's.

"Well, surely Vetch won't try to force his church here after what happened last night; that would seem to be a sign that the gods disapproved."

"I hope you're right, but I'll be happy only when Vetch is a long way from this part of the country."

By nightfall the news had spread through the village, and from nearly every house there floated on the night air songs of thanksgiving for the curious miracle that had occurred at Old Oraibi.

•

XXXIV

THE NEXT DAY dawned clear. The women of Jim's household were hard at work when he awoke. The rabbits brought to Kathleen as trophies of the hunt had to be made ready for the giant stew that would feature the day's feast, after Kathleen was robed in the garments woven by the men. The *pikami,* the white corn meal mush which had been readied the day before, must be baked for some hours in the underground oven.

"Haven't you time to say good morning to your husband?"

"Too busy!" she said.

He pulled her down to him.

"Oh, Jim, please! My hair's got to last through the day!"

His mother laughed aloud as Kathleen scrambled to her feet.

After breakfast Jim went to the *kiva* where he smoked and talked with the men. Late in the morning Sequa-Honau came to say that the *pikami* was about baked and the rabbit tender. A smart youngster, Jim commented to himself—he certainly knows the right time to be around. At this word the men made ready to take the wedding garments to Kathleen. Jim felt a bit self-conscious as he led the formal procession to his house.

Kathleen received the men with grace and poise, and he was proud of their admiration for her. It was Lololomi who made the presentation.

"My daughter, the wife of this my son, we present to you these garments to assure you of a life of happiness. It is our hope that you will both have long lives of great contentment, that you will have children who will honor, respect, and have affection for you. We have woven these with constant prayer, and in this your husband has joined us. Our every thought has been for your happiness and for your peace."

He paused for a moment; when he resumed, his words were directed to them both.

"You have both lived for many years among white people. Their ways are often different from ours. Some of them have brought sorrow and trouble to the Hopi. But, although you have both lived like white people and still often think as they do, with good hearts and honest minds, you have been married as true Hopi are. This is good.

"We have ever prayed that the white man might not be permitted to destroy our Hopi way of life. You have had proof of how our prayers are answered. You have seen how the gods can destroy the work of a man who was filled with bitterness and anger toward us. Many times we have been prompted to lift our hands against him, but we are Hopi and so we quieted the anger in our hearts and united our thoughts in the Hopi way.

"In your life together you will face many difficulties, but if you are steadfast Hopi your thoughts will ever be strong thoughts and your life will be rich with rewards."

As Kathleen bowed her head in gratitude, thankful for the chance to hide the tears that welled to her eyes, Jim recalled with shame the time he had thought Lololomi a dirty old Indian.

The garments were carried to the storeroom as the women bustled about preparing to serve the feast. The men from the *kiva* were being joined by many men and women from the village. The house fairly burst at its seams. As was customary, the men formed a group to themselves and were served generous portions of stew and cupfuls of steaming coffee. The women would eat later. Now their interest lay in admiring the wedding garments. While the men enjoyed the feast, the women crowded into the storeroom to help Kathleen get into her white cotton robe and the white buckskin boots which had to be wrapped to the knees like puttees. Nothing was missing from the outfit; even the cord of human hair with which she would bind her own had been carefully twisted in readiness. No, she must not wear the belt, they said; that would be carried in the roll, the reed roll that Jim had made. Its fringes must hang down, rain falling from the pure white cloud which she now represented.

At last she was ready for the return to her mother's house. Nasayungti would precede her, bearing a great bowl of mutton stew. Kathleen stepped into the room and timidly looked about. To Jim she seemed as she had in her nurse's uniform, stiff and untouchable – he was almost glad that he was not expected to accompany her. The men's pride in their handiwork shone in their eyes. Many of them offered her words of advice. With great ceremony Lololomi sprinkled a trail of corn meal out of the house and onto that of her mother's, the path upon which she would walk. She hesitated just a moment, then looked to Jim. He rose and watched her set out on her return.

The scene in Kathleen's house was gay and lively. Her mother greeted her with every evidence of great joy. Her women relatives took turns trying on her robe and attempting to get their feet into her small boots. Chattering and laughter filled the air. As the day wore on all of the women of the village came to congratulate her, even Mary came with Allan's mother, for a brief talk.

"Did Jim tell you what happened yesterday?" Mary asked.

"He couldn't keep it to himself when John Vadas told us about the church at Old Oraibi!"

"Did he tell you how he faced that old Vetch? He was wonderful!"

Kathleen's heart warmed at the praise.

"Is the ceremony hard?" Mary's voice was almost pleading. "I want to go through with it soon; Allan wants it so."

"Oh, I'm sure you can soon – it's long – it's not hard – not hard. . . ."

"You better come now." It was Allan's mother speaking. "We wish you well, Kathleen. Jim's mother and I have good daughters."

A group of younger women crowded around Kathleen as Mary and Allan's mother left.

"How much corn meal did you have to pay for your husband?" "Is he worth it, do you think?" "How many children will you have?"

They teased her with endless questions. She finally silenced them with gifts of earrings of cotton yarn left from the weaving, and they listened soberly as she thanked them for their help with the grinding.

"Get married soon – and I'll help all of you," she promised.

A knock at the door proved to be Dr. Cummings.

"I'm not sure I belong here, but I sort of felt it wasn't legal without my coming in some time," the doctor said.

"You are always welcome, Don." Kathleen's words were echoed by her mother.

"You should go to Jim's house and join the men," remarked an aunt.

"I'll do that – but I'd like just a word with you, Kathleen."

She walked with him to the door.

"You look happy – I'm glad. I hate to ask this, but can you get back soon? Superintendent Lyons is coming back the day after tomorrow. You know his prejudice against our using Indian nurses – I don't want him to find any irregularity in things just now."

"Tomorrow is the end. I shall be there the first thing the next morning."

"Good. I'll talk to Jim about it, too, so he won't think

we have plotted against him. I like Jim; I hope you'll both be happy."

By Hopi custom Kathleen and Jim would spend that night apart, she in her mother's house, he in Nasayungti's. The following morning she would return to make the final "payment" for him. She knew how Jim must be fuming inwardly over all this – and she had to confess she herself found it all a bit trying, but one more day and their lives would be their own. Was that true? She wondered.

It was late the next morning when a solemn procession started in single file to the house of Jim's mother. Kathleen's mother was first with a great bowl of beans. Kathleen followed, carrying high above her head a tray piled with rolls of blue *piki*. Four of her male relatives followed her, holding a blanket by its corners, in the center of the blanket a basket plaque heaped with white corn meal. This was the great plaque, her mother had explained earlier, on which Jim would be carried, at his death, over the Great Canyon to the place where the dead abide.

Nasayungti met them, all smiles. Various aunts of Jim came forward and received the beans and the *piki* and the white corn meal. Prayers were said silently as the men blew smoke in the six world directions. Suddenly the solemnity was at an end. For the first time since the day before, Kathleen saw Jim in a far corner of the room. He was looking at his mother, a troubled look on his face.

"Something wrong?" she asked softly.

Jim started.

"Oh, I thought you'd never get back! Yes, there is something wrong. It's my mother. She will be alone again – I just realized it."

"Well, it's up to us to see that she isn't – except when she wants to be. We women sort of like to be by ourselves."

"Oh, you do?"

He pulled one of the loops of her hair and the onlookers giggled.

"As I told you – I sort of like it this way."

"Well, it will be gone tomorrow. I'm going back to the hospital. Did Don tell you?"

"Yes, he did. It's all right, I suppose. He said that he was trying to work out some sort of plan for you to be a visiting nurse, so you could have a car and end each day's work here."

"He told you that? He didn't tell me."

"Well, we men have our secrets."

Guests came to offer their congratulations once more before they left to prepare supper in their homes. Jim wondered how they could eat any more. Kathleen's mother paused to say she would go on home and take Nasayungti with her.

"We shall come soon," Kathleen called after them and then, turning to Jim, "Let's go to our spot on the edge of the mesa – it's easy to talk under the stars."

She tucked her arm in his and they walked slowly to the rim. Kathleen propped herself up comfortably and Jim sprawled out with his head in her lap. She ran her fingers gently through his hair.

"Kathleen?" there was question in his voice. "You told your mother we would be along soon. Do we not go to our own house?"

"Just for a few nights we will stay at my mother's. She wishes it; it used to be the custom to stay a whole year – or even longer – for good."

"I know, you told me that. But – your aunt went with us when we decided on our own house. It must be all right for us to live there."

"Our people have been good to us, Jim. Let us be good to them, too, when we can. A few nights at my mother's house will not hurt us, and it will make her feel that we are trying to do things the right way. She knows we want to go into own house soon, and I will talk with her about it tomorrow."

I wonder why I keep bucking these things, he thought. It's not important – Kathleen's right – we must consider the customs of our people when we can. I'll be glad to get back into my own routine again though.

"Are you glad to go back to the hospital in the morning?"

"Yes — and no. I love my work, Jim. I'd hate to give it up, but I'd like more time with you, too."

"I guess I wanted you to say that. But I'll be busy, too."

They talked of his sheep and of the cattle he would be getting soon, of the silver work at Old Oraibi, and of the house of their own they would have one day.

"You know," Kathleen spoke slowly, "you know, I feel as if we had been married a long time."

"Is it as bad as that?" he asked rather ruefully.

"No," she said quite seriously, "it's just that I feel settled — content. But we must get back."

They rose and the night gave their embrace the blessing of its darkness.

XXXV

WITHIN THE WEEK, Kathleen and Jim had established a regular pattern of living. In spite of mild protests by a few of Kathleen's more conventional aunts, they moved into their own house. For the time, their furniture consisted of the barest necessities – blankets and sheepskins, a small stove, a kitchen table, and boxes for seats. But Kathleen had a way with the lovely Hopi plaques and blankets, and their designs and colors and fine workmanship were displayed to the greatest advantage.

One day, as they were discussing plans, Bill Lanta knocked on the door.

"I have never told you how much I like the ring that you helped Jim make for me," said Kathleen as she let him in.

His pleasure at her remark glowed in his face.

"He did well with it. I helped him very little."

"Come, sit with us for a while," said Jim. "I am always so busy working when I come to your place at Old Oraibi that we never get a chance to talk. How do you like our house?"

"I certainly don't want an iron bed such as most of the houses have," said Kathleen. "I'll stick to the blankets and sheepskins first!"

The men laughed at her, and Lanta took up her challenge.

"Some time you two must drive with me to Ildefonso in New Mexico. There you can see some handmade furniture that is very beautiful, and right for a house like this. I tell you, you can write to the Indian who makes it. He would be pleased to make some for you. It is his dream that we shall make furniture that is fitting to our Indian pueblos."

"It must be good," said Jim. "I've never heard you say so much in one breath!" Kathleen sought pencil and paper to write down the address.

Again a knock sounded, and the door opened to admit Lololomi and Nemtaka. The village chief did not often make an appearance in one of the homes of the village; they wondered what might bring him here today.

"I bring you these *pahos* for your ceiling rafters. They will protect your house and assure you of happiness."

Lololomi beamed as the prayer plumes were presented.

"Come, my son, we will place them now where they belong." To everyone's astonishment, the old man jumped on the kitchen table with amazing agility and hung the plumes from one of the ceiling beams.

As he was leaving, Bill Lanta remarked to Jim, "Just a little more work on that necklace and pendant you're making and they'll be ready for the show at the museum in Flagstaff. They'll take a prize, I'm sure."

"Jim, how exciting!"

"Thanks, Lanta. I'll be over nearly every morning now. I'm getting some tools and once the cattle are all set I'm going to get a bench and set up a shop here. Kathleen and I have already decided where it will go."

The visitors gone, Kathleen busied herself with preparing supper.

"Did I tell you that I've arranged with one of the girls to pick me up here every morning? She says she can do it easily. Then if you can come for me every night, everything is all set."

"What makes you think I want you home every night?"

"Well, I just suggested it."

"Any more news of your becoming a visiting nurse?"

"Don's put in the application and it ought to come through any day now — that is, if it does come through. I'll probably plan a couple of rooms in the school as a dispensary if everything goes as we hope."

"Won't the old men be against that?"

"Maybe, at first. That is one of the things we have to work for — their interest and confidence in us."

"You can do it if anyone can," Jim said.

Three days later Dr. Cummings met Kathleen at the hospital with the news that her appointment had gone through and that he had arranged for the rooms in the school.

"That's fast work. You must have been anxious to get rid of me."

"You know better than that, I hope. How's married life working out?"

"Don't get me started on that."

"O.K., eh? Would Jim say the same thing?"

"Well, I certainly hope so. Are you trying to break up our home?"

They both laughed at that.

"You'll start at Second Mesa school, tomorrow," Don said. "The place will need some work on it to get ready for business. The older kids at the school will be glad to help."

"I can always count on Sequa-Honau," Kathleen replied. "He's growing into a really husky youngster. Jim says he's a first-rate sheepherder."

"Plan the place the way you want it and keep a record of the costs. I'll probably assign Martha to help you."

The project was challenging and Kathleen went to work with a will. Martha Honani came daily to help her. At the end of two days the rooms were scrubbed and in order with the minimum of proper equipment for the usual work of a dispensary.

"It looks sort of drab to me," said Kathleen as she surveyed their work. "I think I'll get some of the children in the art class to decorate these walls."

Her scheme worked well, and soon half a dozen youngsters were spending their playtime on murals depicting Hopi ceremonies. They had their reward when one of the old men dropped in one day and exclaimed, "This room's going to look just like a *kiva!*"

One afternoon, a few days later, Nemtaka, Lololomi, and two other village patriarchs came in. It was the first time they had visited or exhibited any interest in the new program. Kathleen felt her chance had come. She explained in careful detail what they were doing on this particular afternoon.

"Much of the sickness that has come to us in the Hopi country has been brought to us by the white man." She hoped she was telling the truth. "And so we must use the white man's methods to cure the white man's diseases."

There was no comment from the old men as they turned from the table to give their attention to the children's paintings. Kathleen was pleased to hear exclamations of approval. At that moment some of the children came in to continue their work. The visitors watched with appraising eyes and soon were explaining to the youthful artists the significance of the markings on some of the *Kachina* masks they were painting.

Suddenly there was some confusion at the door, and it was opened to admit a terrified woman who carried a small child. He had been badly burned, she explained between moans, when he knocked over a pot of mutton stew. The boy sobbed pitifully as Kathleen lifted him onto the table to examine the extent of the burns. One leg was indeed in bad condition, the burn extending down from the waist. The youngster had every symptom of extreme shock.

Kathleen's first inclination was to send out everybody

except Martha – but the old men were crowding around the table. If she forced them to go, they might very well believe that she was performing some kind of witchcraft on the child. This might be an opportunity to prove her own efficiency and competence, as well as the value of the dispensary in such an emergency.

She gave the child a sedative, and then slipped a gauze mask over her mouth, to the astonishment of the gaping audience; she started to wash the areas surrounding the burns. Assisted by Martha, she worked carefully and with great gentleness for twenty minutes or more with sterile gauze compresses, sterilizing powder, and medicated petroleum jelly. The boy grew quiet under her ministrations; the mother was calmer.

Absorption in what she was doing caused her to completely forget that she had an audience. When the job was done she looked up to find the attention of the group riveted upon her every move. She broke into a smile. They smiled too. The tension relaxed. There were mutters of astonishment. It was Nemtaka who addressed her.

"That was indeed well done. It was wonderful to see how fast you worked and how kind your fingers were. You are a great healer."

Suddenly she was conscious of the strain she had been under, of the foul air in the crowded room, and of the whiteness of Martha's face. She hurriedly threw open the door and took in great lungsful of cold air. Now she could hurry them all out without mystifying them. She thanked the men for coming, gave the woman some pills to guard the child against infection, promising to look in on the boy on her way home. Within the hour she and Martha were back examining and weighing babies.

It was Jim who crowned her achievement. She was at the stove when he came in to supper that evening. He went directly to her and turned her about so that she could see the pride in his face.

"What a hit you've made with the old men! I stopped

at my mother's house for a minute and old Lololomi and Nemtaka had been there for hours telling her what a smart girl her son had married."

•

XXXVI

"WELL, DOC, I haven't seen you in a long time!" The hearty voice of John Vadas greeted Dr. Cummings.

"You've not been around much lately, have you?"

"I don't know where the days go. I'd rather be on this mesa than anywhere else, but I don't get here nearly as much as I'd like to, or as I should."

"I certainly was glad to have Vadas come today," put in Jim. "I was just at the point where I needed some advice about those ewes of mine."

"There certainly isn't much advice I can give you. You're doing all right — there's going to be a fine lot of lambs or I miss my guess."

"Why don't we go inside? Maybe you'll stay for supper?"

The questions were Kathleen's. The four had met at the house quite by chance. The doctor had walked up with Kathleen to talk over matters at the dispensary and Vadas had returned from the range with Jim to pick up his car in the village.

"I really shouldn't – in fact, I can't stay long enough to eat supper. But I would like to come in for a bit."

"Same with me, Doc."

"We can have a cup of coffee, at least. Sorry I have no *piki* for you, John."

"What kind of Hopi are you, Kathleen?"

There was a half hour of banter and some serious talk, too.

"I've an amusing story to tell and then I must go," the doctor finally said. "We X-rayed a youngster who was having some trouble with his stomach the other day and found he had a penny in it. I wasn't too sure that was the only trouble so I sent him into Flag – and they found two pennies in his stomach! He's quite all right now, but what do you think the kids have nicknamed him? Piggy Bank!"

"I don't know where anybody ever got this wooden Indian idea." remarked Vadas when the laughter subsided.

"Nor I," said the doctor." But I do have to go. It's been good to see you, Jim. Kathleen's doing a fine job at the dispensary."

The two men left and Kathleen prepared supper while Jim made some notes of supplies he had to get for his sheep.

"Supper's ready, Jim. Are you? It was good to have them drop in, wasn't it?"

"Yes, both of them have a way of making a fellow feel better. I saw Allan for a minute today."

"I looked in on Mary today, too. She does look better, I think. Dr. Cummings wants her to come down to the hospital soon for a complete check-up."

"Allan says that some of Vetch's converts don't have the faith in him they had before the lightning destroyed the church. They don't like the business about those prayer sticks. A lot of them are sure it was Vetch who stole and hid them. A few have already left New Oraibi and others talk of having a *Kachina* dance there once more."

"They couldn't have been very good Christians if they are so easily changed. I only hope it won't stir up a lot more trouble."

Kathleen's hope was doomed to disappointment. When

Superintendent Lyons heard of the actions at New Oraibi he hurried there and forbade the leaders to plan any such dance. While there he heard that an anthropologist by the name of Walter Jacobsen had been talking with the old men on the mesa top, urging them to let nothing interfere with their ceremonials. This news further inflamed his wrath, and he called for a mass meeting at Oraibi school to be attended by the people of both Oraibi villages.

The school was filled to capacity. There was little talk as the people assembled at the time appointed, but many dark looks were exchanged between the Hopi of the mesa top and the Christian dissenters below. On the platform sat Superintendent Lyons, the principal of Oraibi Day School, the Reverend Vance Vetch and his sad-faced wife, and three policemen. Lyons rose to speak. He was a tall, thin man with bigotry stamped on every feature of his unsmiling face. Someone whispered *"Chee-va-to"* and hands went quickly over mouths. It was hard to tell whether or not Lyons heard it but his face flushed as he began to speak in a sharp intense voice. He recounted all that he and his staff had tried to do for the Hopi, of how much better their lot was than it had been when he first came among them, of the help of the Reverend Vetch in bringing to them the Christian faith; with all this, he said, many of them had been uncooperative, even disloyal. He was demanding, therefore, that each person present should sign a pledge of loyalty to "Washington," and he held up a long typewritten document.

His listeners gave little response. The policemen began to clap and were joined by Vetch and his wife and a few of their New Oraibi followers, but the majority of those present looked on unmoved. Then the superintendent singled out individuals and demanded that they come and sign the statement. Embarrassed, brow-beaten, fearful, they came one by one and put their names or their x's at the bottom of the typed paragraphs. Almost all had signed when a woman of Old Oraibi was called upon.

She was the wife of the village chief on the mesa top. It was in her house that Walter Jacobsen was staying. She could not read English but with great solemnity she took time to look carefully at each word on the sheet. There she recognized the name of Walter Jacobsen — and sensed at once that something was wrong. She was sure Jacobsen was a good man — his interest in the Hopi was real. If this was, as the superintendent said, just a pledge of loyalty to the government in Washington, why should Jacobsen's name be there? She did not understand, but she refused to sign, and she called out to all present her reasons for doing so.

A young Hopi who could read English rushed to the platform, seized the paper before anyone could stop him, and in a loud voice read its contents:

"We, the citizens of both New and Old Oraibi, pledge our loyal support to the government of the United States. We have come to realize that Walter Jacobsen, who is visiting in Old Oraibi, has given us bad advice and we herein state that we wish him never to visit the Hopi reservation again. We furthermore pledge our loyal support to Superintendent Virgil Lyons who has been such a benefactor to us that we have adopted him as a member of the Hopi tribe."

As he finished reading, the principal tore the paper from his hands. There was a roar of protest from the crowd and someone towards the back of the room shouted, "*Chee-va-to.*" The superintendent whirled about to identify the offender. At that moment the anger of the group turned to laughter. The offensive name echoed and re-echoed through the room, "*Chee-va-to! Chee-va-to!*" Lyons and the others on the platform could do nothing to stop it. Since the paper had been signed by nearly all present, they decided to get out with it as quickly as possible.

Jim, on his way to Old Oraibi and unaware of what was happening, passed the door of the schoolhouse just as the superintendent and the principal bolted out of the building, followed by the policemen. Jim heard Lyons saying bitterly, "Just wait until I get my hands on that son-of-a-bitch of a Lololomi at Shongopovi!"

Jim waited only long enough to learn what had happened, then started on a run to his village. It was evident that Lyons was avoiding Second Mesa for the present, for he headed for Keams Canyon by the lower road. There would be time to warn Lololomi. The threat of trouble that hung over them was increasing. Would they ever be free of it?

He dashed into Lololomi's house and breathlessly told him of Lyons' threat and of all that had transpired. The old man smiled and said nothing for some minutes. Then he spoke gently.

"Some of the young people have been talking to me about a Butterfly Dance. This is not the customary time for one, but maybe it would be pleasant to have one now. There is time yet before we start to plant the corn. Nothing lifts my old heart as do the lovely costumes and the beautiful songs of this dance. Yes, it would be a pleasant thing to do just now."

"Hadn't you better hide out until this business blows over?" Jim pleaded.

"Hide? I?"

Once more Jim marvelled at this wrinkled little old man who had strength and courage enough to pit himself against the anger and the might of the official representative of the government of the United States. He started to plead with him again, but Lololomi seemed to have forgotten his presence. He sat with a faraway look in his eyes as he hummed a snatch of the mockingbird's song.

XXXVII

ACTING UPON LOLOLOMI'S suggestion, the village set a certain Saturday for the Butterfly Dance, a day when the children would be free from school and could take part in the ceremonial. All looked forward with pleasure to a final festival before corn-planting time. As a bride, Kathleen would not make her appearance in a ceremony until the *Niman Kachina* Dance in midsummer, and so Jim decided he would not participate in this one. They joined in making ready the costumes, particularly the elaborate headdresses worn by the women dancers.

It was Friday morning. Most of the able-bodied men of Shongopovi had gone out to their corn fields to prepare them for the spring planting. The women were busy preparing food for the feast that would follow the ceremony. The older children were down at the day school at the foot of the mesa, and the toddlers were seriously engaged in engineering operations with sand and pebbles. Jim was spending a few hours in Oraibi working on the necklace and pendant that Bill Lanta had praised; he would join the rest of the men in the fields later in the day. Kathleen, at the dispensary, was making ready to go over to Shipolovi where some children had come down with what she thought was measles.

It was a beautiful clear day and the sun was pleasantly warm. The doors of nearly every house were open and neighbors called to each other freely across the narrow streets. It was about ten o'clock in the morning when cars could be heard laboring up the steep road on the east side of the mesa. Some of the women looked out to see who the visitors might be, and then dragged their children into the houses as four government cars pulled up back of the village. On one of the trucks was a deep galvanized trough used for dipping sheep, and with it two large cans of sheep dip and three barrels of water.

As the motors were cut, sixteen men piled out of the trucks, six white men, among them Superintendent Lyons, and ten Navajo policemen. They carried the trough into the dance plaza and with five-gallon cans began filling it with water from the barrels. To this they added the cans of sheep dip, stirring it into the water with remarks that occasioned bursts of laughter, although there were curses when some of the mixture stung their hands. From one of the trucks they then produced back pumps, such as forest fire-fighters use, and these they filled with the sheep dip mixture.

"Well, it's time for our little ball game."

Lyons spoke with a sneer. The Navajo policemen went to the cars and came back swinging baseball bats. One of the white men who knew a few words of Hopi yelled out that all the people in the village should come to the plaza. Within a few minutes a frightened but curious crowd of women and small children gathered around. In the background a few very old men stood in rather fearful wonder.

"Where is that damned Lololomi?" demanded Lyons.

No one answered. No one seemed to know whom he was talking about. Lyons decided to forget the old man for the time being and go ahead with what they had come to do.

"Now, look here. There is a bad epidemic of sickness in Arizona and we have reason to think that this village is one of the worst spots."

There were guffaws from the white men at this, as Lyons continued.

"We have come here to disinfect the place. We're going to spray all the houses, and all you women and kids have to take a bath in this tank of disinfectant."

There was consternation when he spoke of the spraying; shock when the women and girls realized they would have to take a bath publicly. A moment's horrified silence ensued when he finished. One young woman let out a scream and dashed for her house, and then every woman and child in the crowd ran for cover. Lyons barked an order to his men and they ran after the fleeing villagers, leaving their pumps by the trough. At this point Nemtaka stepped forward, surrounded by other old men and boys.

"This is no way to treat our women and children." Nemtaka spoke sternly. "You would not dare do this if our young men were here. You have come like cowards when you knew they were in the fields. You will not do this to our people!"

Nemtaka and his companions spread out across the entrance to one of the covered passages so as to block the route of the superintendent. At an order from Lyons one of the Navajo policemen tried to knock Nemtaka to one side. The old chief threw off the policeman's grip and was instantly surrounded by his fellow Hopi who sought to protect the head of their village. The policemen then began to pull the old men to one side. Lololomi ran in and stood directly in front of the superintendent.

"You have come to make trouble for the people of this village because of me. Therefore, why not beat me with your clubs? Why not throw me into your sheep dip? I am the man you want!"

With a curse Lyons hit the old man across the face with such force that Lololomi went reeling back into the passageway and fell to the ground, his mouth bloody. Exclamations of anger came from the Hopi and they charged upon the whites and Navajo policemen with unleashed fury. The superintendent had been waiting for this. As the old Hopi and the boys came forward, the policemen swung the baseball bats like war clubs and many of the Hopi were knocked senseless. Short bits of rope came from the pockets of the intruders and with these the victims were securely bound, then carried over to the automobiles, where, after being doused with cans of water, they were thrown roughly into the trucks with a Navajo left to guard them.

Through a crack in her barricaded door one of the women witnessed this; she called out a warning to the others to hide wherever they could. Allan's mother ran with Mary to an unused dry cistern that had been carved out of the rock near her house. There they were secure. There was hardly time for the others to seek out the darkest corners of storage rooms and underground chambers before the men were pounding at the doors. Ruthlessly they battered them down, searched out the places where the food was stored and into them pumped the acrid-smelling spray. Then the houses were searched for women and children and those captured were herded into a corner of the plaza. Particularly rough handling was given to any woman who guarded her door or showed any sign of resistance.

The white men tore off their clothes and threw them into the trough. The women and the children screamed and fought, but they were no match for the strong-arm methods and the lascivious manhandling of the attackers. Crying with shame and rage, the women seized their clothes and, covering themselves as best they could, they crept to their houses to cower in terror.

Lyons watched the proceedings with glee. "I hope you belong to that old bastard Lololomi's clan!" he shouted as he helped to throw a screaming, kicking young woman into the sheep dip.

While the ugly scene was at its height some frightened children made their escape and ran down the mesa trail where Kathleen saw them as she was on her way to Shipolovi. The little girls were hysterical; thinking her car might contain more policemen, their screams mounted in terror. Kathleen stopped the car and ran toward them, but they sped off like deer. She was breathless when she finally came upon them cringing under a scrub peach tree.

"What has happened? Tell me!"

It was some time before she could learn what had transpired. Surely the children imagined all this. They were exaggerating. She must see what it was all about. If only Jim were here!

"Tell Martha I am going to the village!" she called. She sped up the steep road. At the top she saw the government cars and she could hear screams coming from the directions of the plaza. It took her but a minute to get to the plaza. There she stopped in unbelieving horror — it was as the children had said!

For a moment she could not speak. An old woman was being dragged to the trough. Kathleen's first thought was one of thankfulness that it was not her mother or Jim's. She recognized old blind Kelwuthi as they tore off her Hopi dress and tossed her into the burning sheep dip. Behind her one of her daughters screamed as a policeman pulled off her clothes, and made some remark to the man next to him that provoked a howl of laughter. The young woman turned and, wrenching one hand free, hit him in the face. The second man knocked her into the trough with one swing of his arm, dragged her through it, then tossed her to one side.

As Lyons took hold of one of the smaller girls, Kathleen seized his arm.

"What do you think you're doing?" she demanded.

"Well, well, if it isn't the cute little squaw nurse from the hospital!"

As he spoke he began to strip the clothes from the little girl. In fury Kathleen swung him around to face her.

"Take your filthy hands off that child. What right have you here? What is the meaning of all this? What are you doing to these people?"

Lyons gave her a contemptuous look.

"Look here — over at the hospital you may be of some account, but here you're just one more dirty squaw and you're going to be disinfected."

He made a lunge for her, but she was too quick for him. Terror struck her. She turned and bolted for the car. She jumped into it and drove frantically, almost blindly, over the mesa road. She had gone more than a mile before she came to herself.

She must not run. She must find some way to help. She could not desert her people. But one woman could not stand against all those men. Maybe Jim was still at Old Oraibi.

She drove at breakneck speed over the rough road and up the ruts to the old village. Bill Lanta, Myron Mansa and the other silversmiths looked up in astonishment as she burst in on them. They stopped work when they saw her terrified face. Jim was just coming in from another room. He went to her quickly and took her in his arms as she collapsed in sobs. He comforted her as best he could, and in a few minutes she managed to blurt out the story.

"Bill," commanded Jim, "you take my pickup and get all the Shongopovi men you can from the fields. We'll meet you at the coal mine. You better go with him, Myron."

Kathleen and Jim waited until they saw the pickup jerk forward. Then she climbed in beside him.

"What can we do when we get there? Bill can't bring in enough of the men to drive Lyons and his gang out. What can we do?"

Jim did not reply to Kathleen's impassioned question. Tense with anger, he gave his attention to driving. Near the top a dirt road turned off to the old mine and there they waited for the others to come.

"Come on, Bill. Come on." The words came from between Jim's clenched teeth.

"They are coming, Jim. Look!"

The truck, crowded with men, was lurching out of a wash onto the gravelled road. In a matter of seconds it was with them, and then the two cars made their way up the road and parked in a place where they could not be seen from the plaza.

"Kathleen, you better try to find out how things are with our mothers. We men will go to the plaza."

As Jim spoke the men were arming themselves with

pieces of wood that lay about. Myron pulled an old gun from his pocket.

"I got no ammunition for this thing, but it might be a good bluff."

As they entered the plaza Jim was horrified to see his mother being pulled out of the trough. Nasayungti sobbed and cowered in shame as she picked her cotton dress from the ground, pulled it around her, and stumbled in the direction of her house. With a cry of rage Jim started forward to where Lyons was standing with his back to him. He turned just as Jim came up. Jim caught him squarely on the shoulder with a faggot, just missing his head by the fraction of an inch. The white man gave a cry of pain.

The fury of the swinging blow threw Jim off balance. Before he could recover himself two policemen were upon him and the three of them went sprawling onto the rocks. Lanta and Myron Mansa tried to come to his assistance. One of the white men caught sight of the gun in the Hopi's hand. He let out a yell, whipped open his shirt, and produced a small automatic from a shoulder holster. He took quick aim and fired. Myron pitched forward on the ground.

There was a moment of terrible silence. All looked toward Myron, who lay sprawled on his face. Lyons began to realize that things had gone further than he had intended. He had planned to write a report that would cover everything they had done with an aura of innocence, but killing a man was another matter. He went to the Hopi and turned him over. The wound seemed too high for the heart.

"Where did that squaw nurse go to?"

One of the policeman yanked Jim before the superintendent.

"This guy's her husband—he ought to know."

Jim called sharply for Kathleen to come; she bent over the stricken man. She quickly tore the shirt aside and disclosed an ugly shoulder wound. As she wiped away the blood, Myron stirred and murmured something. A cry of relief went up from the Hopi looking on.

"Jim, give me a hand. Get someone else, too. We'll take him to the dispensary."

They carried him to Kathleen's car.

"You drive him down and have Martha dress the wound, then see that he gets to the hospital." Kathleen was poised and professional now.

"What about you?"

"I have a few things to say to Lyons – and I'm going to say them now."

She turned to the superintendent.

"Now will you explain what this is all about?"

"There is an epidemic – necessary sanitary precautions –"

"I am a nurse, and I know there is no epidemic here. If you thought there was one, why didn't you advise Dr. Cummings?"

She was interrupted as the rest of the men from the fields rushed in. Lyons thought it a good time to retreat. Still, he'd show them.

"Come on fellows, let's go. We'll take a few of these Indians along. They can cool off in the Keams Canyon calaboose for a few days."

He directed the Navajo policemen to arrest Lololomi, Nemtaka, Allan Lemtewa, and five others.

"Pick up this Jim fellow at the dispensary. I guess things will be a little quieter around here now."

Confused by what was happening, the men submitted to the arrest with little protest. There'd been bloodshed enough for one day. There was nothing to do now but wait. Lyons' men emptied the trough and hurriedly loaded the rest of the stuff on the trucks. The prisoners were jostled into one of the cars. The sullen-faced villagers looked on in silence.

There were no songs in Shongopovi that night. The indignities which had been forced upon the women etched into their very hearts. The men ate scant suppers and drifted over to the *kiva* as soon as they could, although the Crier Chief made no announcement of a meeting there. They sat and smoked in gloomy silence. Nothing like this had ever happened to the Hopi before; there were no words to voice the indignation and the hurt. As the stars swung slowly across the sky the thoughts of the entire village united in deep, heartfelt misery.

In Kathleen's house, she and the two mothers brooded over the events of the day. Her mother had hidden in a little crevice under a large slab of rock which projected over the edge of the mesa not far from her house. She had left the door of her house ajar when she slipped out and so escaped the policemen. Her storeroom had escaped the spraying, so she had brought over food for the others. Jim's mother sat with fixed eyes, looking, it seemed to Kathleen, as if she were contemplating *Masau-u,* the god of death, himself.

Such things didn't happen — had they picked up Jim? Kathleen didn't see how he could have escaped. She wished she had sent him right to the hospital. The men in jail — what could they charge them with? Those old men — they couldn't stand that awful place at Keams Canyon. What could she do? Whom could she go to? The white people she knew would surely be horrified that their agents could do such dreadful things. She jumped as a knock came at the door, which opened to admit Dr. Cummings.

"Kathleen! I came as soon as I heard."

XXXVIII

THE JAIL at Keams Canyon was nicely contrived to depress and break the spirit of Hopi prisoners used to the great sweep of open mesa country. The nine prisoners were divided among three cells lined up along one stone wall. Open bars made it possible for them to converse with each other, but only occasional words had been spoken so far, for each was too dejected to feel like saying much.

Jim was still at the dispensary when Lyons' party came down, and he was put under immediate arrest despite his violent protests.

Lololomi was the first to break the oppressive silence.

"We had no cages like this — no jails — until the white man came. It is because of me that this has happened to us. When I gave that bad name to Superintendent Lyons I thought only that it would make him foolish and without power to sway the minds of our people. I did not give thought to the power that would remain to inflict punishment on our bodies. I have been a poor leader among my people."

The old man sat bowed with remorse.

Then Jim spoke, softly, but loud enough so that he could be heard throughout the jail.

"This has all been confused. Let us see who we are here in these cells. I am Jim Talastewa and with me are Lololomi, Allan Lemtewa, and Nemtaka."

Those in the next cell then identified themselves, followed by those in the third cell. It was Nemtaka who voiced the thoughts of them all.

"Who will plant our corn if we are kept here? Who will conduct the ceremonies?"

No one could answer his questions. Then Jim heard a dry and bitter chuckle next to him. It was Lololomi.

"I do not think the Butterflies will dance in Shongopovi tomorrow."

Their despairing thoughts made sleep impossible. Jim had no idea what time it was, or how long he had been there. It might have been only one hour or it might have been five when a light appeared down the hall. The front door of the jail was unlocked and two men entered. One was a Navajo policeman who had participated in the raid. The other was a short, bow-legged Hopi known in the villages as "Christian George." He had been one of Vetch's earliest converts, one of the very few at Walpi. The cloud of displeasure that had enveloped him in his own village had persuaded the superintendent to give him a job as a sort of errand boy and general flunkey around the agency at Keams Canyon. Whenever there was a task no one wanted to do, it fell to the lot of Christian George.

When the prisoners saw who had come in there was a muttered *"Kahopi!"*

The poor drudge winced at the word. No matter how often it was applied to him, it still cut. With lowered eyes he helped the policemen carry slop pails to the cells and serve the bread and stew which they had brought for the prisoners. Before Lololomi, he looked up, and spoke softly.

"This *Kahopi* can still speak Hopi. This policeman cannot speak it. You were once my father. When I was a child my mother brought me to you for a curing. You were kind to me then. I will be kind to you now."

He lowered his eyes again as he handed the food to the others in the cell. Just as he was leaving, he addressed the old man once more.

"I shall return later, my father. Maybe some day you will believe that the *Kahopi* can still be a Hopi."

All who could hear his words wondered at them. Could this poor creature offer them any hope? They laughed at the idea. They had little taste for food. With the closing of the main door, silence settled down over the jail. Jim's thoughts were on Kathleen. What courage she had! If he only knew she was safe. And his mother –! Could she ever be released from the shame she had undergone this day? Every man here must be having thoughts like his.

He dozed and then woke with a start. Someone was opening the front door again, but this time there was no light. The door closed and someone walked softly up to the bars of Lololomi's cell.

"This is the *Kahopi* who has come back to be a Hopi."

Jim pushed the old man closer to the speaker.

"I cannot sleep, remembering that you, my father, are here. The superintendent is so angry with you that you must not remain here. You must return to your village."

The cell door was opened and Christian George signalled for Lololomi to leave, but the old man at first refused to go.

"Let Nemtaka go. He is our village chief. Our people need him much more than they need me."

"No. It is you who are in the greatest danger. It is you who saved me when I was a child. I must not let two go. Even that stupid policeman would notice that, but I think it may be many days before the superintendent would know if only one escaped."

The men urged Lololomi to take his chance and return to their village. Nemtaka was especially insistent. Finally the old man rose.

"My mind is twisted and dark. I do not know if what I do is right, but I shall do as you wish. My prayers and the prayers of our people will be with you all. Maybe because I once healed this man I may have the chance to be of help to all of you — to all our people. This I wish with all my heart and mind."

In a few moments they heard the door close behind him and Christian George.

XXXIX

"FIRST OF ALL, Kathleen, the chap who was shot is O.K. It was a nasty wound, but Martha did a good job. She's been well trained."

"I'm glad of that. And Jim?"

"They arrested him at the dispensary – he's in jail with the others."

"I hoped that he had gotten away. What shall we do? What *can* we do?"

Kathleen's voice broke.

"That's what I've come to talk to you about," said Dr. Cummings quietly. "Could you ask a few of the villagers to come in and discuss it with us – some of the younger ones, as well as the old men?"

Kathleen's mother rose as the doctor spoke and signified her willingness to assemble some of them.

"Thank you, my mother. You will know the ones."

The room was lit by only one candle. Even the window light had been blocked out by blankets which Kathleen had hung there. Security seemed to lie in staying hidden. Kathleen made coffee as they waited for the others to come.

She smiled her gratitude as the doctor used the time to feel Nasayungti's pulse and to rest his hand upon her forehead.

Two old men of the ceremonial societies were the first to arrive. They were soon followed by Martha Honani, Jack Palakvi, Tom Nesviki, and several others.

"If you don't mind, I'll talk first," the doctor began. "I think it is important that we get word of this affair to all the white people who are friends of the Hopi. We have a new president, and there are many new men in Washington. There may soon be a new commissioner of Indian Affairs. Now is a very good time for us to try to get rid of Lyons and get a decent superintendent and a humane deal not only for the Hopi, but for all Indians. Who, of the people you know, do you think might help us?"

Tom was the first to reply.

"I went to school in Santa Fé for two years and I used to work for Mr. Jed Harris who runs a grocery store there. When I delivered groceries I talked to many white people. They were always friendly to me. Some of them have come out here to the Snake Ceremony. I know they would help."

"That's fine, Tom. We'll get you off to Santa Fé in the morning. Martha, you better go to Phoenix. We both know people we can count on there and, Jack, you better get word to Dr. Jacobsen, if he's still at Old Oraibi — he can get some anthropologists interested. I'll talk to Vadas — he'll get us backing from Salt Lake."

"But," Kathleen protested, "where can we get the money for all this? And who will get the planting done if everyone is away?"

"I know the planting is important, but the people here will just have to work that out as best they can. This is our one big chance, and everybody must take on the job."

"I still don't see where we'll get the money, although I have two hundred dollars that —"

"That's fine. And I've got about five hundred. Now I don't know of any better way to spend it."

"Thank you, Don. I won't forget this — none of us will."

Candle after candle burned down. It was dawn before their plans were complete. They would pick up Dr. Cummings and take him into Holbrook where he would telephone to Phoenix to see if his old friend, Hal Talbot, could relieve him for a week or two. This would make it possible for Dr. Cummings to go to Chicago and on to Philadelphia and Washington, cities where his church had many connections which he could use to advantage.

"You're the only one who speaks fluent English who was an eyewitness to this raid." The doctor was speaking to Kathleen. "An old fraternity friend of mine is with the Coconino *Sun* in Flagstaff, Jake Norcross. You must go there right away and tell him the whole story – I'll give you a note to him. He can put the story on the Associated Press wire, and by the next morning it will be in a hundred or more newspapers throughout the country. That ought to get us some action!"

A man of middle age, Tewayestewa, spoke at this point, in a mixture of Hopi and English. He would one day take Lololomi's place as ceremonial leader.

"In Flagstaff Kathleen should see Dr. Donaldson. He is at the College there. He has been out in this country. He studies rocks. He is a good friend."

"That's another good lead. It begins to look as if everybody might be our friends – except Lyons and Vetch!" There was triumph in the doctor's words.

Tewayestewa, encouraged by the success of his first remarks, now stood and addressed them all.

"When I came through the darkness to this house my heart was heavy and without hope. Dr. Cummings has brought hope back to me and strengthened it in my heart. When I see our young men and our young women who have been away come back and be good Hopi and help their people, then I know that our Hopi way will live. We will plant our corn, even though many of our men can not be here. Our boys will become men and our little girls will grind corn meal like women." A faint smile came to his lips. "We will even have our Butterfly Dance when our brothers who are now in darkness at Keams Canyon walk with us again under the warm light of our great sun."

As the group left the house the first rays of the rising

sun flowed over them and through the doorway. The light rested upon the blankets Kathleen had hung over the windows. Slowly she went over and took them down. The warm beams played over the face of Nasayungti, as she sat sleeping on a bench in a corner of the room.

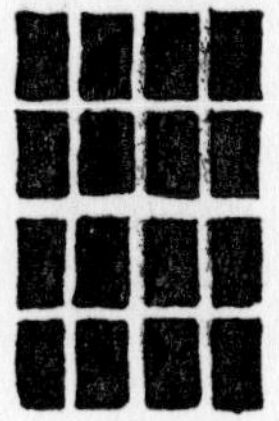

XL

TO KATHLEEN, the next few days were like some fantastic dream. Her natural diffidence made it hard for her to face strangers in a world alien to hers, and Don's friend Norcross greeted her with a cool, appraising stare. His attitude changed to one of interest when he read the doctor's note.

"Look. We can't talk here. Let's go over to the coffee shop at the Weatherford. There's a quiet corner there where you can tell me all about this."

An hour later he laid down his pencil and his pad of paper.

"My God, girl, it's a good thing you brought that note from Don – I'd never believe a word of this otherwise! Let's go see the boss."

Kathleen went with him back to the newspaper office where he introduced her to Austin Gable, publisher of the Coconino *Sun*. He greeted her courteously and listened without comment as Jake Norcross outlined her story.

"There are probably all kinds of political angles on this," the latter said as he finished, "local and state, and maybe even national ones. Some missionaries are like royalty – they can do no wrong. And what that old bird of a superintendent has in the way of connections outside the reservation, the Lord only knows. Our biggest advertisers are good churchmen here in Flagstaff. If the superintendent stands in with the traders association and with some of the bankers around here they can put the squeeze on every advertiser who needs their good will."

"Before we do anything, let's try out some of the big boys," the publisher put in. "If this young lady will stall around town for the next hour we can have lunch with any of them we can reach, and we'll see if we can get a few of them on our side. It'll make it easier."

He turned to Kathleen. "Don't get the wrong idea, youngster. Even if these men won't play along with us we're going to run the story. Be back here about one and you can tell all this to them, firsthand. And, Jake, write it up right now for the AP, then we'll be all set to send it at around two this afternoon. Now that the inauguration news is off the front pages, we ought to get a break in every AP newspaper in the country."

Kathleen had dreaded the luncheon meeting, but, thanks to the tact and skill of Austin Gable, it went off very easily. One of the men who attended was George Livingstone, a grizzled old man in his late seventies. She remembered that Jim had told of meeting his son Ted the day he went into town with Vadas. George Livingstone was the oldest of three brothers, influential businessmen of the state who wielded no little political influence, in northern Arizona. It was he who came to her when the meeting was over and took her arm.

"In my dealings with your people I've found them shrewd bargainers, but men of their word. I'll be glad to do what I can to help. Only last week a Gallup friend of mine told me about this man Lyons – said it was likely only a matter of days until the county attorney would charge him with complicity in an arson case. The end of your troubles may be closer than you think." He started to walk away and then turned back. "Where are you staying in town?"

Kathleen suddenly realized that it was too late for her to drive home that night. Her face showed her confusion. Livingstone took her by the arm.

"My wife will be glad to have a guest – not many young people around our house these days."

Before she knew it she was being driven to a comfortable-looking old house a short distance from town. That night a group of Livingstone's friends came in to hear her story. It was evident that they were men and women of importance in the community, members of clubs with national connections, of civic, church, and cultural organizations. Kathleen went to bed with her mind buzzing with their pledges of support, and their plans for winning national interest in the Hopi.

During the night's discussion at Kathleen's house in the village, Dr. Cummings had suggested that she turn over the dispensary to one of the hospital nurses for a few days and make the hospital her headquarters, a sort of clearing point for all involved. After breakfast the following morning she talked further with the Livingstones and then said she felt she should get to the hospital that day.

"You've been so very kind to me, both of you. I don't know how to thank you."

"Well, don't. It's time we old folks began to do something useful. Good-bye and remember to come again."

She stopped at the office of the Coconino *Sun* to express her thanks to Austin Gable but he was not yet in the office. She was writing him a note when Jake Norcross came in.

"Tell Don he sent the right person when he sent you."

She blushed, somewhat at a loss for words.

"I mean it. You made a great hit with the Livingstones. You're real and all these old guys sensed it. Tell Don I'll be out to see him one of these days. I hope I see you, too!"

His breeziness embarrassed her; she tried to switch the subject to the news story.

"Sure, it went out. We'll be hearing from it soon. It's a little early in the morning for people to be excited yet."

She finished the note and he laid it on the publisher's desk.

"Thank you," she said. "And I know Don would like to see you."

"And wouldn't you?"

He never quite knew whether she heard his question. It seemed but a minute until she was in the car and on her way.

It was late afternoon when the girl in the office at the hospital greeted her.

"It's good to have you here again. Dr. Cummings telegraphed from Chicago — said you should keep an eye on Dr. Talbot."

"Talbot?"

"He's from Phoenix, you know — he's here till Dr. Cummings gets back." Then in a whisper, "Did you hear? Lololomi escaped — he's on his way back to Shongopovi."

"Wonderful! How did he manage it?"

"No one seems to know, except that he's free."

"Well, that's good enough. I'm dusty and tired. I'll get a bath and then I'll feel better. Leave word for me here if any messages come in before you leave."

XLI

THE FOLLOWING DAY was a quiet one. Kathleen found it rather pleasant to be back in the routine of the hospital. There were no serious cases to worry about, the nurses were all capable, and young Dr. Talbot took hold with quiet efficiency.

"Don's done a fine job here," he said. "The place runs itself. Any news of him?"

"No. I imagine he's in Washington by now. Can I do anything to help you while I'm here?"

"Don't know of anything, but I'll certainly call on you if anything comes up."

"Has Superintendent Lyons been in?"

"Not that I know of."

"Good – I hope he's a long way off."

She wished there were some way to get word from Jim. The jail wasn't far away, but she could not risk trouble by going there. Surely someone would know something about them. Maybe Lololomi was at Shongopovi by now. She guessed she'd drive up later and see how things were.

At noon Martha Honani came back from Phoenix.

"Everyone I met was wonderful," she reported. "All the people at the hospital said they'd back up anything we did, and they're going to flood Washington with letters. Have you been up to the dispensary?"

"No, I got back too late yesterday. This morning I felt I better stay here in case there was news."

After lunch the two of them started off together in Kathleen's car.

As Kathleen reached the mesa top she saw a car surrounded by a number of the villagers. I hope this doesn't mean more trouble, she thought. Maybe I better turn back. I've got to stay free until all these people get in touch with me. While she debated this, a familiar voice hailed her and Tom Nesviki came toward her.

"What's the trouble? What's the crowd for? Have you heard anything about Jim? Did you hear that Lololomi got out?"

Kathleen asked the questions all in one breath.

"No, I just got back – I've heard nothing. The crowd?" And he started to laugh.

"That's a lot of people from Santa Fé – funny lot but they want to help us; insisted on coming back with me to see the village and people and find out what it was all about. Probably wanted a trip, but we can use 'em. Come on with me; they'll want to meet you. I've been telling 'em all about you."

Kathleen parked her car and walked over to them with Tom. The villagers made way for her.

"This is the girl I've been telling you about. This is Kathleen."

Tom's introduction was met with a profusion of "Oh's" and then one young white woman came forward with outstretched hand.

"We think you're wonderful. We've read all about you. The story's in all the papers. Don't mind us – we're all a little balmy, but we love this country, and we think the Indians are pretty swell, too. The story got us excited and we made Tom bring us over to see what we can do to help."

Kathleen was surrounded by the visitors, all talking at

once. There were three men in the group and five girls, accompanied by a Navajo man and woman whom they had picked up somewhere along the way. The white girls were dressed like Navajo women in long full skirts of cotton print and velvet blouses, and the clish-clash of their Navajo silver reminded Kathleen of dish-washing time back at boarding school. Two of the girls had tried to dress their hair Navajo style, which caused some merriment to the young Navajo woman. The obvious friendliness of the group as a whole, their generous gifts of candy for the children, their enthusiasm for the really charming aspects of the village, and their constant ejaculations of delight over the magnificent views, won over many of the curious Hopi.

Kathleen found herself rather touched by their sincere interest in her cause. For an hour or so they seemed to flow through the village; then one of them said, "Oh, we want to see the hospital and maybe go over to Oraibi before we start back."

"I'll give you a note to Dr. Talbot," Kathleen said.

"You mean Hal Talbot?" asked one of the youngest of the group. "He's wonderful – I met him in Phoenix."

At this point one of the most attractive girls in the party came to Kathleen.

"Could we talk somewhere by ourselves for a minute before we leave?"

"My house is just there," Kathleen pointed it out. "We'll have it to ourselves."

Quite to ourselves, she thought, and wondered if Jim would ever be back there.

"You must think we're a crazy lot dressed up like this – I feel sort of foolish here, but back in Santa Fé we all do it."

"I guess it's no worse than we Hopi getting all dressed up in your clothes." Kathleen tried to spare her embarrassment.

"You know it is – but you're kind. I'd give anything to manage the dignity you have; you never seem foolish."

Tom looked in and said he thought it was time to be off.

"Just a minute, Tom, and I'll be right there." Then the girl said very seriously, "We do want to help, Kathleen. My father publishes a paper back in Pennsylvania. I send him a column of news and stories from time to time. I could write up all this business and he'd print it right off — it might help."

"Of course it would. There isn't much time to tell you about it, though. I tell you — I've an extra copy of the Coconino *Sun* in my car. I'll get it for you. It has the whole story with all the facts straight."

The two made an interesting picture as they walked together to the car, the tall Hopi girl in her severe nurse's uniform and the tall white girl in her swishy Navajo skirts.

"I'd like to see you again some time, Kathleen," the white girl said almost shyly.

"Jim and I want to come to Ildefonso some day to see some furniture an Indian there makes. Maybe you'd still be in Santa Fé."

"Swell! But who's Jim?"

"My husband — he's one of the men in jail at Keams Canyon."

"Oh, I'm sorry — I hadn't realized —" She halted in embarrassment. "But I must go now, Tom has them all organized. He certainly handles that truck of his well. Good-bye. I do hope everything turns out all right — and that you and Jim will come to Santa Fé."

"Thank you. I hope so, too, — oh, I'm sure so. Good-bye!"

"I'll be glad to get 'em all safely back," Tom whispered. "I hate to think of the joking I'll get when I get back here."

"Don't worry, Tom. They're all right."

There were gay good-byes from the whites, echoed in less boisterous fashion by the Hopi villagers. The remarks of a few of the old Hopi would have brought blushes even to the sophisticated faces of the brashest of the young girls, if they could have understood them. Kathleen watched them down the road. "Indian lovers," — the disparaging phrase came to her mind, but in the next moment she rejected it. We can use a few people who like us, she pondered. I'd rather have them than Vetch or Lyons any day.

•

XLII

LATE THAT SAME AFTERNOON a car drove into Keams Canyon and a worried-looking white man with a newspaper in his hand pushed past the clerks in the outer office of Superintendent Lyons and threw open the door of Lyons' private quarters.

"Have you seen this?" he asked.

Spread across the front page of a leading Los Angeles daily was the story of the raid on Shongopovi. Lyons was suddenly aware of the silence in the outer office; he knew that every clerk was listening. In fury he strode over and slammed the door. His face was pale as he slid down into his chair and his hand shook as he handed the paper back to Bill Reed, the district commissioner of Indian Affairs. The latter looked down at him with utter disgust.

"I must say you've asked for this. I'd have fired you a year ago — that time I warned you — if the Indian commissioner had not been your friend. But he's on his way out and then you'll no longer have a backer in Washington."

The stammering Lyons could not get in a word.

"And I've got other news for you, too, Lyons. They

signed a complaint against you in Gallup this morning — you'll have to explain that Shongopovi deal as well as some of these other things."

The superintendent got shakily to his feet.

"You son-of-a-bitch! What about the things I know about you! That timber deal you put over in the Zuñi forest, for instance!

Reed was prepared for this.

"With all that's against you, who's going to believe anything you say! I've been in some raw deals but I don't go around beating Indian women and throwing people into jail without reason."

"Suddenly turned noble, haven't you?" Lyons spoke contemptuously. "Los Angeles is miles away — what harm can that story do?"

"Harm!" Reed banged the crumpled paper on the desk. "The guy who owns that paper hates the Indian Bureau. This story will give him his chance to crusade. We'll have all kinds of investigations going on. Besides, it's in every Associated Press paper in the country. What's more, I hear that Doc Cummings is already in Washington working to get you kicked out. This morning I passed a truck load of those Santa Fé Indian lovers that Tom Nesviki was bringing over — they'll probably raise a stink when they get back. And they've got a lot of pull."

"Well, as long as I've got my job . . ."

"Well, you don't have it. You're fired right now. Do you hear me? Fired! You're on your way out, and I'm not afraid that you'll take me with you."

Reed threw the paper in Lyons' face as he stalked out of the room, slamming the door behind him. The clerks looked up rather sheepishly as he addressed them.

"I'm the district commissioner and I've just fired that old bastard in there. Where's this jail of yours?"

At that moment John Vadas entered the office.

"What's going on here?"

The district commissioner looked him over.

"And who are you?"

"I'm John Vadas from the Bureau of Agriculture."

"Well, I'm Bill Reed, district commissioner of Indian Affairs. I've just fired that old fool Lyons. I don't know where you stand in all this, but take me to the jail if you know where it is. Why didn't you report this situation to me, Vadas?"

"You know why," replied Vadas. "I send my reports directly to my superior in Washington. I have nothing to do with the administration of the reservation — thank God!"

"You, at least, have some guts — we'll need some to get us out of this mess. Did you read the AP story?"

"No, but I heard about it. It's rotten business. I know those Shongopovi people. They're mighty good Indians."

"The first thing is to get these men out of jail. I can't stand this sort of thing."

They had come to the jail door. Nobody was in sight.

"Hey, George!" called Vadas, and in a few minutes Christian George came around a corner of the building.

"Open up here," commanded Reed.

With a grin of delight George unlocked the front door and led them within.

"Lololomi not here," he said. "Lyons, he just found out. He come this morning very angry."

"You needn't worry about Lyons. Where are the men?" asked Reed.

The cell doors were opened in a matter of minutes.

"Come out, you fellows. It's all right," Vadas voice reassured them, and, as he noted Jim, "I didn't know you were here. Why didn't you get word to me?"

Somehow Jim found himself unable to look at any white man, even John Vadas. With eyes averted, he followed the others into the sunlight. The men stood blinking, dazzled by the bright rays, as Reed spoke.

"I'm Reed, the district commissioner. I just heard of your arrest, and I came over right away. I've fired Lyons and you're free; you can go home at once. Our government does not condone arresting men without due process of law."

He finished pompously and rather gruffly.

"Jim!" It was Kathleen. "I just heard!"

She was in his arms, and over her head Jim looked

directly at John Vadas. The latter came to him and extended his hand.

"I think I know how you feel, Jim. I've an idea things are going to be better."

Kathleen turned her tear-stained face toward him and smiled as she said simply, "I think so, too."

"Reed, these are friends of mine, Jim and Kathleen Talastewa."

The introductions were interrupted by the noise of a car swerving down the road with the motor wide open. It took the curve by the jail with a screech of rubber and in a cloud of dust.

"Who in hell is that?"

John Vadas smiled.

"Our late superintendent seems to be in something of a hurry!" he said.

XLIII

DOWN THROUGH the pale white trunks of the Aspen forests high on the shoulders of Mount San Mateo, in western New Mexico, a solitary old Indian walked as if guided by some deep animal sense of direction. His square-cut bobbed hair with its bright *banda,* his short squat frame and his worn rust-colored moccasins proclaimed him a Hopi, but a Hopi nearly two hundred miles by trail from the nearest village of his people.

On that dark night when Christian George had opened his cell door, Lololomi had first set his feet in the direction of Shongopovi, but prompted by some inner compulsion he had turned south instead. He reached the top of Awatobi mesa in time to contemplate the dawn. But the rising sun brought him no comfort; its warmth did not penetrate. A sense of guilt oppressed him. It was his ridicule of Superintendent Lyons that had set in motion the chain of circumstances that culminated in the cruel raid upon his village. He could not return there without some word, some message for his people that would reassure them in this time of crisis.

At his feet lay the ruins of what had once been one of the greatest of Hopi villages. A wall with cracked and pealing blotches of plaster right where he was standing attested that this had been the site of an old *kiva.* Some power had directed him to this spot, of that he was sure. Here a people had gone back upon their pledge, and welcomed back the Spanish missionaries after the great rebellion that swept the Spaniards and their priests from the entire Indian Southwest. Here that same people had paid the penalty for their transgressions when the Hopi of Oraibi and Shongopovi descended upon Awatobi and destroyed it. Lololomi knew every detail of that historic event. Nearly every man and woman had been killed, and the young children were later adopted by the avenging villages. The village had been levelled within a few hours and left in ruins – an everlasting reminder that the Hopi expect their people to keep their word.

Surely this page of Hopi history had some meaning for him, else why had he been led here? The old man sat down upon a rock facing the east and, without seeing it, watched the sun mount into the sky. His mind searched for a way to help his people – he must find a way. Then he rose and spent the morning wandering through the ruins, convinced that here he would find the answer he sought, the sign that would direct him. By noon hunger and thirst were making their demands, and still there had come to him no hint of what he could say to his people to make amends for the great disservice he had done them.

He remembered that once many years ago he had come to this place with his ceremonial father and they had drunk at a spring on this side of the mesa. It was good to find the spring still flowing, and he breathed a prayer of gratitude as he drank. Near the spring lay a stick; it proved easy to kill one of the rabbits that scurried now and then across his path, and he found some shade to shelter him as he skinned and cooked it. From a small leather billfold, which some tourist had traded him for a *kachina doll* years before, he took a pocket knife and matches. With them were a few downy eagle feathers and some string. He had put them there, he recalled, when he was making a prayer plume for Kathleen's house.

As he cooked the rabbit, he noticed a great mass of clouds piling up far off to the southeast. Over Mount San Mateo near Acoma? No, no, San Mateo was too far away – the clouds must be over the red mesas near Gallup. The rabbit was ready now and he ate it with satisfaction. As he was finishing, he noticed that one of the fluffs of eagle down had fallen on the ground. A breath of wind caused it to circle his feet and then, slowly, it was carried away from him in the direction of the clouds piling up in the southeastern sky.

Was this the sign he had been waiting for? From time immemorial in periods of drought or of other distress the Hopi had made pilgrimages to distant high mountains in the four directions to plant prayer sticks in shrines on their summits. For centuries Hopi ceremonial leaders, accompanied by their neophytes, had journeyed over mesas and washes and lava flows and desert stretches to place their prayer plumes, made with many prayers and decorated with care, in hidden sanctuaries upon the topmost heights of Navajo Mountain, of the San Francisco Peaks, of Mount San Mateo, and even of the White Mountains which loomed up in the land of the enemy, the Apache. There was now not a vestige of doubt in the mind of Lololomi – he had cotton twine and eagle feathers for making prayer sticks and, more than to any other summit, the cloud masses had carried his thought at once to Mount San Mateo, the mountain where the leaders of Awatobi and of his own Shongopovi had journeyed for guidance and help in the days gone by.

He set forth at once. He would go by way of Zuñi and there, from an old and steadfast friend, he would secure food, a water jug, and an extra pair of moccasins. The prospect cheered him and for the first time in many days he felt a song in his heart and he gave voice to it as he trotted along the trail.

He scarcely noted the passing of the hours or of the days. As if in a trance he sought out his Zuñi friend, made known his simple needs, offered his thanks, and continued on his way, his face ever toward the peak of San Mateo. Up its rugged trails he climbed with unerring feet. He reached the top one afternoon when the sun was low on the western horizon.

The summit was heavy with snow, but on the western face the sun had bared the rocks, and here he sought the ancient shrine. An hour of search disclosed a pocket in the rock, and in a deep, protected recess of it he scraped out the disintegrating fragments of some old prayer sticks. The string and the feathers were gone, but the crumbling bits of wood attested to their having been there. Thoughtfully, prayerfully, he brought from his pocket the cotton twine and the eagle down and, with wood picked up along the trail, he fashioned his own prayer sticks, and with fitting prayers placed them in the secret niche. Then, slipping and sliding on the hard-packed snow, he started the long trail homeward.

The sun, now nearly out of sight, the beautiful trunks of the aspen, the invigorating air of the high forest, all challenged his imagination. No vision had come to him, no sign had been given him on the peak, but here there was peace and, as the sense of it flooded over him, he felt a great upsurge of faith, of confidence that he had done what was expected of him. Now he could return to his people.

It had grown dark and the night's chill was stealing into his bones. He stopped and sought a sheltered spot in which to spend the night. When he found it he lit a fire and made a frugal supper of meal from roasted corn mixed with water and Zuñi bread. Then he lay down by the warmth and dozed fitfully through the night.

He was awake long before dawn and stirred the nearly dead embers of the fire as he waited for the light. He would get well started on his homeward journey today. He had little food left, but there were Indians everywhere who would respect his mission and his need. He would not starve, he knew that. With dawn he could see smoke rising from the New Mexican village of San Ventana. There was little love lost between the Hopi and the New Mexicans, but these

Penitentes were people of the mountains and that set them somewhat apart. He would pass through their village. There he would not ask for food, but he would not refuse it should it be offered to him.

The barking dogs of San Ventana proclaimed his coming. The little village had but six huts and a small *Morada.* On a high lava outcropping back of the village three tall, heavy crosses angled against the horizon. The simple, isolated people greeted him with friendly curiosity and they set before him such food as they themselves were eating. One old New Mexican noted that his moccasins were frayed and worn. He signaled for Lololomi to take them off, and with a cobbler's skill he fixed to them heavy rawhide soles. These kindnesses gave to the old Hopi added assurance that all was well and that he was following a trail set for him by the gods.

By nightfall he was high on the western side of the Continental Divide. From there the trail led down through a wide valley almost filled with a rough broken lava flow. The Navajo with their heavy wagons had followed the ancient foot-trail as it serpentined to avoid the higher, rougher masses of lava. At one place a pair of ruts joined the trail from the south, and on them Lololomi was surprised to note the fresh marks of automobile tires. Surely not even a Navajo would bring a car in here. The trail in many places had been almost impassable, even for wagons, and the sharp lava would tear tires to shreds. The road ahead was no doubt little better, and it would probably divide and re-divide as wagons turned off to the various hogans of their owners. He examined the tire marks carefully and felt sure they had been made within the past few hours.

But he must find a spot for another night's camp. The good rabbit stick, carved a few days before, had again provided him with a rabbit, and from the Penitentes he had gotten matches to replenish his scant supply. Looking about for a site for his fire, he turned off the trail. He climbed a few feet up a small, cinder-floored arroyo and found a place where the lava flow overhung the dry stream bed. A quantity of pine wood lying about afforded ample fuel for the night.

He built a fire and propped his rabbit before it on a green stick. Then he lay back, at ease, content, even happy, and waited, occasionally reaching forward to turn his improvised spit.

Suddenly there flowed over him an awareness of Vance Vetch. He felt no fear of the missionary, just an overwhelming sense that he was near. Those tire tracks – he was somehow glad that he was not camped near where he had seen them. As he squatted in front of the fire he knew that this consciousness of Vetch was tied in with his own presence here and with his pilgrimage – that it was part of the whole maze through which he had been guided by the same powers that had guided him ever since he walked out of the jail at Keams.

He was in no hurry to eat – he was in no hurry for anything. Whatever was going to happen would happen in spite of anything he might do. He was not eager, not curious to know the future – he was simply resigned and content to let the powers direct him as they would. He ate in leisurely fashion and then composed himself by the fire for such sleep as might come to him during the night.

•

XLIV

NEWS THAT THE KEAMS CANYON prisoners were free spread quickly to Shongopovi, and the returning men were given a jubilant reception at the mesa-top. Foremost in the happy throng was Mary Lemtewa, who threw herself upon Allan with a little cry of joy.

"I guess we better see to that Hopi wedding soon," said Jim, to break the tension.

Mary looked at him over Allan's shoulder and giggled.

Allan was interrupted by the arrival of clan members of Lololomi's family and leaders of the ceremonial society of which he was chief.

Where was he? Why had he not returned to Shongopovi? What had happened? Had he been caught and again imprisoned? The questions were many and insistent. Finally Nemtaka stilled them. He sounded old and tired.

"Lololomi has not been with us since our first night in jail. We hoped he had come back to the village. We know only that he has gone. But he is not dead, I feel sure of that—he is not dead."

The sobbing of Lololomi's wife halted him, and he turned to her gently.

"He is working out some plan for the good of us all. Hold him in your thoughts and in your prayers. He will come back. And, now, the planting — there is much to be done."

For fully an hour they stood and talked of when they would plant and of how the work should be divided. The question of the Butterfly Dance came up and all agreed that it must be held soon. They could not quite believe that Lyons was gone, and they wondered aloud what Vetch's long silence might mean. Night had fallen by the time they returned to their houses.

"It is good to be home again," said Jim simply as he and Kathleen entered their house.

They clung to each other wordlessly for a few tense minutes.

For an interval Jim's thoughts seemed elsewhere, then he sat down with a great sigh and buried his face in his hands. Kathleen waited, then, quietly, she began to tell him of all that had happened — of her days in Flagstaff — of Dr. Cummings in Washington — of the Dr. Talbot who was taking his place — of Martha's luck in Phoenix — of Tom and his funny crowd from Santa Fé — and particularly of the great kindness of the Livingstones.

"Livingstone?" Jim looked up for the first time.

"Livingstone — I must get my cattle soon. My sheep — I wonder how they are."

"Sequa-Honau says they are fine. I saw him this afternoon just before I went back to the hospital, just before I heard they were letting you out."

Gradually the sense that he was really at home came back to him.

"Don't I get anything to eat after all this time?" he laughed.

Kathleen thrilled to the change in his voice.

"I'm not so sure — I've gotten out of the habit of cooking."

But she busied herself at storage shelves and stove, and

soon the smell of coffee permeated the room.

"I bought bacon and eggs this morning. I don't quite know why — I thought you might like a Navy breakfast when you got back."

"Breakfast! Let's have it right now. I'm beginning to feel hungry enough to eat everything in sight."

Later they turned serious again.

"You were telling me about all you have been doing. I hate to think I was of no use when you most needed me."

"Don't say that. You were having a much harder time."

The thought of those dark days overcame her for just a moment, and then she went on brightly.

"I didn't tell you that late today there was a letter from Don. He'd sent some directions to Dr. Talbot and then added a postscript for us. I cut it off; I'll read it to you.

" 'Tell Kathleen I'll soon be on my way back and to take heart. Everybody is talking about her story to the Coconino *Sun*. The president is to appoint a new commissioner of Indian Affairs soon, a man I know. There's a better day coming! — Don.' "

"I hope he's right. I'd feel better if I knew about Lololomi."

"Where can he be? Nemtaka seems to feel sure that he will come back. Do you, Jim?"

"Yes — yes, I think I do. Nemtaka's a wise old man. I've come to know him better these days."

"You know, Jim, when I first came back after working in the hospital at Phoenix I found it hard to look upon these old chiefs of ours as men of intelligence and wisdom. They'd come in from the fields reeking with sweat and dirt. They'd walk about the dirty streets with dirty children tagging at their heels. I often thought I could not endure it. As a nurse I often had to talk with them, and I came to realize that they knew and felt more than I ever gave them credit for. I suppose that because for generations — for centuries, really — they have been adapting themselves to this land, they feel more in harmony with it than people in towns and cities feel with their environment. Well, that's quite a speech. You're probably not even listening."

"Yes, I'm listening," but again his thought seemed far away. "I think I am becoming a real Hopi at last. I can't help feeling that something final will have to be worked out about both Lyons and Vetch before . . ."

"Before what, Jim?"

"I don't know exactly – before this whole situation ends. There are some things we can't do ourselves – some power beyond us will have to take over. Nemtaka knows that, Lololomi knows it; and now I think I know it, too."

Kathleen got up and started to clear away the dishes. Jim sat there motionless for a moment or two, then he pulled out a package of cigarettes and lighted one. As Kathleen looked over at him from the stove she saw him blow little puffs of smoke in the six world directions.

XLV

FOUR DAYS passed with no word of Lololomi. He was not mentioned in the village, but his name was in all their hearts. The nightly gatherings in the *kivas* with their silent prayers were witness to that. Nemtaka, worn out by the strain of his imprisonment, stayed in his house, and left to Tewayestewa the affairs of the people. The men went to the fields daily, and the planting was well started. On the surface life was tranquil.

Jim planted his mother's fields, and one she allowed him for his use. His energy was beginning to return. He went with Tom to the range and was happy over the condition of his flock — and by the pleasure Sequa-Honau showed at his return. It was the middle of the afternoon, the fourth since his return, and he stood idly in his doorway breathing in the warm spring air.

A thought struck him; it was too good a day to be in-doors; he'd bring out a table and work on silver for a while. He was glad he had chosen this work for his more leisurely hours; he must finish up that necklace and pendant. If Lanta thought it might earn a prize — well, it really *might*

— and he and Kathleen could use a little prize money. How soon would she be home from the hospital? It was early yet — Dr. Cummings ought to be back soon. Then she'd be back at the dispensary every day — not so far away.

He carried out the table, and for some time worked steadily on the silver for the Flagstaff exhibit.

"May you walk in beauty, my friend."

Jim looked up into the face of a Navajo who was observing his work with interest from the saddle of his horse.

"You are a good craftsman — for a Hopi," the stranger continued, as he slid from his bony steed.

Jim thought he had never seen such a dirty human being. The man's face and hands seemed to be complete strangers to water. His battered trousers and faded shirt gave no hint of what color they had been. He wore the usual tall-crowned, broad-brimmed hat of the Navajo, but it was so caked with dust that its original black was quite unrecognizable.

He grinned and repeated his greeting, "May you walk in beauty."

The poetic words seemed out of place coming from such an unromantic-looking Indian. The Navajo squatted by the table, his horse standing quietly a short distance away. Jim went on with his work and the Navajo continued to observe him. Then a movement from the horse caused Jim to look toward it, and his eyes caught sight of the most beautiful saddle he had ever seen. It was liberally encrusted with silverwork of exceptional craftsmanship, made by an artist, Jim knew, of high caliber. Instantly he decided he wanted that saddle.

Jim was aware that the eyes of the Navajo were constantly returning to Jim's left wrist on which he wore a watch that he had bought during his Navy days. He wouldn't buy such an expensive one now, but he was in the money then. I wonder if this Navajo would trade it for that saddle? he thought. What was it John Vadas had said one time? — something about the Hopi being the shrewdest bargainers on the desert. Well, he'd see how good a Hopi he was!

Jim stopped work and looked at his watch with great

care, then wound it very slowly. Next he took out his handkerchief and, after breathing on the crystal, he polished it with painstaking deliberation. The watching Navajo fairly drooled. Jim turned back to his silver work just as Tom came by and paused for a bit of gossip. As the three of them smoked, Jim spoke to Tom in Hopi to see if the Navajo understood. The puzzled expression on his countenance showed clearly that he did not, so in the same tongue Jim explained to Tom what was happening.

"How much do you think our friend's saddle is worth?"

Tom looked at it for the first time and his eyes lighted up.

"At least a hundred dollars – the silver work is well done."

"He likes this wrist watch of mine. I think we will make a trade."

Tom laughed, "I think you said you paid twenty dollars for that watch. Is it right for a Hopi to give such an expensive watch to a Navajo for a saddle worth only a hundred dollars?"

It was Jim's turn to laugh as he replied, "You think I should get the horse, too?"

Tom got slowly up from his haunches.

"It's not much of a horse. Don't cheat yourself!"

Tom walked away, but before he was out of sight he called back, in English this time, "I bet you two bucks you don't get both of them."

"It's a bet!"

A few minutes later Jim nodded to the Navajo, lifted the bench into the house and closed the door. The Navajo's face fell as he turned to lead his horse across the street where he squatted in the lee of a house from which he could watch Jim's door. There Kathleen passed him as she came home from the dispensary.

"Who's the stranger?" she asked as she entered the house.

"The Navajo? I've got a wrist watch he'd like to have – and I wouldn't mind owning that saddle."

Kathleen took a quick look at it through the window.

"It is a beauty. How much does he want for it?"

"I told you – my wrist watch."

"Oh, Jim!"

He could not quite tell what her tone meant, and she had disappeared into the storeroom before he could say anything further. He could see that the Navajo was still there, his eyes fastened upon the house. He waited a few more minutes and then walked to the doorway where once again he looked at his watch intently. The Navajo half rose, but Jim gave no hint that he knew he was there. He started to close he door when the Navajo called to him.

An hour later Jim had the saddle, the horse, the saddle blanket, and a rather good bridle with silver conchos. The Navajo had the wrist watch. By this time all of Shongopovi knew what was in progress and from every corner and window they watched with curiosity. When the trade was completed they praised the wrist watch, some of them with a few words of Navajo, and caused the stranger's face to beam. Jim then graciously threw in a lesson on how to wind it. The Navajo went through the same motions, then held it to his ear and turned to Jim in consternation, for there was no sound from his newly acquired instrument; he had wound it too tight. Jim's knowledge of mechanics stood him in good stead and in a short time the watch was again ticking away the minutes.

Kathleen turned when Jim came in.

"Jim, not all that!"

"I just couldn't resist it – it was so easy."

"But – it isn't right."

"I know it isn't. I'll figure a way to really pay him before he gets off. I am a Hopi, I guess – that trading was more fun than anything I've done in a long time."

A knock at the door startled them both, and the Navajo timidly poked in his head. In broken English he explained that it was time to go to his hogan and he had no horse and he could not walk.

"Why not?" asked Jim.

The Navajo shrugged his shoulders and simply explained that Navajo always ride. He was hungry, he said, and it was late, and he had no horse.

"Come, Jim, that's enough," said Kathleen, although laughter welled up within her as she looked at the man's mournful face. "We have plenty of food. Tell him he can have supper here."

The Navajo needed no second invitation and he squatted in a corner of the room as Kathleen busied herself at the stove. The simple meal was soon ready, and the stranger ate with gusto all that was set before him.

"Your hogan is a long way, you say? How can I help you?"

Jim's questions elicited no reply from the Navajo, who sat back contentedly and smoked the cigarette Jim had offered.

"I'll be a friend to you," Jim went on. "I'll return your horse to you and give you one of my saddles so you can get home without walking."

The simple-minded Navajo beamed and rose to go. He turned the full force of his smile upon Kathleen and gave her a ring from his little finger. She smiled and bowed her thanks as Jim led the way out.

"Come for our Butterfly Dance," invited Jim as he helped the Navajo saddle his horse.

Again the latter beamed.

"You are good Hopi," he said. "I bring you wood when I come."

A crowd of children had gathered to see him off, and to all of them he called as he started down the trail, "May you walk in beauty always, my friends."

Jim shooed the laughing children away and turned into the house.

"I'm not sure I like strange men giving my wife rings!"

"One Navajo – one ring. I'm not sure but I like it better than the one a certain Hopi made!"

She gave him a quick kiss and went on with the work of putting the room in order as he put away the afternoon's booty.

"I left the hospital at noon and spent the rest of the day at the dispensary. That's why I was home fairly early."

"Is everything going all right there?"

"I think so—not many have been in lately—too much upset, I guess. We'll get back on schedule soon, I hope."

"When's Dr. Cummings getting back?"

"I didn't have a chance to tell you—he *is* back." She opened the door to the cool evening air as she spoke, and then came back to where Jim was sitting. "Martha was at the hospital this afternoon and he came in just before she left; he said he had a great surprise for us but he'd come and tell us about it himself."

"That's exactly what I said." They looked up to see Dr. Cummings and John Vadas looming in the doorway. They jumped to their feet.

"We weren't too sure you'd want to see any white people for a while." John spoke in his usual hearty fashion.

"Well, this is one white man you'll want to see, I know."

The doctor spoke somewhat mysteriously and hesitantly. Then he turned to the two young people.

"Kathleen—Jim—shake hands with your new superintendent, John Vadas!"

They almost shouted their incredulous delight, each seizing a hand, but Vadas had grown grave.

"I'm as surprised as you—and I'm not even sure I want the job. But I'll certainly do a damn sight better than Virgil Lyons did—I guess I can promise you that!"

XLVI

"THERE'S ONLY three dollars and forty-two cents —" The woman's voice trailed off as she slid the small pile of coins into a dirty white cotton bank sack and looked over at her husband. Vance Vetch sat in a broken arm chair, his head bowed almost to his knees.

A week before they had begun a series of revival meeting in Holbrook which they felt certain would pay for themselves and also bring in money enough to rebuild the church at Oraibi — enough, too, they hoped, for the new one at Shongopovi. They could not fail, Vetch maintained, for they were on the side of God. His wife had made no comment.

The meetings had begun auspiciously enough. The tent was crowded the first night, and there was more than fifty dollars in the collection plates, but thereafter the crowds had dwindled — every night there were fewer and fewer people in the congregation and less and less money in the collection. Tonight the tent had been almost empty, and those who had come were the curious, for the most part, rather than the devout. Although neither had said it as yet, they both knew it was hopeless to continue.

The woman handed Vetch the small sack of change and he put it into his pocket without looking up. She stood behind him quietly, her hand on his shoulder. There was no need for her to say anything — everything had been discussed in the days since they left Oraibi. The lightning flash that had destroyed their church and broken the faith of so many of their hard-won converts had also destroyed something in her husband. Some power had gone out of him. No longer could he play upon the emotions of people who came to hear him preach; the words were hollow and brought no response even from those who sought the refuge of religious belief.

Her mind went over their years together — not so many years, at that; they were not yet middle-aged, but the years had been long and hard — meetings in cold, windy tents and in hot, bare makeshift churches. Two months here, a month there — home, children, security, happiness; they had had none of these — until New Oraibi. She had come to love her little house there, the gentle people, the few plants that flourished in her window boxes, her half dozen chickens, the first pets she'd known. Now that was all gone — and gone for good, she felt sure, and they'd be on the move once more. Suddenly she felt very old and terribly alone.

His wife's hand upon his shoulder brought no answering gesture from Vetch. Over and over he reviewed the week's failures. Just that day on the main street in Winslow a Hopi had laughed at him and another had called out to him — right in front of the post office — "Is Jesus still coming?" The laughter of the people standing about still made him flinch. Then a corrosive doubt began to work into his mind. Never since his ordination had he for one minute doubted his mission — until now. Now he looked back over the years, and especially over the recent months, and found himself re-examining with misgiving action after action that had seemed entirely justified at the time. He tried to pray, but the well-remembered words had no meaning for him — they no longer brought him that moment of ecstasy in which he felt in true harmony with God. In his heart he realized that this was gone — and gone forever.

The tent had grown cold. Mrs. Vetch began to pick up the things that were theirs as her husband got slowly to his feet. She slipped her arm through his and guided him out to their nearby car.

The improvised beds in the back of the car afforded them no sleep that night. They talked intermittently, of what, they scarcely knew. At dawn they rose and washed at a nearby gas station, unaware of the sleepy attendant's curious glances. Over a cheap breakfast they tried to plan their day. A couple of Mexicans would help them take down the tent and they could return it to the company. Vetch knew a place on the highway, a second-hand place, where they'd take the lumber in the benches – he guessed he could knock them down. Breakfast was about over before he mentioned anything of the future, and then the words tumbled out.

Over at Fort Defiance his church conducted a mission to the Navajo. It was in charge of young Grant Graham, whose father had been president of the seminary where Vetch had been ordained. Old Dr. Graham had been his youthful inspiration – to him more than to anyone else he owed the deep religious conviction that had been the foundation of his faith. He'd heard the old man was still alive – perhaps even at Fort Defiance. If he could only see him and talk with him maybe he could get back his self-assurance, his hope, his inspiration, his faith.

His shaking voice and trembling hands told his wife how great was the conflict within him. They must be on their way – people were coming in – they would wonder at his flushed face. And his voice had risen with his passionate intensity. Pity for him lent decision to her movements. Fortunately, she had the right change for the check, so it was but a matter of minutes until she had him safely outside. He had grown quiet once more and as they walked toward the car he told her to go on and he'd be back in a few minutes with the Mexicans. With doubt in her mind she watched him go, yet he was as good as his word, and somehow the day saw his plans carried out. By mid-afternoon they were on their way to Fort Defiance.

"Yes, Dad's here with me, he'll be glad to see you."

Young Grant Graham was friendly in his greeting. "Come in. I'll call him."

They waited in a pleasant little living room until old Dr. Graham shuffled in, his eyes unseeing, his hand unsteady. His face lighted up when he heard Vetch's voice.

"Of course, I remember you. Vance Vetch! What have you done all these years? You gave great promise — great promise."

Vetch launched into an account of how badly the years had dealt with him, of how hard he had worked, and of how few the rewards had been. His wife noticed that old Dr. Graham was not listening — she wished her husband would say no more. Within a very few minutes the son returned and took his father by the arm.

"I think you will find that my father tires easily. If you will wait here just a moment I will take him to his room."

At the door the old man hesitated and said, "I'm glad that you have been so successful, Vance."

Vetch was about to protest, but his wife put her finger on her lips.

The younger man returned shortly.

"You can see how it is with my father — you realize how it is at his age. He can remember little and his mind wanders. Perhaps you will stay here tonight. The mission has a small guest cabin, and we shall be glad to have you."

They murmured their thanks and said they would be glad to go to it at once, if they might, and refresh themselves.

"Good! We have dinner at seven — we shall expect you. Jeff!" — this last to an Indian lad — "please show these people to the guest cabin and at seven bring them to the dining room."

The unexpected kindness on the part of the young minister touched Mrs. Vetch deeply, but her husband was disheartened at finding that old Dr. Graham had failed to understand his problem and had given no word of spiritual reassurance.

"But, you can see that he is very old," she said. "I think it remarkable that he should have remembered you at all. And we are lucky to be invited to stay here. If we can rest for just a few days, maybe –"

"Maybe what?"

"Oh, nothing. Hush – there's the boy to take us to dinner."

Dinner was given over to another monologue by Vetch which obviously interested young Dr. Graham very little. He was a busy, modern young preacher who seemed much more interested in his social welfare work among the Navajo than in listening to Vetch's endless stories of Hopi ingratitude. Occasionally he tried to tell of his own interests and to suggest a different approach to the Hopi, but Vetch ignored him and continued his harangue. Mrs. Vetch was glad when dinner was over.

"You are probably tired and want to go to your cabin early," the young man suggested. "My own family are away for a few days, so I shall have to leave you pretty much to yourselves. You are welcome if you wish to stay for a day or two before going on."

On where? Graham wondered. They're a pathetic pair. I must keep Dad out of this fellow's clutches – how could he ever convert anyone, this worn-out fanatic? They really are not so old – but God pity the Indians he tries to convert! A bell rang and he bade them good night.

After breakfast the following morning they walked about the mission grounds. Most of the day they spent in their room, pretending to sleep and rest, but both with minds too restless to find any peace. Somehow the hours passed and at seven the young Navajo boy came to announce dinner. Once more only young Dr. Graham awaited them. Tonight he managed to dominate the conversation, starting in at once to recount some interesting experiences of recent weeks.

His church had asked him to explore the possibilities for a mission among the Penitentes in the mountains of northern New Mexico. The childlike simplicity and religious fervor of the people around Cubero and Marquez had especially interested him. He spoke with enthusiasm of a little settlement beyond Satan Pass. He became eloquent as he described the ecstatic preoccupation with death and everything pertaining to it that pervaded this region, symbolized at every turn by the cart of death with its skeleton rider, the *carreta de la muerte,* as he said they called it.

These stories stirred anew the fanatical mind of Vetch. These people had faith, perverted, it was true, but faith such as he thought he could understand. Here were people he might work with. By morning he had convinced himself this was a real call. If he could only talk it over with old Dr. Graham.

At breakfast he brought up the subject with the son.

"No," said the latter with the gentle tone he used in talking of his father, "no, that would do no good — you saw that."

This last was said to Mrs. Vetch, who had sat silently, torn between doubt and loyalty to her husband. She knew there was no deterring him, once he had made up his mind.

"It is isolated country," continued the young minister. "How much one could accomplish there, I really don't know."

To himself he thought: this man would be the wrong one for the job. And he's in no state now to attempt it. But to say no would only make him more determined. The wife's against it, one can see that — sometimes, though, a fanatic like this can do more than some of the rest of us. We need a mission there — oh, I don't know —

Aloud, he said, "Why don't you drive over through there and get some idea of the place, and then come back and we'll talk it over?"

"How long will it take us?" Mrs. Vetch asked.

"I wish to go alone," Vetch said firmly, "and at once."

"But, Vance — " Mrs. Vetch began.

Sorry for her, young Graham interposed, "You can stay here until he comes back, Mrs. Vetch."

"Thank you," she faltered.

Then she looked at her husband, but he gave her no answering glance.

XLVII

TWO DAYS LATER Vetch drove into the Penitente hamlet of Sebyoteta. Only that morning there had come to him the realization that this was Holy Week and the day Good Friday. Worn by the long, rough journey from Fort Defiance, he felt that he could go no farther, that somewhere in this region he must find the people among whom he would continue the work of his Lord. This rather stark landscape appealed to his soul. These "Brothers of Light" needed guidance toward the true faith, and that must be his burden. The sun was high in the sky as he parked his car and joined a small group of New Mexicans, intently watching what seemed to be a sort of parade.

Twelve men were marching up a rocky hill toward a graveyard. They were naked to their waists and over their faces were black hoods. They moved forward with a slow, rhythmic pace, in time to a chant. Each man swung a whip of yucca fibers and with it at every sixth step he lashed his own back. As the procession passed Vetch, who was observing it with fascinated intensity, he felt something wet splash against his hand. He looked down to find a drop of blood.

Instead of being horrified, he found himself strangely stirred.

The people about him were moving up the hill, and he was carried along with them. As they neared the graveyard he could see, set up in the center of it, a tall crude cross. Before it *Los Hermanos Penitentes* prostrated themselves and automatically Vetch followed suit. He understood no word of the brief Spanish prayer that followed, but he felt uplifted by it. Now the flagellant marching was resumed and the little group of villagers and Vetch followed. This time they proceeded to a small building on the top of a low hill, a *Morada,* he thought young Graham had called it.

The bloody marchers and some of the people entered, but Vetch was barred. They were polite, but firm, in their refusal to let him enter. There were curious glances at him, but no unfriendliness. To their Spanish he could reply only in English, but gestures clarified both their meanings.

The people outside the *Morada* waited patiently while some sort of ceremony was conducted within. Vetch waited quietly, too, accepting it all without question. A half hour must have passed before the door was opened, and again the flagellants and the villagers moved on, this time to a higher hill back of the *Morada.* And now at the head of the chanting procession Vetch could see a man led by rawhide ropes in the hands of four men, being jerked this way and that and at times jerked off his feet and dragged over the sharp rocks. Back of these walked a man with bare and bloody back and behind him two men who flogged themselves without mercy at every sixth step up the steep trail. Midway in the procession was a young man with hands bound to a long heavy pole which he carried over his back. He was followed by two man bearing crude crosses, which were tied to their backs.

"Christ and the thieves," Vetch was murmuring to himself the identifying phrase when he looked up directly into the face of the young man. He felt suddenly transported by the expression of ineffable ecstasy on the sorrowing features, and he completed the torturous climb with no hint of weariness.

Dominating the summit of the hill, stood a gigantic cross

swathed in sheets. The Penitente men knelt before it and behind them a group of women prostrated themselves, their great black shawls almost concealing them. At this moment a tall New Mexican robed in black, his waist encircled by a thick round horsehair rope, strode to the foot of the cross and poured forth a torrent of passionate Spanish as he seized a cord and dropped the sheets to reveal a crude figure of the Christ nailed to the heavy beams of the great cross. Bedlam broke loose—women screamed and wailed and men shook crude rattles—tin cans filled with pebbles. As the din continued, the cross was lowered and the figure removed from it, and then the largest man in the crowd shouldered it. The clamor lessened, and once more the procession was under way.

Back to the *Morada* they went this time, the self-flagellation continuing. As they neared the little church, the man being dragged by the ropes gave a great cry and pitched forward on his face. The man with the bloodied back was suddenly lashed with fury by the two Penitentes behind him and he, too, gave a cry and fell to the ground, whereupon the floggers dropped their whips and carried the two senseless men into the *Morada,* followed by the entire procession. The huge man with the cross stood it against the wall and, falling to his knees, crept slowly through the door, which closed behind him.

Vetch, shut off from whatever final rites were being carried out within the *Morada,* finally went back to his car. He did not know how long he sat there, reviewing the terrible, but fascinating, performance. Usually the sight of blood nauseated him, but today he had been deeply, inexplicably quickened by it. He loked down at his hand and gently touched the spot where the red drop had fallen. Then, to his amazement, he found that his clothes were spattered with crimson, as were both his hands. Still there was no revulsion. He started the car. He let it idle for a few moments as he recalled the Christlike face of the young man.

Surely, he thought, belief that could illuminate like that could not be wholly evil. Yet such barbarism could not stem from God. Somewhere long ago he had heard some anti-Catholic zealot use the phrase "Black Mass." Maybe this was what he had seen today. He began to think of the words he would use to describe the frightful pageant, but as the sentences came to his tongue they served only to conjure up in his mind the beatific countenance of the young New Mexican.

Still pondering the events of the day, he put the car in gear and started back upon the road by which he had come. What could he bring to these people? He had not a word of their language. Had he a faith that could be a substitute for theirs? — a faith that could bring to the face of any one of them the ecstasy that burned on the features of that radiant youth? One more he faced the sterility of his tenets, and in his heart there arose the words, "My God, why hast Thou forsaken me?"

Suddenly Vance Vetch realized he had lost the trail. He had been following, with no conscious thought, a pair of wagon tracks through a wide, high, desert valley filled with a rough, broken lava flow. The sun was setting and the brief twilight would be quickly gone. He stopped the car and looked about him. There was no landmark that looked even vaguely familiar. He felt faint and hungry, and suddenly panic swept over him. What if he were in Navajo country? He had never liked the Navajo — he feared them. He recalled the many stories he had heard of solitary white men being murdered as witches in the back-of-the-beyond reaches of the reservation. He must get out of here!

He began to drive ahead furiously, wildly. It was no road for such speed — he knew that, but he could not slow down. He swerved the car this way and that to try to follow the twists and turns of the wagon ruts. Time after time his front wheels crashed against chunks of lava — he knew a tire might blow any minute, but he dared not stop. There must be a trading post ahead or a sheep camp! If only he could see a light!

He failed to see a tongue of lava projecting out upon the road, and there was a sudden crash. Vetch felt himself flung against the windshield. The steering wheel broke against his ribs. There was a blinding flash of burning pain, and he knew no more.

XLVIII

"ONWARD CHRISTIAN sol-ol-diers—marching as to war . . ." the words ended in a sobbing fit of coughing, punctuated by a gasping cry of pain.

Lololomi jumped up from where he had been sleeping by the embers of his fire. What had wakened him? For a long moment there was silence. Then, a feeble "Help!" came from up the road. He threw some wood on the fire and watched the flames eat into the brittle juniper, then quickly, but cautiously, he went in the direction from which the sound had come.

Two hundred feet up the trail he came upon an overturned car. Nearby where it had been pitched into a pocket in the lava, he discovered what looked like a pile of torn and dirty rags. From it came a whimpering sound, a hint of movement. As the old Indian bent over it he knew that he was looking upon the bloodied features of Vance Vetch.

His first instinct was to get away from him as quickly as possible. Why should he stay to help this man who had so often sneered at him and who had brought such grief to his people? He might even be a witch. Let his own God rescue him!

Vetch was too weak and dazed to recognize the Hopi. All he knew was that he was no longer alone with terror. His prayer for help had been answered. Feebly he raised an arm and extended a pathetic hand as he muttered, "I thank God! Water — Water . . ."

As he contemplated the broken man, pity flooded over Lololomi. As gently as possible, he reached under Vetch and lifted him from the ground. How light this enemy of the Hopi was! The movement tore a groan from the injured man, and he continued to cry out as the Indian carried him down the trail and up to the fire. He was chilled to the bone from loss of blood and shock and the cold night air, and he opened his hand toward the blaze with a barely intelligible "Fire — warm — good."

Lololomi made him as comfortable as he could on a bed of soft cinder in a recess between the lava flows. Fortunately, there was about a cupful of water left — he let the missionary sip it slowly. Then he sat beside the moaning white man. As the night wore on Vetch became delirious and seemed possessed by overpowering fears. When Lololomi got up to add wood to the fire Vetch screamed and clutched at the air; he was comforted only when the gentle old Indian returned to his side. His defenselessness completely broke down the red man's antagonism. He ran his fingers through Vetch's matted hair and patted him as he would a small child. Vetch clasped one of Lololomi's hands and held it tightly, although this little movement stabbed him with pain and he cried plaintively. The fire's warmth and the human companionship at last seemed to banish the fearful nightmares, but then self-pity took hold. Tears flowed down his cheeks, making white streaks through the dirt. By dawn, he had lapsed into unconsciousness.

Surely there could be no evil left in this poor, childlike, shattered man. Lololomi no longer felt any revulsion or hatred for him. In his mind there was only a great wonder that in this hour of supreme need the white man's gods were of no value to him. It would be a poor Hopi indeed who could not face death with dignity and composure.

Lololomi made no plan for the morning. The powers that had directed his footsteps to Awatobi, to the shrine of San Mateo, and to this old trail in the lava flow had guided him also to Vetch. These powers would not fail him now.

Daylight found him sitting quietly by the dying fire with Vetch's head lying in his lap. The ravaged body stirred restlessly from time to time, but quieted when it felt Lololomi's soothing hand. Suddenly the silence was broken by the sound of a wagon being driven slowly along the rutted road. Lololomi laid down the white man's head as gently as he could and went to seek help from the passers-by.

They were Navajo, on their way to Fort Defiance. Yes, there was room for the two of them — but what if the man should die in the wagon and so bewitch it?

"I shall know if he is to die," said the Hopi, "and we will then take him from the wagon."

The Navajo accepted this as simply as Lololomi had uttered it. It took a matter of minutes to lift the almost lifeless body of Vetch into the wagon. Then Lololomi took his place by the broken body of the white man and thus they rode throughout the long day. Occasionally a babble of sound and a few childish sobs would come from the inert figure, but it was obvious that for him life was near an end, and that a few hours would bring him release from all doubts and fears.

It was late afternoon when Lololomi called to the Navajo that Vetch was about to die. They stopped the wagon instantly and got out and stood to one side. They did not help the old Hopi, and they looked on in silence as he took down the tailgate, lifted the sprawling figure from the wagon, and carried it to the shade of a nearby juniper. Then they jumped in and drove off as fast as they could without one backward glance.

Again the Hopi made the white man as comfortable as possible and then took up his vigil. As death came ever closer Vetch once more seemed to be beset by fears and cried out with increasing terror in his voice. With each assault upon the dying man's broken defenses the old Indian redoubled his efforts to allay his fears. As the soft hands and the gentle voice, singing *Kachina* songs, worked their soothing magic, the terror somehow departed. Again the Hopi wondered at the missionary's lack of comfort from his religion – why he should die frightened, without pride, without comfort from his gods.

There was a quick gasp and Vance Vetch was gone.

Throughout the night Lololomi sat by the lifeless body. It was nearly noon of the following day when a car came from the direction of Fort Defiance. As it neared the tree under which Lololomi waited, it stopped and two men got out.

"Some Navajo told us that you have a dying white man –"

The old Hopi did not wait for the man to finish the sentence, but pointed to the body at his feet.

A woman who had remained in the car now jumped out and, running toward them, fell upon the dead man, sobbing bitterly. Then she straightened up and faced Lololomi.

"They tell me you took care of him – you did unto him as –"

She could not finish and buried her tear-stained face in her hands. With infinite kindness and dignity, Lololomi took her arm and led her back to the car. The men pulled a blanket over Vetch's white, pain-wracked face.

"We will be back soon for the body – we better get Mrs. Vetch to the mission now. I am Dr. Graham. Can I arrange for you to get back to your village?

Lololomi shook his head.

"No; I know my way. I can go to my village now."

They watched his bowed old figure start slowly in the direction of Shongopovi.

•

XLIX

"I'M GOING IN for my cattle tomorrow." Jim tried not to sound too happy about it. "Tom's going in with me, and we're taking Sequa-Honau, too."

Kathleen looked up from the table where she was working on a report.

"I bet he's excited—and I am, too. I got my check today, and it's thirty dollars more than I used to get at the hospital!"

"Better let me buy you a cow or two."

"Not a bad idea. I'd rather like to be the first Hopi woman to own cattle! No, we'll start to save for that furniture we're going to get some day. Listen!"

The voice of the Crier Chief rang out on the evening air, and they listened without comment to the end.

"A rabbit hunt tomorrow? Another marriage maybe?" Kathleen asked.

"I think it may be the beginning for Mary and Allan. I passed him on the road today and he called something to me I could not quite hear."

"I know Mary went down to the hospital this week for

a final check-up. I haven't had a chance to ask about it. We must see them soon."

"I'd like to go on the hunt tomorrow, but I've arranged all this and I can't get out of it very well."

"Tell Mr. Livingstone how grateful we are to the others. Don said today that the people they interested in our trouble wrote more letters and saw more people than anyone else. Some day we'll go into Flagstaff together and thank them."

"Maybe they'll come to the Butterfly Dance."

"I don't know if they'd want to make the trip. And, besides - - -"

"Besides what?"

"I know all the reasons for having the dance now; they're good reasons, too. But still, I sort of wish they'd waited until we know what happened to Lololomi."

"He would want us to go on as usual."

"I know he would. Maybe he'll be back by then – if he's coming back."

"Let's not talk about him."

Jim got up abruptly and Kathleen sensed that the old man's disappearance had affected him deeply. She turned back to her work. Jim went to the door and opened it. Then he stood looking out into the darkness as if he would penetrate its depths and find somewhere in them the old man who had been more than father to him in these months since his return.

"I'm going to the *kiva* for a while," he said at last. "There may be some work on the costumes that I can help with."

"You haven't changed your mind about taking part?"

"Since you can't, I think I won't this time. No," as she started to protest, "that's not the only reason. I'll feel more a part of these things once I am initiated – if I ever am."

She knew he was thinking of Lololomi's promise to sponsor him in the initiation ceremony.

"He'll be back in time, I'm sure."

She went to where Jim stood in the doorway and put her arm through his. He gave it a quick pressure and left without a word.

She was asleep, or feigning to be, when he returned from the *kiva.* When he awoke the next morning she had gone. On the breakfast table he found a note.

"I forgot to tell you I have to be at the dispensary early this morning. Some members of the church board are coming today and I want to get some of my jobs out of the way so as to be free for them. See you tonight. Don't be too late. Kathleen."

How could I have slept so hard? he wondered. I guess I'm just getting caught up with those sleepless nights in jail. He heard the motor of Tom's car, bolted down a cup of coffee, and rushed out to his own car to find Sequa-Honau waiting for him. They were well down the mesa road before the sun rose above the eastern horizon.

Getting the cattle was a long day's work and it was dusk when he came in from the range. The house was dark. Strange that Kathleen should be so late. It was the first time he had come home to an empty house, and its loneliness oppressed him. Then he heard her voice and she burst in.

"Jim! He's here! I told you he'd come back. He's here!"

He took her by both arms and held her firmly. "You mean Lololomi?"

"Yes."

"Here? In the village?"

She poured out the story.

"I was late at the dispensary because of the visitors. Don and I were checking over some records when I heard a sort of scraping sound outside."

She paused for breath.

"I went to the door and saw a figure reach toward the wall but fall to the ground before his hand had touched it. I called Don and we carried him inside. It was Lololomi."

"Is he – is he all right?"

"Don thinks he fainted from exhaustion. He brought him to and was having him drink some warm tea when I left. He wants to keep him there for a few hours. But I had to tell you and I am going to drive his wife down. Come on back with me."

Lololomi's old wife was reluctant to get into the car – she

didn't like them, she declared quite firmly; and Lololomi might come – she must stay home.

"I don't want to tell her yet and get the whole village excited," whispered Kathleen. "What shall we do?"

"I'll get my mother," Jim replied. "Wait a minute."

Nasayungti came at his bidding and he explained to her what had happened as they hurried to Lololomi's house. Although his mother's excitement was great, he knew he could count upon her.

"Come," Nasayungti said to the reluctant wife of the old Hopi. "We are to go to where Kathleen works. Dr. Cummings wants us both. Perhaps he has word of Lololomi."

The name was all that was needed to persuade her to join them, her trembling lips and hands witness to her hopes and fears.

"You drive, Kathleen," said Jim. "There'll be room for the two of them with you, and I'll just hang on."

There was but one light in the dispensary as they neared it and that was in the little waiting room. Kathleen wondered if that meant something had gone wrong, but Dr. Cummings came to the door when he heard the car.

"He's awfully tired," he whispered to Kathleen, "but all right. The light hurt his eyes – too much sun and sand – but he's all right. Oh, I'm glad you came, Jim; I want to talk with you later."

The voices brought Lololomi to the door. There was a hushed moment and then, with a little cry, the old woman rushed to the worn figure and put her arms about him, stood off, then rushed to him again. Lololomi stood motionless, the tears pouring down his cheeks.

"Let's go inside," said Dr. Cummings gently.

He closed the door after the old people had entered, and signaled to the others to wait.

"They'll be all right," he said. "I want to ask about getting him to the village. He can't stand much excitement – he's completely worn out. Yet he keeps repeating that he must speak to his people, that there is no more evil, and some other things I don't quite understand. He'll be more content, I know, if he can go there tonight, but as I said,

I don't want the whole village clustering around him, asking him questions, and getting him all wrought up. Yet, he needs a chance to talk it all out."

It was kind old Nasayungti who turned to him.

"It is late. The children are in bed, the rabbit hunt has tired many — only the chiefs and a few young men are in the *kiva* tonight. Let him go there — his wife can come with me. I shall see that she understands."

Jim and Kathleen both looked at her with pride.

"Vadas and I always maintain that your mother is the best of them all, Jim."

"Thank you," said Jim. "Will you come with us?"

"No, the committee is waiting for me at the hospital. I'll leave it all to you. I'll run up in the morning to see how the old fellow's coming along. The other car's around here somewhere; you better use it as well as that little one Kathleen has."

He remained long enough to see that Jim found the car and had the key.

"Good night. He's an amazing old man. Take care of him."

Again it was Nasayungti who took the initiative. She opened the door gently, then flung it wide. The old people sat there together, their eyes closed. She touched each of them and motioned to the car. They rose, and for the first time the old man saw Jim. He said no word at first, and Jim found himself tongue-tied as he went toward Lololomi. Then they found themselves clasping each other tightly as the old man murmured, "My son, my son!"

Kathleen never quite knew how they got started up the mesa road. Jim took the old people with him, and Nasayungti, all smiles, climbed in with Kathleen. Jim drove as close to the *kiva* as he could and helped the old man out to a place in the shadows. He took the old woman to his mother's house, parked the car, and came back to where he had left Lololomi. He literally carried the wasted old man down into the *kiva*.

Of the young men, only Tom was present, working on a bit of dance gear. Drowsing to one side were Nemtaka and a few ceremonial chiefs. Varying expressions of unbelief passed over their faces as they saw Jim and his burden. They came forward and helped to make Lololomi comfortable in one corner. The old man sat with eyes closed for some time while the watchers exchanged troubled glances. Nemtaka pointed to another pile of sheepskins and blankets on the floor and, following the unspoken suggestion, Jim picked up the weary Lololomi and laid him down on them gently. The old Hopi opened his eyes, held up his hand as if in greeting, spoke the words, "butterflies" and "tomorrow," and then he rolled over on his side and was silent.

Nemtaka put his ear to Lololomi's chest and with one hand marked the beat of his heart. His breath came regularly; he lay utterly relaxed. Satisfied at last that he was deep in health-giving sleep, they moved quietly to the far end of the *kiva.*

Jim slipped out to reassure Kathleen. He returned with a bowl of water and a soft cloth. With gentle skill he took off the sweat-stained *banda,* washed the dirt-streaked face and hands, brushed the matted hair, removed the ragged moccasins and bathed the swollen feet. Occasionally the old man stirred and great sighs came from him, but he did not wake at any time.

At the bottom of the *kiva* ladder the men held whispered consultation. Lololomi would be all right after a long sleep, and Jim told them that Dr. Cummings had said he would be up on the morrow. Jim and Tom would stand watch, and the others would bring food at dawn. Tom turned back to where Lololomi lay as the others climbed the ladder. Jim followed them, remembering Lololomi's grim chuckle that night in Keams Canyon jail. This time the chuckle was his own.

"I think the Butterflies *will* dance tomorrow," he said aloud, and then he turned and went slowly down the ladder and joined Tom by the sleeping Lololomi.

L

JIM AND TOM DROWSED off as the long night hours passed and Lololomi continued to sleep as if drugged. The village activity at dawn woke the watchers completely but caused not even a stir in the blanket-covered form of Lololomi.

"The dancers – they will be coming in soon," whispered Jim. "What shall we do? He should not be disturbed."

"Today's dance is not like some of our other ceremonials," Tom explained. "Only the young men will come here to put on their costumes. The little girls and the older ones will dress in their homes. The young men will keep our secret until we are sure that he is strong enough to stand the excitement."

"I'll go to his house now while not many are about and bring back clothes and moccasins," suggested Jim.

"Good! I'll watch until you return."

As Jim left the *kiva,* two men were entering with a plaque of *piki,* some stewed peaches, and a pot of steaming coffee. "Is he awake?"

"No, not yet, but he slept through the night as if he

felt no pain or worry. When he wakes he will be hungry. Tom is there. Go on down. I'll be back soon."

By the time Jim returned, many of the young men who were to take part in the Butterfly Dance had arrived to prepare for it. They looked down with happy smiles at the still sleeping figure of Lololomi. Others came in and were cautioned to keep silent. With smiles and gestures they made ready for the dance.

In the houses of the village, girls of all ages were fitting their fragile, decorated headdresses over their black hair. The thin flat boards formed a towering crown vividly painted in red, green, yellow, and blue, with fluffs of eagle down arranged to hang from the cloud symbols at the top. Their foreheads were almost obscured by bangs into which were stuck little tufts of brilliant parrot feathers. The old-style Hopi dresses of black or brown were held at the waists by red sashes, and vari-colored capes were draped over their shoulders, hanging down their backs in graceful folds. Bright-colored embroidered bands adorned wrists and ankles. The costumes were complete with the family treasure of silver, coral, and turquoise. Cheeks were carmined, and in each hand was a small cluster of fir twigs.

By mid-morning the plaza was gay with color and laughter, but the house of Nasayungti held two silent women, fearful of what news might come from the *kiva*. They looked up expectantly when Kathleen came in.

"Jim says Lololomi is still sleeping. They have taken food to the *kiva* and Jim has gotten him some clean clothes. When the dancers start I'll come for you and we'll all go to watch as if nothing had happened. Oh, this is going to be a wonderful day."

She gave Nasayungti a kiss and patted Lololomi's wife on the hand.

"Thank you, my daughter." The warm smile of Jim's mother spoke her love for this wife that Jim had chosen.

Back in the *kiva* the men participants had donned their glossy velvet shirts of many colors and their wide embroidered *kachina* sashes and had wrapped their square-cut hair in bright new *bandas*. Silver necklaces, bracelets and rings had been borrowed from families and friends to make a rich display on this occasion. They were ready to leave the *kiva* now for the first part of the Butterfly Dance. All looked affectionately at the sleeping Lololomi. Who would guide their steps through the intricacies of the movements of the Butterfly Dance, as he had done for so many years? They picked up their gourd dance rattles and held them so they would make no sound, then silently climbed the ladder.

In the plaza, men and girls of all ages faced each other in two long lines headed by the best dancers of the village. The spectators, Kathleen and the old women among them, lined up beside the houses. The dancers began to move toward each other in a slow-moving, shuffling trot.

Back in the *kiva* Jim alone was left to maintain the vigil. He busied himself by putting the room in order. The pot of coffee stood unused as yet — a cup of it would help; no matter if it was cold. He poured it carefully into a tin bowl and was raising it to his lips when he heard, "The Butterflies — they dance!"

Lololomi was sitting upright, his eyes wide and clear, his

hands steady. Jim went to him at once and the old man seized his hands and pulled himself to his feet.

"I must go to them – help me."

Jim hesitated. He feared that the old man might be delirious. But a direct look into the bright eyes assured him that Lololomi was quite himself. They both turned at a sound from the entrance.

"I don't belong here, I know, but Kathleen sent me down." Dr. Cumming's words came haltingly as he awkwardly negotiated the *kiva* ladder. "What's all this?"

Lololomi smiled at him and patted his hand.

"You're a tough old man," said the doctor admiringly, as he examined him. "No, you don't need me. He's all right." This to Jim. "I'm going up to watch the dance. Vadas will be along any minute.

Jim managed to get the old man to swallow a cup of coffee and a bit of *piki*. Then he helped him into the clean clothes. The excited old Hopi could hardly wait to button his loose cotton shirt before he ran to the foot of the ladder and started up.

"Wait!" called Jim, "I'll be right after you."

He had difficulty catching up. As they turned from the *kiva* toward the plaza Lololomi took his arm, and the two of them advanced to the line of dancers.

The drum was stilled, the gourd rattles were silenced, the crowd was hushed. Lololomi took his place as leader of the ceremony as if nothing unusual had happened. With unfaltering steps he went up and down the lines of dancers, sprinkling them with pinches of sacred corn meal from a pouch handed him by Tewayestewa, urging them to go on with the dance.

The mood could not be sustained. There were shouts from the crowd of onlookers, the dancers broke their lines, and Lololomi found himself unable to move in the pressing crowd. Voices demanded to know where he had been, what had happened, when he had returned.

"I would not have missed this for anything," said Dr. Cummings to Jim, "but I am afraid of all this excitement."

"Well, I thought I'd get a chair for him so that he can

sit down and talk to them. We'll have to forget the dance for a while, I guess."

Between them they managed to lead Lololomi through the excited crowd to a place in the shade. He sat down slowly, then with a smile waited for the crowd to settle itself. The oldest men of the village squatted nearest to him, and all the others stood or squatted in a semi-circle facing him. Even the children were quiet as they waited for him to speak.

Nemtaka, as village chief, felt that a formal welcome was in order. All turned toward him as he slowly stood up.

"We are happy to welcome you to your home and to your people. You have come back at a favorable time. One by one the troubles of our people have dropped away like the shadows of the night before the morning sun. Now that you have returned, the last shadow has gone."

Lololomi thanked him gravely. Then he began the narrative they were waiting to hear. He was a natural storyteller with a fine sense of the dramatic. He gave them in great detail the account of his journey, of his meditations, of his finding the missionary, of his decision to see Vance Vetch through his last hours, of the homeward journey which had ended the night before on the *kiva* floor.

He spoke without interruption. When he finished he sat back and accepted a cigarette from one of the chiefs near him. Ceremoniously he blew the first whiffs to the north, the south, the east. the west, and up, and down. Then he listened to the questions and he answered them with directness and simplicity.

Finally, one voice shouted out, "Why should you care for Vetch? It would have been better had he died long ago — there would have been less trouble for all of us!"

Lololomi answered him gently.

"It was right for me to do as I did. At the end there was no evil in him. He was like a child — I could not leave him to his loneliness and to his fears. He could get no comfort from his gods. I thought how much better our old people die. At death the Hopi is not alone, he is not frightened, he leaves in dignity on his journey to the Underworld, to the beautiful painted cliffs always bathed in a soft blue haze –"

Lololomi puffed silently away for a little time before he spoke again.

"Yes, our Hopi way is indeed a better way of death – and of life. But I wish the Butterflies to dance. This day must be a happy one. I shall go for a time and then come back and watch. Tewayestewa, you keep the dancers in step while I rest in my house."

He stood up and took his wife by the hand. The crowd parted to make way for them and watched until the door of the house closed behind them. The dancers once again lined up, the drum began to sound, and from along the walls the villagers watched with added pleasure the shuffling figures in their bright beautiful costumes. Particularly their eyes dwelt upon the little girls, like painted dolls as they gestured in the dance. Later there would be feasting and joking and laughter, but now the minds of all turned back to Lololomi's story and ahead to prayers for the future.

When Jim returned to his house he found Kathleen sitting at the table with her face hidden in her hands. He went to her quietly and put his hand on her shoulder. With a swift gesture she rose and flung her arms about him and held him tightly as she sobbed, "That wonderful old man!"

Through the window came the voices of the Butterfly dancers as they rose in the happy chant of mockingbird's song. "I now sing of the whole far earth – I sing of all things that bear fruit – I sing of life itself – life everlasting –"

Epilogue

T*HE FLAME OF THE NOVEMBER sunset lights up the village of Shongopovi high on its mesa top. In the west a crescent silver of moon shines briefly on the quiet landcape. It is the month of the Wuwuchim.*

The summer rains have been bountiful. The fields have yielded of their abundance. Storerooms are filled with piles of corn—blue, white, red, yellow, vari-colored. Storage baskets are piled high with squash, beans, dried peaches. Watermelons and cantaloupes are ripe for eating. Under the projecting roof beams of the dwellings long strings of brown-red mutton dry in the high desert air.

Two figures make their way across the plaza to where the poles of the kiva ladder are like long, slender, imperious fingers against the brilliant sky. The face of the old Hopi is serene and he walks with calm dignity, his thin cotton pants and loose shirt flapping in the evening breeze. His companion is a young man of intently serious mien. Only the ends of a Kachina dance belt give any touch of vivid color to the black and white woolen blanket in which he is tightly wrapped.

At the entrance to the kiva the young man takes from a pouch a pinch of corn meal. With a muttered prayer he sprinkles it upon the ceremonial emblem tied across the ladder poles. Then, in traditional descent, he is guided step by step down the kiva ladder by the older man.

In the kiva the ceremonial fathers, with ancient implements and many prayers, kindle the New Fire. Upon its rising flames the young man sprinkles another pinch of corn meal.

Throughout the night the great drum throbs in the kiva. All night long the ceremonial fathers instruct, in the secret lore of the Hopi, the young men who are about to assume the status of full adulthood. Old songs are sung. Old legends are recounted. Time-honored laws and customs are impressed upon young minds.

Old Lololomi speaks, his words directed to the serious young man whom he had guided down the kiva ladder.

"With this night the ceremonies of your rebirth begin. The life you led far away among the white men is now over. The months that have passed since your return to us have proved well that you are now truly ready to walk the Hopi way.

"With the passing of five days you will have died as a boy and a youth and will have been reborn as a Hopi man, a leader among our people. The name Talastewa which you have borne as a boy and as a youth will be gone. You will have a man's name henceforth, a name that you will still carry with you on that day when you set out to the Underworld.

"As your ceremonial father I have watched the sun make his journey across the sky many times as I waited for this day to come. I am proud that it has come, my son."

As the first grey light is visible on the eastern horizon the old man and the young one go forth from the kiva to the edge of the mesa, there to await the yellow dawn. In the direction of the rising sun they toss corn meal and silently bless the warmth and light bestowed upon them as the great orb starts another journey across the arc of the heavens.

Their silent prayers mount with the climbing sun – prayers of thanksgiving for the bountiful crops so recently harvested, for the peace and security now granted them after years of schism and dissension.

The young man feels his heart soar in spiritual exaltation – as if he were rising out of himself – above himself – in unity with all mankind – one with the hard rock at his feet – one with the sun above. For red man and for white man his prayers go up.

Lightly old Lololomi touches his arm and they turn back to the kiva.

•

TUBA CITY
MOENCOPI
ORAIBI
CAMERON
LITTLE
HUBBELL
LOWER ORAIBI
TOLCHACO
FLAGSTAFF
SUNRISE
LEUPP
EAT
D.P.